Praise for Melanie Dickerson

"This book will have you jumping out of your seat with anticipation at times. Moderate to fast-paced, you will not want this book to end. Recommended for all, especially lovers of historical romance."

—*RT Book Reviews*, 4 stars,
for *The Silent Songbird*

"When it comes to happily-ever-afters, Melanie Dickerson is the undisputed queen of fairy-tale romance, and all I can say is—long live the queen! From start to finish *The Beautiful Pretender* is yet another brilliant gem in her crown, spinning a medieval love story that will steal you away—heart, soul, and sleep!"

—Julie Lessman, award-winning author of
The Daughters of Boston, Winds of Change,
and Heart of San Francisco series

"I couldn't stop reading! Melanie has done what so many other historical novelists have tried and failed: she's created a heroine that is at once both smart and self-assured without seeming modern. A woman so fixed in her time and place that she is able to speak to ours as well."

—Siri Mitchell, author of *Flirtation Walk* and
Chateau of Echoes, on *The Beautiful Pretender*

"Readers will find themselves supporting the romance between the sweet yet determined Odette and the insecure but hardworking Jorgen from the beginning. Dickerson spins a retelling of Robin Hood with emotionally compelling characters, offering hope that love may indeed conquer all as they unite in a shared desire to serve both the Lord and those in need."

—*RT Book Reviews*, 4½ stars, on
The Huntress of Thornbeck Forest

"I'm always amazed at the way Melanie Dickerson creates a world. Her writing is as fresh and unique as anyone I know, and I am always pulled into the story and taken far away on a wonderful, romantic, and action-packed journey."

—MARY CONNEALY, AUTHOR OF *NOW AND FOREVER*, BOOK TWO OF THE WILD AT HEART SERIES, ON *THE HUNTRESS OF THORNBECK FOREST*

"Melanie Dickerson does it again! Full of danger, intrigue, and romance, this beautifully crafted story will transport you to another place and time."

—SARAH E. LADD, AUTHOR OF *THE CURIOSITY KEEPER* AND THE WHISPERS ON THE MOORS SERIES, ON *THE HUNTRESS OF THORNBECK FOREST*

"Melanie Dickerson's *The Huntress of Thornbeck Forest* is a lovely, romantic read set during one of the most fascinating time periods. Featuring a feisty, big-hearted heroine and a hero to root for, this sweet medieval tale is wrapped in a beautiful journey of faith that had me flipping pages well after my bedtime. Delightful!"

—TAMARA LEIGH, *USA TODAY* BESTSELLING AUTHOR OF *BARON OF GODSMERE*

"Melanie Dickerson weaves a tantalizing Robin Hood plot in a medieval setting in *The Huntress of Thornbeck Forest*. She pits a brave heroine with unique talents against a strong, gentle hero whose occupation makes it dangerous to know him. Add the moral dilemma and this tale makes a compelling read for any age."

—RUTH AXTELL, AUTHOR OF *SHE SHALL BE PRAISED* AND *THE ROGUE'S REDEMPTION*

"*The Huntress of Thornbeck Forest* is a wonderful romantic tale filled with love, betrayal, and forgiveness. I loved this book and highly recommend it for readers of all ages."

—CARA LYNN JAMES, AUTHOR OF
A PATH TOWARD LOVE

"*The Huntress of Thornbeck Forest* reminds me of why adults should read fairy tales. Author Melanie Dickerson shoots straight to the heart with a cast of compelling characters, an enchanting story world, and romance and suspense in spades. Reaching The End was regrettable—but oh, what an ending!"

—LAURA FRANTZ, AUTHOR OF
THE MISTRESS OF TALL ACRE

"For stories laden with relatable heroines, romantically adventurous plots, once-upon-a-time settings, and engaging writing, Melanie Dickerson is your go-to author. Her books are on my never-to-be-missed list."

—KIM VOGEL SAWYER, AUTHOR OF *WHEN MERCY
RAINS*, ON *THE HUNTRESS OF THORNBECK FOREST*

"Ms. Dickerson deftly captures the flavor of life in medieval Germany in a sweet tale filled with interesting characters that will surely capture readers' hearts."

—KATHLEEN MORGAN, AUTHOR OF THESE
HIGHLAND HILLS SERIES, *EMBRACE THE DAWN*,
AND *CONSUMING FIRE*, ON
THE HUNTRESS OF THORNBECK FOREST

The Noble Servant

Other Books by Melanie Dickerson

The

NOBLE
SERVANT

MELANIE DICKERSON

THOMAS NELSON

Since 1798

The Noble Servant

© 2017 by Melanie Dickerson

Published in Nashville, Tennessee, by Thomas Nelson. Thomas Nelson is a registered trademark of HarperCollins Christian Publishing, Inc.

Thomas Nelson titles may be purchased in bulk for educational, business, fund-raising, or sales promotional use. For information, please e-mail SpecialMarkets@ThomasNelson.com.

Scripture quotations are taken from the Holy Bible, New International Version®, NIV®. Copyright © 1973, 1978, 1984, 2011 by Biblica, Inc.® Used by permission of Zondervan. All rights reserved worldwide. www.zondervan.com. The "NIV" and "New International Version" are trademarks registered in the United States Patent and Trademark Office by Biblica, Inc.®

Library of Congress Cataloging-in-Publication Data

Names: Dickerson, Melanie, author.
Title: The noble servant / Melanie Dickerson.
Description: Nashville, Tennessee: Thomas Nelson, [2017]. | Summary: "After being betrayed and cast out, Lady Magdalen and Steffan the Duke of Wolfberg must work together to reclaim their rightful titles"-- Provided by publisher.
Identifiers: LCCN 2016052625 | ISBN 9780718026608 (hardback)
Subjects: | CYAC: Nobility--Fiction. | Love--Fiction. |
Impersonation--Fiction. | Identity--Fiction. | Middle Ages--Fiction. |
Christian life--Fiction.
Classification: LCC PZ7.D5575 Nob 2017 | DDC [Fic]--dc23 LC record available at https://lccn.loc.gov/2016052625

Printed in the United States of America

17 18 19 20 21 LSC 5 4 3 2 1

Chapter One

The year 1365, Barony of Mallin,
the Holy Roman Empire

Where do you think you are going looking like a beggar?"
Mother asked.

Magdalen's hand was on the door. "Just walking."

"I'd think you would be ashamed to be seen in such clothing."
Mother narrowed her eyes at Magdalen.

Magdalen wanted to say, "Even Hegatha allowed me to go for a
walk in my oldest dress," but Mother did not like it when she spoke
of the dead.

"Just don't let anyone see you, and if you are not home before
dark, I will send Hans with his dogs."

Magdalen hurried out the door before her mother changed
her mind.

The path led away from Mallin Park House across a gentle
green hill. The village of Mallin was visible in the valley over
her left shoulder. The farther she went, moving away from both
her home and the village, the more grass grew on the once well-
worn path.

1

Vegetable plots lay on either side. A middle-aged man stooped over a row of cabbages with his hoe. He looked up as Magdalen approached.

"*Guten Morgen,*" Magdalen greeted.

"Guten Morgen, Lady Magdalen." He smiled and nodded. His frightfully skinny legs in baggy, thigh-length hose showed below his tattered woolen shirt that hung over his bony frame.

A pang of guilt twisted inside her, as it did every time she thought about her people being in need. If only the mines had not run out of copper. "God, please provide for them," she whispered.

She kept her gaze on the path that led down one grass-covered hill and up another, looking for interesting rocks to add to her collection, such as the rock that hung around her neck on a gold chain. It was the last gift her father had given her—a necklace made from a red jasper stone found in the copper mines.

As she neared the first of the three abandoned mines, the trees became thicker and the hills rockier. She stepped up to the narrow entrance, barely wide enough to admit a broad-shouldered man but plenty wide enough for Magdalen. Two large tree limbs lay across the opening. Magdalen lifted her skirts to step over them.

"Magdalen!" Jonatha called out.

Magdalen stopped, dropping her skirts back over her ankles. "I am here," she called out, catching sight of her sister's bright-blonde hair and Lenhart's tall, lanky frame through the trees.

"Mother wants you home right away. She sent Lenhart and me to fetch you back."

Lenhart's brown eyes widened as they did when he was excited or confused.

"Is something wrong?"

"A missive arrived just after you left." Jonatha's normally loud voice was slightly hushed. "Mother started screaming for you as soon as she read it."

What could this mean?

Magdalen started back down the narrow path toward home with Jonatha skipping in front of her and Lenhart striding behind.

While Jonatha sang a song, Magdalen's thoughts raced to that letter. She couldn't help but wonder if it was from the Duke of Wolfberg.

She had danced with the duke at Thornbeck Castle two years ago. Her mother had hoped he might seek to marry her, but that was unlikely. She was only a baron's daughter from a poor region.

She entered the house and could hear Mother's strident voice giving orders to one of the servants.

"Magdalen, you must make haste and pack your trunk." Her cheeks flushed, Mother motioned her forward. "The Duke of Wolfberg has sent for you. He wishes to marry you."

Her stomach fluttered and sank at the same time. It took a moment before she could speak. "He does? But why?"

Mother shook her head. "He probably heard about your brother and knows you will be the heir to Mallin now. What does it matter? He is rich, he can do as he pleases, and he has chosen you." Mother's eyes lit as she clasped her hands in front of her.

Jonatha danced around in a circle, squealing. "Let me come for a visit!" Jonatha threw her arms around her. Her other sisters ran into the room and joined the commotion.

"Be quiet!" Mother shrieked. "You'll make me go deaf."

Magdalen absently patted her sister's shoulder. "But I thought the duke studied in Prague at Karl University."

"He has come home, then." Mother held up a crisp parchment and shook it, making the ribbons dance from where they were sealed into the wax. "Because here is his seal and his colors on the letter. He wishes you to come to Wolfberg at once."

Her duty to her family and to her people required that she marry the wealthiest man she could to save them from extreme poverty. Indeed, she had hoped the duke would want to marry her. He was young and handsome, unlike most of the wealthy unmarried men in the Holy Roman Empire. Two years had passed, however, since she had seen him, and marrying him had sunk into the realm of the impossible.

But the impossible was happening. She, Magdalen of Mallin, was to marry the Duke of Wolfberg.

She took the parchment from her mother's hand and read it. It seemed to be in order, but the missive contained no reference to meeting her at Thornbeck, no expressions of eagerness to see her again, and no sentiment of any kind. Her heart sank. He barely knew her, but she'd hoped . . .

"He doesn't say why he wants to marry me. He must know I have no fortune."

"You will marry him, and do it quickly." Mother shook her finger at Magdalen. "Don't you dare tell him you are poor either. Lady Thornbeck, whose father was nobody, managed to get herself a margrave, and now you'll have a duke."

Mother's lip curled in that way of hers that always made Magdalen's insides squirm.

"And you had better not think of going to Wolfberg and being mousey and submissive. After he has made you his wife, you will demand he live up to his responsibilities to your family. Make him think there is still copper in our mines, but insist that he send money and livestock. He can well afford it. Everyone is depending on you."

Mother jabbed her finger one last time in Magdalen's face. "Now make haste and pack your things. You shall leave at dawn tomorrow."

What if he'd heard false information about her fortune? She had been betrothed to an earl three years ago, but he had the betrothal annulled when he realized how poor she was. Her face still felt the sting of that humiliation.

Magdalen had hoped her mother would want her to be joyful in her marriage. A lump formed in her throat as she went to her room and began to collect her things.

Her desire was for true love, but perhaps that was selfish. And yet, the thought of having the same kind of marriage as her parents felt akin to a boulder sitting on her chest.

At least her marriage would save the people she loved from starving.

Steffan rode his horse between the two men his uncle had sent to escort him back to Wolfberg.

The road heading north from Prague was frequently shaded by large oak and birch trees in this verdant part of the Holy Roman Empire, but Steffan hardly noticed his surroundings. He had begun to doubt the honesty of these two guards. His suspicions had grown the farther down the road they traveled.

"Do you know Sir Burgen?" Steffan asked them just as a hawk took flight from the tree several feet in front of them.

"Oh yes, Your Grace," said the tall, dark-haired guard. "He was well when we left Wolfberg a few days ago."

"And Sir Ruger? He was in good health as well?"

"Yes, Your Grace." The stockier blond guard answered this time. "He sends his greetings to you."

Steffan felt a twist in his gut as all his senses heightened. Breath rushed into his lungs and energy flowed through his limbs as he noted the sword on each man's hip. What other weapons did they carry?

His own dagger was in his saddlebag. He had a smaller knife in the sheath on his belt, and his sword hung at his hip.

The dark-haired guard said, "Let us leave the road and enter the woods to find a place to sleep for the night."

Darkness had not yet descended, and they had only been riding for a few hours. Steffan eyed the two men. "There is an inn a few miles ahead."

The guards glanced at each other. "Very well, Your Grace."

They approached a stone bridge over a swift-flowing river.

"I believe my horse needs a drink," the dark one said. "And truth be known, I am thirsty myself."

Steffan slowed his horse to let the two men move ahead. When they reached the river, the guards dismounted from their horses. Steffan approached the water's edge. The men didn't even look his way, so he let his horse drink. He dismounted, keeping his hand on his sword hilt.

The men stared and slowly started moving toward him and away from each other. They flanked him, preparing to attack from both sides.

Steffan took a step to the left and one back, to shift nearer to the short guard. "Who sent you?"

"We told you," the tall one said. "Your uncle, Lord Hazen." A devious smile stretched his thin face.

"You said Sir Burgen and Sir Ruger were well." He continued

to move to the left and back. "Sir Burgen died ten years ago, and Sir Ruger fifteen years ago."

"Everyone must die sooner or later." The tall one drew his sword with a metal-on-leather sound.

The short one followed suit, but Steffan beat him to the draw. He leapt at him and hit the man's wrist with his sword blade. The short, blond guard dropped his sword with a screech.

Steffan crooked his arm around the man's neck and jerked him around, holding the short one in front of him like a shield.

The tall one struck at his sword, but Steffan parried his strike. The tall one brought his blade down for another strike. Steffan shoved the short guard at him. The tall one struck his companion instead, slicing through his neck. The short guard made a gurgling sound as he fell face-first on the ground between them.

Steffan kept striking at the tall guard, beating him back several steps. He refused to look at the river just behind his opponent so as not to reveal its proximity.

Steffan gripped the sword hilt with both hands, wielding one overhand blow after another. He forced his enemy back one step at a time until he stood at the very edge of the bank. Only then did the man's gaze dip to the river below.

His eyes went wide and he hesitated, giving Steffan one extra moment. Steffan struck the man's raised sword and pushed him. The man threw his arms out wide as he fell.

He cried out just before he hit the water and went under.

Steffan watched and waited. The man bobbed to the surface several yards downriver, flailing his arms, then went under again.

Steffan walked back to where the first man lay in a puddle of blood. "Oh God in heaven," he breathed, lifting his head and gazing downriver. The attack had hardly lasted five minutes, it happened so fast.

"I just killed two men. Forgive me." He made the sign of the cross with his right hand. The two men had intended to kill him. He'd had no choice, but the thought made him so sick he sank to the ground.

Home. He would think of Wolfberg Castle. The chalky-white shore next to the sea behind the castle. The grassy-green pastures and the roar of the crashing waves.

Who had wanted him dead? Could his uncle have sent assassins? Even if Steffan were dead, Lord Hazen would not inherit his title. Since Steffan had no heir, the title would become extinct, and yet it was likely that King Karl would bequeath Wolfberg Castle and all of Steffan's properties to his uncle, unless the king had another loyal subject on whom he'd rather bestow this favor.

Before she died, his grandmother had warned him about Lord Hazen's greed and lack of feeling. Still, it was difficult to accept.

Steffan walked to his horse and sheathed his sword. His two would-be murderers' horses had shied away, but Steffan was able to catch them. He tied them to his horse and started toward Wolfberg and home.

But what would he find when he arrived?

Chapter Two

What would life be like in her new home, married to the Duke of Wolfberg?

Magdalen's cart jolted as they hit another hole in the road, knocking her nearly into the wooden side rail. She had begged her mother to let her ride her horse, but Mother said riding a horse all the way on a three-day journey was not appropriate for a lady. Did she think it was ladylike to ride in a cart for twelve hours a day, rattling her teeth every time a wheel found a dip in the road?

But no one argued with the Baroness of Mallin.

Erlich, who had served Magdalen's family for years, rode his horse while his daughter, Agnes, walked. And Lenhart made up the fourth member of their group as he walked beside the mules who pulled Magdalen's cart.

Wolfberg Castle stood on a hill overlooking the sea. She'd never beheld the sea. What would it be like to hear the waves crashing against the shore? What kind of rocks might she find there?

"Rosings Abbey is just ahead." Erlich pointed to the lane off to the right.

Darkness closed in on them. Erlich reined in his horse as he waited for Lenhart to turn the mules, drawing Magdalen's cart into the lane that would carry them to the abbey. The tall convent buildings, with their steep roofs, were visible above the rows of trees.

At the abbey a young nun greeted them with a bow. She led Magdalen and Agnes to a long, low building, then to an austere room with two small cots. Magdalen's legs were like jelly after using them all day to brace herself as she rode in the jarring cart.

Agnes set her bundle on the floor. She turned one way then the other, her tight blonde braid swaying as she stretched her back. "I shall go and speak with my father and return soon." Agnes did not ask permission but simply walked out before Magdalen could reply.

Gretha, who had been her constant companion since Hegatha had died of a sudden apoplexy, had been all set to come to Wolfberg with her. The day before they were to leave, Gretha told Magdalen she would not be going with her, but Agnes would be taking her place.

Not wanting to hurt Agnes's feelings, Magdalen had agreed.

Now as Magdalen prepared to lie down and sleep before the third and final day of their journey, she wished she had inquired more particularly about how this change had come to pass. Every day Agnes had done something—given Magdalen a shrewd look or spoken more sharply to her than any servant should—to make Magdalen regret allowing her to accompany her.

And now, instead of asking her mistress if she needed anything, Agnes had left Magdalen to struggle alone to take off her heavy overdress.

Magdalen didn't want to embarrass Agnes in front of her father, but as soon as they arrived in Wolfberg, she would have a stern talk with Agnes about her duties as a lady's maidservant.

And if her attitude did not improve, she would replace her with someone from Wolfberg.

Magdalen lay on the narrow cot, covered with a thin blanket since it was still late summer and warm, and thought of her future husband.

Good sense told her it was strange that the Duke of Wolfberg would ask to marry her when Magdalen was only the daughter of a poor widowed baroness. He had seemed sensible when she met him and a man of integrity as well. Every time she closed her eyes and recalled his face, his smile, the kindness in his eyes, her heart fluttered.

But truly, she knew very little about him. She had talked to him, all total, for only two or three hours.

Agnes opened the door, then shut it behind herself, interrupting Magdalen's musings.

"When you are ready for bed, you may blow out the candle," Magdalen told her.

"I will." A snide tone infused her cheerful voice.

Magdalen said a prayer to quell her uneasiness and closed her eyes.

The next morning when Magdalen awoke, Agnes was gone. Magdalen gathered her things, dressed herself, and was ready to go when Agnes came back in.

"Here is your breakfast, Lady Magdalen." With bold eyes she handed Magdalen a warm bundle. Inside was a bun stuffed with meat and cheese. "I also snagged us some apple pasties. Are you ready to go?"

Soon they met Erlich and Lenhart with the cart, mules, and horse and set out on the road to Wolfberg.

When they halted for their midday meal, Magdalen climbed down from the cart and took a drink from the small spring nearby. She splashed some of the cold water on her face, then wiped her cheeks and forehead with a cloth.

When they had finished eating, Agnes and her father kept glancing at each other. A nervous flutter in the pit of Magdalen's stomach caused her to watch them closely. Agnes clutched a small bag to her midsection as she turned to face Magdalen.

"This is how things are." Agnes's eyes were hard and dark as she stood five paces away. "I want to be married to a duke, to be rich, and you are going to change places with me." Agnes pulled her hand out of the bag withdrawing a knife. Her father stepped behind her.

A cold tingling crept into Magdalen's face and spread to her fingertips. Her gaze flitted from Agnes's knife to her father. "Erlich?"

"Do as she says, if you wish to live." He skewered her with a dark, hard look.

Agnes held the knife higher, at the level of Magdalen's chest.

Just then, Lenhart came out of the trees after relieving himself and gasped. He halted and stared.

"Boy, stay back." Erlich glanced at Lenhart. "Agnes is your new mistress. From this day on, Magdalen is no better than you are. Do you understand?"

Lenhart continued to stare, his eyes big and round, his mouth hanging open. He shook his head.

Magdalen tried to think of how she might defend herself and Lenhart, but she had no weapon. What could she possibly do?

"Take off your outer dress." Agnes motioned with the knife. "I will wear yours and you will wear mine. From now on, your name is Agnes and mine is Lady Magdalen of Mallin."

Lenhart grunted, an angry sound, as he stepped toward Agnes.

"I said stay back, boy." Erlich faced Lenhart with clenched fists.

Lenhart shook his head at him and grunted again. He lunged at Agnes's arm. She screamed and Erlich grabbed Lenhart's shoulder. Erlich drew back his fist and slammed it in Lenhart's face, knocking him to the ground.

"Stop it!" Magdalen rushed to Lenhart's side and fell to her knees. "How can you be so cruel?" Blood oozed from a cut over his eye.

"If he tries to interfere again, he'll get worse than that." No hint of remorse tempered Erlich's voice. "Now do as you are told."

Magdalen pulled a clean cloth from her sleeve. She pressed it against Lenhart's eyebrow to stanch the bleeding.

"Get up!" Erlich yelled.

Lenhart took the cloth and nudged her away. Fear and compassion shone in his eyes—he was worried they would hurt her.

Magdalen stood to her feet.

Both Erlich and Agnes glared at her out of narrowed eyes and hardened faces. But the knife Agnes thrust at Magdalen's face was shaking.

"Agnes, you cannot be in earnest."

"I am. And if you do not make haste to remove your dress, my father will rip it off."

Erlich stepped around Agnes and stalked toward Magdalen.

"Very well." Magdalen reached under one arm to untie the

laces at the side of her overdress. "But I do not know how you think you will get away with this. The duke knows what I look like. Do you think he will believe an imposter?"

"He will have no choice. I will show up saying I am you. I do not look so different from you. While wearing your clothes, I will be just as good as any baron's daughter."

Magdalen could do naught except comply. Underneath her overdress she wore a long-sleeved, ankle-length chemise. She untied the other side of her sleeveless blue overdress.

"And you had best not get any ideas about telling the duke who you are, or I will kill you and the boy. At least we don't have to worry about him telling anyone." Erlich alluded to Lenhart's muteness.

Magdalen's hands began to tremble. If Agnes and her father killed Lenhart and her, how would anyone know what had happened to them? In fact, Erlich and Agnes might decide they were safer if they did. Should Magdalen try to fight them?

Her friend Avelina knew what to do in a fight, knew how to think and plan and devise a way of escape. But Magdalen had been raised gently, taught little more than how to dance and greet dukes and princes and embroider tapestries. She had no idea how to contend with rebels and fiends.

Erlich snatched the dress as soon as Magdalen pulled it over her head. He held Agnes's knife pointed at Magdalen's heart while Agnes took off her own dress and threw it on the ground. Then she donned Magdalen's blue silk.

Agnes and Erlich still stared at her, so Magdalen picked up Agnes's brown woolen kirtle and pulled it on, letting the stiff material fall to her ankles, then tied the laces at the top of the bodice.

"Now give me your necklace." Agnes pointed with her knife at the rock pendant her father had given her. "Do it or I'll cut it off."

Magdalen's hands were steady as she unclasped her precious necklace, which represented the bond she and her father shared, all the times they had gone to the mines together and he had carefully taught her about copper ore and how it was mined, stories about the beautiful countryside around Mallin.

Her blood was ice-cold as she handed the necklace over to Agnes and watched her put it around her own neck. Magdalen would bide her time and watch for an opportunity. She would get her necklace back from the usurper.

Magdalen was a baron's daughter. She could get help from one of the noblemen and women who knew her mother. But they were headed in the opposite direction of her friends in Thornbeck, and no one who had met Magdalen lived anywhere near here, except the Duke of Wolfberg. His sister, Gertrudt, had been at Lord Thornbeck's two-week party, but she had married and moved far away.

What if she told the duke she was Lady Magdalen and he didn't believe her? Agnes had the same pale skin and similar hair coloring, though Magdalen's was reddish-blonde and Agnes's was more of a yellow-blonde. Magdalen's eyes were green and Agnes's were hazel. But he still might believe Agnes was really her.

"Now I shall ride in the cart the rest of the way to Wolfberg while you walk beside it." Agnes smirked in a way that made Magdalen clench her teeth.

She would plan a way of escape, just as Avelina would have. Even when she was afraid, Avelina had worked hard to stand up to the evil that had been afoot in Thornbeck Castle. Did Magdalen have that kind of strength and determination?

She was about to find out.

Chapter Three

Steffan had slept at the inn a day's ride northeast of Prague, but he awoke with the same heavy feeling he'd lain down with.

He traveled an hour before coming to a village. The church's bell tower rose above all the other buildings, and he turned his horse in its direction, with his attackers' horses following behind by use of tethers.

He tied the horses to a stake just outside the church and went inside. "Is the priest here? I need someone to hear my confession."

"I am here," a voice called from behind the chancel. "Go in and I shall be there in a few moments."

Steffan stepped into the wooden confessional box and closed the curtain, then lowered himself to the kneeling bench, focusing his mind on the Lord Jesus' death on the cross.

The priest shuffled into the box.

Eager to get this done, Steffan blurted out, "I have committed a great sin against God and against humanity."

"There is no sin the Lord cannot forgive," the voice said from the other side of the slatted window. "What have you done that you wish to confess?"

"I killed two men."

The priest made a strangled sound, as if he'd choked on his own tongue. He coughed, drew in a loud breath, and coughed again.

"Shall I go get some water for you?"

The man cleared his throat. "No need. I am well. So you killed two men?" His voice rose higher as he spoke.

"They tried to kill me."

"Why did they try to kill you, my son?" His voice almost regained the peaceful tone he'd had at the beginning of the confession.

"They said my uncle sent them."

"Why would your uncle want to kill you?"

"I don't know. He probably wants my inheritance."

"So these men attacked you?"

"Yes. They attacked me with swords."

"And you killed them both?"

"Yes." Steffan had never had a priest ask so many questions. "Have you had anyone confess to murder before?"

"You are my first murderer. But Jesus says when we hate someone, we have committed murder already in our hearts. You did not hate these men?"

"No, I never saw them before."

"I see. Since it was in self-defense, your penance shall be light. You must spend today and the next day in prayer for these two men's families."

"Very well, I shall."

"And you may sleep tonight on a cot at the back of the church. Then if you will promise never to kill again, you will be absolved."

Steffan was silent as he thought about it. "If I am attacked again by my murderous uncle or his henchmen, I shall be forced to defend myself. I am not sure I can promise that."

The priest made a clicking sound, as if with his tongue against his teeth. "Well then, you must vow never to kill unless out of necessity to save yourself from being killed. And you must remember, vengeance belongs to the Lord."

Vengeance? It wasn't something he'd ever thought much about, but he did want to make sure his uncle was brought to justice if he was found to be guilty. His uncle deserved the greatest punishment for causing Steffan to kill two men.

"I shall do as you have said."

"Very good. Now seek peace, my son."

Steffan spent the two days at the little village church, kneeling in prayer. He prayed so much and so long, his mind sometimes wandered. And when the assigned penance was over, he was not sure if the heaviness on his shoulders was any lighter. Had his prayers made a difference? Had he prayed fervently enough to receive God's forgiveness?

It seemed only right for him to feel guilty for taking two lives. Was praying for two days enough penance for two men who would never have a chance to repent and ask for the remission of their sins?

Regardless, Steffan had had little choice. He had killed the men in self-defense. And now he rode toward the home he had not seen in almost two years.

Erlich and Agnes moved a bit faster now, and they reached Wolfberg before sunset.

As they neared the gate that led to the castle, Agnes whispered, "Not a word out of you, or Father will kill the mute boy." She glanced in Lenhart's direction.

Magdalen merely glared back. *You and your father will pay for hurting Lenhart.*

The cut over the boy's eye was still crusted over, and his expression reminded her of a stray dog she'd seen once in the village of Mallin when some boys threw rocks at it. The thought of anyone hurting a kindly, innocent boy like him made her blood boil.

She had to be brave like Avelina and watch for an opportunity to right this wrong.

The gate was high and impressive, and the guards wore the gold and burgundy livery of the dukedom of Wolfberg. In the gray twilight, the castle emerged from the trees as they passed through the gate. The five towers loomed over them, one giant round one in the middle and one square tower at each of the four corners of the massive building.

The guards halted their little group, and Erlich made a show of helping Agnes down out of the cart. He told them in a gruff voice, "This is the duke's future bride, Lady Magdalen of Mallin."

He bowed to Agnes, who stepped forward and smiled at the guards.

Their mouths went slack and they bowed respectfully, then stepped back to let them pass.

As Magdalen walked past, their gazes lingered on her and her brown woolen kirtle. One of them gave her a lascivious wink.

Magdalen had to look straight ahead to hide her expression. It seemed these men respected only a woman of noble rank, and nobility was only as deep as one's clothing.

A guard escorted them up the steps toward the door of the castle, while a servant came to lead away their horse, cart, and mules.

"Let this servant boy help with the horse and mules," Erlich said. "He is fit only to serve in the stables, since he is mute."

The guard nodded.

Magdalen picked up a bag of her things from the cart, but Agnes snatched it out of her hands, then shoved her own bag at Magdalen.

A woman appeared in the doorway and bowed to Agnes. "Lady Magdalen, I am Frau Clara, and I am the head house servant. Please allow me to welcome you to Wolfberg Castle."

"Thank you, Frau Clara. Before we go in"—Agnes pointed at Magdalen—"would you please send this servant girl to do some menial task outside the castle? She has displeased me greatly, and I no longer wish her to be my personal servant."

"I believe our most menial task would be seeing to the geese." She looked down her pointed nose at Magdalen.

"Yes, that is the best task for her." Agnes narrowed her eyes. "She cannot unleash her sharp tongue on anyone, gossiping and lying, which is her wont, for there will be no one around except the geese."

The guard hurried up the steps and through the front door, which was guarded by two more soldiers. He disappeared inside, then several moments later he returned, accompanied by four servants who rushed toward the cart, gathered all their things, and carried them back up the steps and into the castle.

A middle-aged man with dark hair mixed with white emerged from the castle door and met them at the top of the steps.

Frau Clara said, "Lady Magdalen, this is Lord Hazen, the duke's uncle."

Agnes smiled at Lord Hazen, a short, balding man with small eyes.

"Frau Clara," Lord Hazen said, "take Lady Magdalen's servants to their quarters while I show the lady to her room."

As Magdalen and Erlich walked away, Lord Hazen said, "The duke is not feeling well this evening, but I believe you will get a chance to meet him in the morning."

The rest of their conversation was lost as Frau Clara hurried Magdalen along.

"No dawdling. And if you think you shall be turning your sharp tongue on me, you shall regret it. We do not accept such behavior here from our servants. You will find yourself without a position at all. You can sleep in the maidservants' quarters and take your meals with the other servants. I expect Katrin will be pleased to let you take her place with the geese. She's been asking to be promoted to the kitchen."

Magdalen said nothing, her cheeks burning at the unjust scolding. What would the woman say when she discovered she'd been speaking this way to the actual Lady Magdalen?

And what if the duke did not realize Agnes was an imposter before Magdalen could convince him he was making a mistake? The thought of the Duke of Wolfberg marrying Agnes made Magdalen's stomach churn. Her people needed her to help them have enough food again. She could not allow Agnes to ruin Mallin.

How furious Mother would be at Magdalen for allowing this to happen.

Frau Clara led her outside. They passed the kitchen, which was a detached brick building only two feet from a side door of the large stone castle. They descended a series of steps built into the grass-covered mountainside until they curved to the right and revealed a gaggle of geese and a young woman beside them.

Frau Clara put her hands up and cupped the sides of her mouth. "Katrin!"

The maiden looked up in the last rays of the bright-orange sunset, herding the geese with a stick toward a small stone structure. The birds waddled right inside. Katrin closed the door and bent to lock it, then ascended the steps toward them.

"Katrin, this is Agnes. She is taking your place as goose girl, and you will go to work in the kitchen forthwith."

Katrin's eyes brightened as the smile stretched across her face. "Truly?"

"I don't know why you are so joyous. Working in the kitchen is hardly better than being the goose girl."

"Oh, it is so much better. Thank you, Frau Clara." She grasped the house frau's hand and grinned up at her. Then she turned to Magdalen and clasped her hand as well. "Thank you ever so much." Katrin darted past them, her feet tapping up the steps.

"You saw where Katrin put the geese. You will take them out every morning to forage in the meadows and along the hillside, wherever you find grass, and put them away every evening at sunset. If you lose any of the geese, you shall be severely punished. Now, come along and you can have your supper with the other servants."

Magdalen opened her mouth to ask a question, but Frau Clara set a fast pace as she climbed the steep steps again. Magdalen hurried to keep up.

They entered a dim room where the only light came in through one window. A man came in behind Magdalen carrying a torch. He lit the torches attached to the wall. Several other servants stood in line, accepting food from a woman handing out wooden bowls and bread rolls. Then they sat at a long wooden trestle table.

"Get in line for your food," Frau Clara said. "Katrin!" She called to the goose girl, who stood in the queue. "Show Agnes to the servants' quarters after you finish your meal, and help her find a bed tonight."

"Yes, Frau Clara." Katrin smiled at Magdalen and waved her over. "You can get in front of me, since you are new. Do you live here in Wolfberg? I've never seen you before."

Magdalen was thinking about how to answer her when a man yelled, "Who do you think you are?"

The man behind Katrin leaned toward Magdalen with a fierce scowl in his eyes. "You cannot cut in front of the rest of us. We were here before you."

"Leave her alone, Hanns." Katrin pushed his shoulder, even though she was a head shorter than he and only half as wide. "She just got here. Can't you see you're scaring her? But you don't scare me, so quiet down." She turned back to Magdalen and whispered, "Don't pay any attention to him."

"What's your name?" The man peered around Katrin's shoulder. He was smiling now and missing at least two teeth.

Katrin scrunched her face and shook her head. Someone distracted the man and he turned around.

"Thank you," Magdalen whispered.

"You don't want Hanns to ever start talking to you. He will make you want to slap his face in less time than it takes to tell him to go jump in the Baltic Sea." Katrin widened her eyes and shook her head again.

They had reached the front of the line. A large woman with a cloth around her hair handed them each a bowl and a roll of bread.

After they sat at the table, Magdalen lifted her spoon. It appeared to be pea porridge thickened with oats.

The woman sitting across from them made a growling sound deep in her throat. "Before the young duke left to get his education in Prague, we had meat in our porridge—a little bacon at least." She looked with disgust at the porridge on her spoon.

Katrin scooped some food into her mouth, then scrunched her face and quickly took a bite of her bread roll.

Magdalen's stomach rumbled, so she took a bite of the porridge, then followed it with a quick bite of bread. It did not taste terrible. But it also did not taste good. After a few more bites, she began to feel queasy, and she just finished her bread. The other servants mopped out their bowls with the last morsels of their bread, then put away the bowls and spoons.

"Not eating that?" Hanns stood behind her, pointing at her bowl.

She shook her head and gave it to him.

"Come," Katrin whispered, "before he asks you your name again."

They hustled out the door of the servants' dining hall. It was nearly dark now, and Katrin led her around the grassy area behind the castle. They proceeded toward a row of wooden buildings.

"Where did you say you came from?" Katrin asked.

"I am from Mallin."

"And what is your name?"

If she told Katrin the truth, word might get back to Agnes, and she might have Magdalen thrown into the dungeon. However, she could not bring herself to say her name was Agnes either.

"You can call me Maggie."

"Maggie? That's an unusual name. I know three other Katrins

in Arnsbaden. One came here with me and works as a servant in the castle—she does things like change the bedsheets for the duke's family. Although he hardly has any family anymore since his grandmother died two years ago. Only his uncle is staying in the castle, and Lord Hazen brought all new indoor servants with him from Arnsbaden. But the young duke has just arrived back in Wolfberg."

"He was in Prague, was he not?"

"Yes. They have a university there where men educate themselves about all sorts of matters. Been there for almost two years. I cannot imagine how there could be enough books to study to keep oneself occupied for two years, can you? He must know so much by now. What do you suppose he studied? I don't even know how to read or write, but it probably would be too difficult for me to learn."

"I could teach you to read," Magdalen said.

Katrin stared at her, open-mouthed. "Truly? And you think I could learn?"

"I should think so, and very quickly too. I enjoy teaching others to read."

"I am not sure Lord Hazen would approve of that." Katrin's brows drew together. "Perhaps you should not tell anyone you know how to read."

Yes, perhaps she had not been wise to reveal that information. She should be asking Katrin for information.

"When did you say the duke arrived back in Wolfberg?"

"Only in the last day or two."

But Katrin must be mistaken. Had the duke written asking her to marry him while he was still in Prague? Why would he ask her to come immediately to Wolfberg if he might not arrive before she did?

They entered the maidservants' barracks and Katrin led Magdalen to her bed. Magdalen stared down at the narrow bed she would have to sleep on . . . for how long? How long would she be a goose girl and herd geese? How long would people think she was a servant and Agnes was the daughter of a baron? Magdalen had thought she would be sleeping on a giant featherbed as the soon-to-be Duchess of Wolfberg.

And she had thought she would see the duke again, would be able to speak to him, to learn why he wanted to marry her and make her his wife. Now she wasn't sure if that would ever happen. What would become of Mallin's people? Would they all starve?

Somehow Magdalen would find a way to get back into the castle and warn the Duke of Wolfberg—in case he did not already realize it—that the woman pretending to be Lady Magdalen was actually an imposter.

Chapter Four

Steffan's beard had grown an inch long and his hair fell almost to his shoulders by the time he reached the northern regions and drew near to his beloved home. He'd traveled many days from Prague. He sold the two assassins' horses along the way, exchanged his fine clothes for those of a peasant, and when he entered the gates of Wolfberg, he was sure few people, if anyone, would recognize him.

The person who knew him best since his grandmother died was Jacob. His father's steward had been like a father to him since Steffan was six. Perhaps he could pay Jacob's sister a visit and she could help him speak to Jacob without alerting anyone at the castle, particularly his uncle.

He walked down *Almstrasse* toward the *Marktplatz* in the center of town. Then he turned down *Rathausstrasse* while trying to go back in his memory to the day when he'd gone with Jacob to visit his sister. The air had been slightly cool, as it was late summer or early autumn, not so different from today. Steffan must have been about twelve years old, as his head barely reached to Jacob's shoulder.

They'd entered an abode with large wooden beams framing

the front door with intricately carved animals and birds, and Steffan distinctly remembered a rooster and a mule by his head as he walked in.

There. Steffan stepped up to the door and knocked.

A young maiden answered the door. *"Kann ich Ihnen helfen?"*

"Guten Tag, Fräulein. Can you tell me if the sister of Jacob Klein lives here?"

"Come in," a woman from inside the house called out. "I am Frau Binder, Jacob Klein's sister."

The young servant who had answered the door hurried away as an older woman stepped forward. She wore a kerchief over her gray hair and smiled out of a round face that reminded him of Jacob.

"May I know your name?" she asked.

"My name is Steffan. I'm looking for Jacob Klein. Does he still live at the castle?"

"Ach, but *nein."* The woman seemed to study him more closely. "My brother died several months ago."

Steffan's heart crashed against his chest, then sank. "I am very sad to hear that." His throat was so tight it was hard to speak.

"You knew him?"

"Ja, I met him when I was a boy. He was very kind."

"He was indeed. Won't you sit down and let me send the servant for some cool water and a bit of bread and butter?"

"Danke schön. That is very kind of you."

He would never see Jacob again. How could this be true? He felt so numb he was not sure he could keep his wits about him.

The servant brought a goblet of water for him and a wooden serving tray with bread, butter, and a knife.

"How is it you have not heard of Jacob's death? Most of the town came to the burial."

"I have been away."

Frau Binder's brow wrinkled. She seemed about to speak, then only stared down at the floor.

"Frau Binder, I know you don't remember me, but I was very close to Jacob. If something is amiss at the castle, I pray you would tell me."

She considered his face, as though discerning his character. "You are the duke."

Steffan sat back. "How did you know?"

"What other young man would be asking for Jacob after being away? Besides that, I remember you as a boy. You have the same brown eyes."

He rubbed a hand down his beard. "I see my disguise is not as effective as I'd hoped."

"I think you will be able to fool most people. Just don't look directly into people's eyes. That is a sure sign you are not a peasant."

He nodded at the good advice. He'd rarely been around peasants enough to observe them. Even at the university in Prague he'd spent most of his time with wealthy burghers' sons. Few people there knew he was a duke, and he'd enjoyed blending in. Everyone assumed he was an ordinary, though wealthy, young man.

"There is another reason I recognized you. My brother told me, not long before he died, that you might come looking for something. He said to give you this note." She went to the hearth, removed a loose stone from the front, and pulled out a small rolled-up parchment tied with string.

Steffan took it from her hand, then untied and unrolled it.

I hid your portrait in the castle in the place where you used to play as a small child.

Jacob's last words to him. But where did he mean? Steffan and his sister had played all over the castle. He would have to think more about this later. "Do you have a cook fire?"

Frau Binder led him to the kitchen. Steffan threw the small parchment in the flames and watched it burn until it was nothing but ash.

"Does anyone know you are in Wolfberg?" she asked as she led him back inside the house.

"No. But you must tell me what has been happening here."

"Lord Hazen came to Wolfberg and sent away all the servants at the castle and replaced them with people from his own town of Arnsbaden. Then Jacob fell down the stairs at the castle and broke his neck and died." She lowered her voice. "I do not think it was an accident. It is very likely that Lord Hazen had him killed because he was too loyal to you. Jacob must have discovered his evil intentions."

"My uncle sent two men to have me killed as well."

"Saints above." Frau Binder exhaled and made the sign of the cross over her chest. "God shall have His vengeance on the man for killing my poor brother. But to have the lack of natural feeling to kill his own nephew . . . And he will try again."

"Only if he discovers I'm still alive. You must not tell anyone you spoke to me."

"*Nein*, of course not."

"But I will need a way to get into the castle. I could work as a servant or guard perhaps."

"I don't know anyone at the castle anymore who could give you work. And wouldn't that be too dangerous? Lord Hazen could recognize you."

"I have to get inside the castle. When Lord Hazen tells

everyone that I am dead, that portrait is one of the only things that can prove I am the Duke of Wolfberg."

"You think he will tell King Karl that you are dead so he can take over Wolfberg?"

"Yes."

She twisted her mouth and stared at the floor. "I do know one person, the steward in charge of the outdoor servants who take care of the livestock."

"Whatever it takes to keep me close to the castle."

Magdalen awoke to her stomach growling. She got dressed and went with Katrin to the servants' dining hall, where they had barley bread and oat pottage. Both were tasteless, but Magdalen ate them, swallowing the best she could and washing it down with the weak fermented drink that came from a large wooden cask in the corner of the room. The drink smelled bad and tasted worse, but she drank it anyway.

She had slept better than she might have imagined, but she had been exhausted from the tense day and the long trip. Now she turned her mind to getting into the castle and finding the duke.

She walked outside with Katrin, who pointed down the side of the castle mount at the little wooden goose pen.

"The geese are mostly gentle and even like to be petted, but stay away from the one with the black spot on his beak. He bites."

Magdalen nodded absently. She'd nearly forgotten she was supposed to take care of the geese.

"Now I must go to work in the kitchen, but I shall try to come this afternoon, if the cook allows it, to tell you all of their names—the geese, I mean. They are very clever and know when you are calling them. Farewell." Katrin waved as she hurried back toward the brick building.

No one seemed to be around the back of the castle. She turned and stared up at the huge stone building, with its five towers and multitude of windows. A door caught her eye. She lifted her skirts and ran up the hill.

She reached the door, out of breath and panting. Waiting for her breathing to slow, she put her hand on the iron handle. She pulled down on it, but it did not move. She tried again, using all her strength to open the wooden door, but the handle did not budge.

If she was to save herself, she had to get into this castle. She continued around to the west side of the enormous stone building and found another door, identical to the one on the back. People milled about in the bailey. A few gathered around the well, and some others stood in front of the blacksmith's little shop.

Magdalen tried to look inconspicuous as she put her hand on the handle. She held her breath as she pulled down. It opened! She pulled the door farther open and stepped inside.

"Who are you?" A guard stood in front of her. "This door is not for servants."

Magdalen's cheeks burned. How dare he speak to her like that? She opened her mouth to scold him but then remembered . . . she was a servant.

"I . . . I need to see Frau Clara."

"Go through the kitchen." He seemed to thrust out his chest, as if to push her back out.

"Very well." She had little choice but to turn around and leave. The soldier slammed the door behind her.

All the people around her—the servants at the well, the men standing about the blacksmith stall—stared at her. She pretended not to notice them and walked back the way she had come.

The brick kitchen building was connected to the main castle by a brick enclosure that provided no outside entry. She'd have to go through the kitchen door.

She walked toward it. "Please don't let anyone see me or ask me what I'm doing," she whispered.

Magdalen stepped inside the kitchen. Immediately, eight pairs of eyes focused on her.

"Maggie." Katrin stood with several other women either chopping vegetables or kneading bread at a table in the center of the room. A fire was burning in the large fireplace.

Katrin came toward her. "Are you well? Are the geese—?"

Magdalen spoke softly. "I need to speak to Frau Clara. I'm just going inside for a moment—" She took a step toward the enclosure that led into the castle.

"Where are you going?" the cook shouted. "You cannot go in there. Who are you?"

"She is the goose girl," Katrin said. "Her name is Maggie, and she has only just arrived."

"If she's the goose girl, then why isn't she tending the geese?" The middle-aged woman looked askance at Magdalen.

She should try to talk her way in, but what should she say? Every person was staring at her, and two young maidens snickered, hiding their mouths behind their hands.

"I shall speak to Frau Clara later. Excuse me." Magdalen went back out the door. A titter of laughter followed her.

Her cheeks burned. She would have to sneak in another way, another time, as more servants finished their morning meal and headed out to work. They stared at her. In a place where people rarely came and went, of course they stared. She was a stranger. It was the same in Mallin. When someone new arrived, everyone whispered about them until they could discover everything about the person. But no one had ever treated her this way. Tears stung her eyes. Was she destined to be scorned for the rest of her life?

Chapter Five

Magdalen ducked her head and ran down the hill toward the goose pen.

The geese started honking. Her hand shook as she unlatched the gate. What did she know about taking care of geese?

The goose girl at home would herd the geese with a long, thin, flexible stick. Magdalen looked around and saw just such a stick lying on top of the low pen. She picked it up and opened the door to let the geese out.

The large gray birds flocked out the door, some of them extending their wings, as if stretching after being cramped. A few of them looked at Magdalen and honked.

What was she to do now? Of course they were surprised to see her and not Katrin. Would they keep honking until people came to see what was the matter?

She slapped the ground twice with the long, limber stick. The geese started waddling one behind the other down the little path of worn grass down the side of the gentle hill, and the honking lessened until only one goose was still raising a ruckus. Eventually the noisy one honked less enthusiastically.

She had to get into the castle as soon as possible. What would she do with all these geese? She had no idea if they could be left alone. At the bottom of the hillside, the geese spread out and nibbled at the green grass with their little orange beaks.

Magdalen became more and more aware of a sound, something like the wind rushing through treetops, but more like a dull, far-off roar. Where was it coming from? But she had no time to chase the sound. She had to figure out what to do with the geese.

Some of them were smaller than the others. Perhaps those were the goslings. She seemed to remember that the geese that nested in the area around the lake near the back of her home in Mallin had babies following them around in the spring and summer. These must be the goslings, as they were a bit fuzzier than the larger ones, while the larger ones seemed to be losing some of their feathers.

The birds seemed restless, occasionally honking at each other or flapping their wings. But at least none of them were trying to run away. Magdalen sat on the grass and rubbed her eyes.

What was the duke doing at this moment? Had he met with Agnes over a large breakfast in the Great Hall? Or was Agnes sleeping late and reveling in her newfound luxury?

Magdalen should probably hate Agnes. She still could hardly believe what she had done. What had driven the maidservant to do something so drastic? If she were found out—and she certainly would be—dire consequences for her actions would ensue. Would the Duke of Wolfberg have her put to death? Magdalen supposed she could beg the duke to banish Agnes instead. Perhaps they could send her and her father away to the Kievan Rus region where the savage Cossacks lived, or even to the north country where it was rarely ever warm. Then they would be sorry for the way they treated Magdalen.

What she needed was a plan to get into the castle and speak to the duke. She had to tell him *she* was Lady Magdalen. Could she disguise herself as an indoor servant? What did they wear? Frau Clara wore a white kerchief on her head. Now that she thought of it, she remembered another house servant wearing the same white kerchief and . . . a green kirtle. Or was it blue? With the gray sleeves of her underdress showing. Perhaps she could find the laundry and snatch some clothing.

She stood and looked around. Should she leave the geese? Though they were pecking at the grass, they mostly stayed together as a group, except for one goose that was waddling away from the others.

She ran toward the goose that had wandered astray. What had Frau Clara said? If she lost a goose she would be "severely punished."

As Magdalen got closer, it looked up and saw her and bolted the other way.

"No, no. Come back." She clenched her teeth. Would more geese wander away while she was chasing this one?

She worked at sneaking around it. When she was on the other side, she slapped the ground with the stick. "Go on, goose. Go back with your friends. Go on." But instead of moving, he stretched his neck toward her and let out a loud honk.

"I'm not afraid of you. Now go!" She slapped her stick on the ground to punctuate her words.

He flapped his wings and honked again.

Oh God, please help me. I have no idea how to make this lackwitted bird do anything I want it to.

The goose put its head down to pluck at the grass.

"Go on, I said. Go." She tapped its tail feathers with the stick.

Gradually the errant goose waddled its way back toward the rest of the flock. They were all intent on eating, their heads bent to the ground.

"Stay." Maybe this would not be so difficult after all.

Magdalen hurried up the hill and found the path that would take her to the castle. She ran, glancing back to make sure none of the geese followed her. They did not, so she kept running.

When she reached the castle, she slowed so as not to attract attention to herself. She was breathing hard as she walked around to the front and watched as people came and went through the gate. A steep cliff and deep ravine around this side of the castle formed a natural barrier, and the only way into the castle yard was a bridge over the ravine, with a gatehouse on the bridge.

A cart rolled through the gate, drawn by a mule with a man leading it. Several people milled around the courtyard. Some maidservants were gathered to one side, standing around a fire and a huge black cauldron. Were these the laundresses?

Magdalen moved closer, skirting as close to the edge of the ravine as possible, hoping no one would notice her. On the other side of the women near the cauldron was a clothesline with several gray underdresses, white kerchiefs, and blue kirtles hanging along it. Just what she was looking for.

Magdalen hid behind a bush. She eyed the garments, trying to decide which kirtle would best fit her. The women were pulling items out of the cauldron and laying them on the ground to cool. Then two women would stretch out a cooled piece of clothing and twist and squeeze it between them. They did not seem to be paying any attention to the apparel on the line.

Magdalen sprang forward. She flipped a kerchief off the line, then a blue kirtle, tucked them under her arm, and raced for cover. She crouched behind the nearest bush.

No one yelled. No one ran after her. She waited until her breathing slowed. Sweat was dampening her underarms. Never had she stolen anything. Surely God would forgive her for trying to save the duke from marrying Agnes—as well as trying to save herself and her people.

Magdalen moved away from the ravine and found a stand of trees. She stared down at the clothes. Her hands were shaking. But she couldn't approach the same guard again, not so soon after he had turned her away. The other back door was locked, and the door through the kitchen was swarming with the maidservants who had snickered at her less than an hour ago. The only other door was the front door, and she would probably get a harsh scolding if she endeavored to go through it.

She would simply hide the clothes under her bed in the servants' barracks until she could get past the back-door guard or enter the kitchen without being seen.

When she neared the long wooden building, she saw several other servants congregated out front. So she steered herself back toward the hill where she'd left the birds.

The geese were still grazing on the grass, but they had spread out. She glanced around. Where could she hide the clothes? A pile of brush at the edge of the woods caught her eye. She approached, lifted the branches, and stuffed the stolen clothing underneath. The blue and white still showed through the cracks. She found a few rocks and piled them on top. There. That was the best she could do.

Magdalen headed back toward the geese. Her hands still shook and sweat tickled her forehead. She wiped her face with her sleeve.

"Oh no." Some of the geese were wandering away. One was almost in the trees, and another was scores of feet away, nearly out of sight.

She couldn't lose the geese, even if she would not have charge of them much longer. They would be easy prey for a fox or wolf or whatever predatory animals lived in this region.

She focused on the long stick, which lay just on the other side of a large goose who lifted its head and took a step toward her.

She moved toward the goose, intent on retrieving her stick. It honked and Magdalen jumped back. Then it lifted its enormous wings and flapped once, twice, then flew at her face. She raised her arm to protect herself. Its beak sliced into her skin as if it were a knife.

Magdalen screamed, flailing at the enormous bird.

"Maggie!" a voice called.

The vicious bird flapped away, still honking at her, as Katrin hurried down the path toward her.

"Are you all right?" Katrin stared at Magdalen's arm where a line of blood was forming. "That mean old Gus. Shoo!" Katrin turned and threw out her arms, flapping them at the goose. "You have done it now!" She chased him away toward the rest of the geese, picked up the long stick off the ground where Magdalen had left it, and went after the goose that had wandered so far across the hillside.

Had Katrin seen her steal the clothes and hide them?

Blood oozed out of the spot on her forearm where the goose had bitten her. She didn't even know geese could bite.

She looked around for something with which to wipe it. Nothing—except for the stolen clothes, and she'd never use them for that.

Katrin was still a long way off, shooing the straying geese back toward the others. Magdalen stared at her bleeding arm and tears filled her eyes. "What did I ever do to you, you stupid goose?" Her bottom lip trembled, and she clamped it between her teeth. What had she done to deserve being thrown out to tend geese? She was supposed to marry a duke.

A tear escaped and ran down her cheek. She hastily wiped it on her sleeve. Her mother would die of shame to see her wiping her face with her sleeve or herding geese. But her mother was not here and Magdalen was glad. Mother hated tears—though she often used them for her own purposes.

Katrin finished herding the geese into a smaller group, then hurried toward her. "Gus is prone to bite. You have to be careful around him." Katrin lifted her apron and dabbed at the blood on Magdalen's forearm. "I'm so sorry. I should have helped get the geese accustomed to you. I wasn't thinking. Come. We'll take the geese to the spring so you can wash this off."

Katrin used the stick to get their attention and then walked in front of them. They followed her as if she were their mother, and she took them down a little path on the side of the hill until they came to a small glade of trees.

A trickle of water bubbled up out of the ground, flowed a few feet, then formed a pool before trickling on down as a little stream.

"This is where I take the geese every day for a drink. I'm sorry I did not show you. I suppose Frau Clara didn't consider that you would need help. It's not as if she has ever concerned herself with me. The indoor servants think they are so much higher than the outdoor servants." Katrin rolled her eyes.

She squatted by the spring and dipped her apron in the clear water, then stood and wiped the rest of the blood from Magdalen's arm. "I wish I had a cloth so I could fashion a bandage for it."

"It is nothing. It will cease bleeding soon."

"You will have to stand up to Gus. He thinks he is the king. You must show him that you are bigger and stronger." Katrin pressed a corner of her apron on Magdalen's wound while she talked. "The rest is easy. Just lead them to the water once or twice a day, make sure none of them wander off, then lead them back to their pen just before sunset."

Magdalen nodded.

"Oh, and Lord Hazen made an announcement this morning. The duke apparently was sick when he arrived from Prague, and Lord Hazen wanted him to have time to rest from his trip and recover his full health before letting people know he had returned."

Magdalen's heart jumped at hearing someone mention the duke.

"And his betrothed, Lady Magdalen, has arrived from Mallin. He only just announced it."

"The duke and Lady Magdalen have seen each other?"

"They have now, I suppose." Katrin sighed. "She is a fortunate woman. Can you imagine marrying the Duke of Wolfberg and living in Wolfberg Castle? It is so grand."

"I can imagine it." The hollow space in her chest seemed to swallow up her hope.

Agnes must have fooled the duke.

Chapter Six

Magdalen rose, dressed, and skipped breaking her fast, since the food was so disgusting anyway.

After the other maidens had left, including Katrin, Magdalen got on her knees, reached under her bed where she had hidden the blue dress and white headscarf, and pulled them out. As she put them on she imagined confronting the duke, telling him that Agnes was not the real Lady Magdalen.

He would look into her eyes and exclaim, "It is you!" He would kneel in front of her and say, "My dear Lady Magdalen. Please allow me to tell you how sorry I am for all that you have suffered at the hands of this woman and her father. I shall banish them forever."

Then he would kiss her hand and promise to love and cherish her always.

She whispered, "Oh, God, Lord above, help me. Don't let me get turned away at the door. Help me find the duke, and let him believe that I am who I say I am. Thwart the plans of the wicked and the deceitful"—she pictured Agnes's and Erlich's faces—"save me, Jesus, from their plot, and give me success today."

She lifted her eyes heavenward and breathed an "Amen"

before she tied the kerchief around her hair at the back of her neck.

She stuck her head out of the barracks doorway and glanced around. A few people mingled around the side of the castle, but no one looked her way. She hurried out and focused on the door where the guard had turned her away the day before. Her heart seemed to tremble as she headed straight for it.

Magdalen grasped the handle, opened it quickly, and stepped inside.

"Who goes there?" A guard advanced toward her.

"I am Maggie, a new upstairs servant. I stepped out to speak with my brother, but I must get back to my duties now. Excuse me." She curtsied and rushed away without waiting for his permission.

The back of her neck prickled as she listened for him to call her back, to call her a liar, but she kept walking. Only silence loomed behind her.

Her heart thumped hard as she hastened through the corridor. Was this the way to the stairs? She had no idea, but she kept going, trying to look confident. Finally, she came to a back staircase made of unpolished wood—the servants' stairs. She practically ran to them and hurried up the narrow steps. When she reached the next floor, she had to decide whether to go up to the next floor or search this one. Not wishing to lose any time, she ventured out into the corridor.

A long hallway stretched out in front of her with doors along either side. How could she know what she might find if she opened a door? Magdalen could be tossed out of the castle before she found the duke.

This was madness. She had no idea where his bedchamber was, and he might still be in bed. But if he was up this early, he might be in the Great Hall breaking his fast, especially since he had a guest in the form of Lady Magdalen. Didn't he realize she wasn't the same woman he had danced with at Thornbeck? Or did he think Agnes was to be his bride?

Magdalen walked a few more feet, listening, hoping to hear the duke's voice. But she heard not a single sound.

She turned and went back down the servants' stairs. Still she saw no one. Apparently the inhabitants of Wolfberg Castle were not early risers. Otherwise, servants would be scurrying up the stairs bringing whatever Lord Hazen, "Lady Magdalen," and the Duke of Wolfberg wanted or needed.

At the bottom of the stairs she encountered another guard. She ducked her head and walked by him as if she knew exactly where she was going. Her throat went dry until she was past him.

She found her way to the Great Hall. It was not hard to find since it was the largest room in the castle. She approached the door carefully and peeked inside—empty of people except for one maidservant cleaning the table. Did she dare ask if the duke would be coming down for breakfast?

She could barely breathe at the thought of being ordered out, so she took a step back and pressed herself against the wall, but her gray underdress sleeves and white kerchief practically glowed, even in the small amount of light in the windowless corridor. She looked all around her, walked a few feet away, and ducked into a doorway.

The room was dark, having no window or candle or torch. She stood just inside and watched the Great Hall door. Soon servants milled around, setting goblets and platters of bread on the table.

Her hands trembled. Would she see the duke? Would he recognize her? What would he say? What should *she* say?

She stood as still as she could, trying not to blink, but still no one came. The servants seemed to disappear as well.

Magdalen leaned her shoulder against the door frame as she continued to watch the entrance to the Great Hall. She yawned, her sleepiness reminding her of the dream she had the night before, of ferocious wolves attacking the geese while she watched, helpless and horrified.

One wolf raced toward her, snarling as he stared at her with hostile yellow eyes. Three or four other wolves attacked the geese, carrying them off amid the most awful honking.

"Please stop." It was futile to beg the hungry wolves not to take them. Finally, they left, having decimated her gaggle of geese. She sat down and cried in frustration, then awakened with tears under her eyes, that helpless feeling almost overwhelming her.

But she was not helpless. She was here in the castle, ready to use her voice to stand up for herself and for Lenhart and all the people of Mallin. She would not let Agnes get away with stealing her identity.

Voices and footsteps sounded on the flagstone floor. Finally, someone was approaching. She took a step back into the shadows of the room and clenched her hands together as she tried not to move.

Two people came into view: Agnes—Magdalen could tell by her walk and the way she held her head and shoulders—and the other was a young man.

The young man should be the Duke of Wolfberg, but somehow she wasn't sure. He was tall, and he was thin, and the duke was both of those things, but something did not look right about him, though she was only seeing him from the side and behind.

The couple entered the Great Hall. Agnes was talking and laughing, and hatred rose in Magdalen like bile in a sick person's throat. It was so strong it seemed to choke her for a moment as she took a step toward the Great Hall.

No. She could not think like that, especially not now. She pushed her rage away, ignoring Agnes and her high-pitched voice, and followed several feet behind them. She had to speak to the duke.

It had been more than two years since they'd seen each other. Could he believe Agnes over her?

But the longer she watched the opulently dressed man walk across the expansive floor, his heels clicking on the polished stone, the more she kept thinking . . .

"That is not the duke." She whispered the words into the empty corridor. His head was all wrong—too round—and his hair hung down on his neck, whereas the duke's hair was perfectly cropped. Still, he could have changed his hair. But this man's manner was hesitant and halting—the way he walked and the way he hovered next to Agnes and moved his hand toward her back, then pulled it away without touching her.

This man's hair was the same brown color, but the Duke of Wolfberg's hair had been thicker and not as straight.

Magdalen crept up to the doorway to the Great Hall and peered inside. Agnes and the young man seated themselves next to each other at the high end of the table on the dais. She could see his face now, and she was more confused than ever. He had regular, even features, but was the duke's skin as white as this man's? Were his lips as thin? She tried to picture the duke as he had looked when she had danced with him. Her spirit told her this was not the same man.

"What are you doing here?"

A man's voice made Magdalen jump. She ducked her head, recognizing the duke's uncle. She curtsied.

"Get back to your duties."

"Yes, my lord." Keeping her head down, Magdalen scurried away.

Over her shoulder she saw Lord Hazen disappear into the Great Hall.

Magdalen hurried toward the other side of the Great Hall where the servants would be coming and going.

A young male servant carrying a pitcher came from the kitchen. He passed through the back doorway into the Great Hall. He had not noticed her. A few minutes later, he rushed back out.

"Please, may I ask you a question?" Magdalen stepped quickly toward the young man.

"Yes? What is it?" Interest seemed to light his eyes as he stopped and gave her his full attention, looking her over.

"Can you tell me"—Magdalen kept her voice low—"who is that man sitting in the Great Hall?"

"The young man is the Duke of Wolfberg and the older man is his uncle, Lord Hazen."

"Are you certain? Forgive me, but I need to know if that young man is definitely the Duke of Wolfberg."

"That is what they tell me. He just returned after being away from Wolfberg for two years."

"Were you here before he left?"

"No." He was smiling now as he seemed to be staring at her lips. "What is your name? I have not seen you before."

"Perhaps I shall see you at mealtime. Thank you for this information." She backed away from him even as she spoke.

"Come to the kitchen with me."

"I must go now. Back to my duties." She turned and fled.

A heaviness settled over her chest. What was happening here? Was there an imposter in the duke's place?

What could she do? Who could she turn to? She hurried back toward the door she had come in through before someone who knew all the indoor servants confronted her.

The same guard who had let her into the castle was still guarding the door. He stared at her as she approached. He opened his mouth, as if about to say something.

"Frau Clara sent me to fetch . . ." She smiled at him and let her voice trail off as she reached the door. She left as the door shut behind her.

She ran to the maidservants' barracks. Inside the empty room, she knelt beside her bed. Tears leaked out as she put her hands over her face. "God, I'm so afraid . . . so alone. What do I do? Where do I turn?"

She had put all her hope in finding the duke and convincing him she was Lady Magdalen. Now she did not even know who the duke was. Had the man at Thornbeck Castle two years ago been a pretender? Or was this man talking with Agnes in the Great Hall the imposter? And how could she ever prove her identity now?

She had to get someone to help her, someone like the Margrave of Thornbeck who was married to her friend Avelina. They would certainly help her figure out what was going on here in Wolfberg and with the duke. But how would she get to them? They lived at least a two-day journey from Wolfberg to the southwest, while Mallin was to the southeast. It was not safe for her to travel alone, but who would she ask to accompany her?

"God, help me. Please. I don't want to be lost and alone, and I don't want to be a goose girl."

Steffan approached the castle, a feeling of anticipation in his heart. He had not seen his home in nearly two years, and he had also not seen any familiar faces. What had happened to all of his loyal servants whom he had grown up with? People he loved and who loved him? According to Frau Binder, the indoor servants had been ousted from their positions, but perhaps he would at least get to see his favorite horse groomer, Ansel, who had taught him as a small child how to ride a horse.

As he approached the stables, a man he did not recognize walked out and gave him a sullen stare.

"I'm looking for Gregor, the man in charge of the outdoor servants."

"He's at the blacksmith's on the other side of the castle." The middle-aged man spit on the ground and gestured with his arm.

"Thank you. And I was wondering . . . is Ansel still working here at the stables?"

"Never heard of any Ansel here."

Steffan nodded and moved on, walking across the bailey and around the castle. How could everyone he ever knew have vanished? Surely his servants had not all been killed, as Jacob had been. Were they living in the village below, struggling to survive? Or had his uncle banished them from the region?

Magdalen had been watching the geese for a week. She was learning which of them were friendly and liked to have their backs stroked and which she should stay away from, like Gus.

She walked behind the waddling birds as she guided them to their little shed, closed the door, and locked it. Then she trudged the rest of the way up the hill to the servants' dining hall.

As usual Katrin joined her as they lined up to receive their food. "There is a new shepherd." She whispered loud enough for Magdalen to hear over the rest of the servants' voices. "I think he is very handsome. See him there?"

Magdalen turned to see a man walking along the far wall of the dining hall, then finding a seat at the table. She couldn't help but stare. He looked so familiar. He looked like . . . the Duke of Wolfberg.

Could he possibly be the duke? This man had a beard, and he wore coarse woolen clothing, the kind poor peasants and outdoor servants wore. Besides that, he seemed larger, broader in the shoulders, and more muscular. It was certainly possible that the duke might have grown a bit larger, since he was only nineteen when she met him, and he could have grown a beard, but he would not be working as a shepherd.

She tried not to stare, especially since Katrin found the man handsome.

They got their food, and Katrin led her to a seat not far from the new shepherd. Again, Magdalen could not help looking at him. Did he have the same eyes? The same brown hair? The same mouth? It was so difficult to remember exact features from two years ago. Were his mannerisms the same? He did sit very tall and straight, reminding her of the duke.

Besides the fact that he wore the clothing of a shepherd, he had a scowl on his face, an angry wrinkle between his brows. The Duke of Wolfberg had nearly always been smiling, a kind, mild expression on his face. Still, that did not prove it wasn't him.

The man's head was down as he stared at his food. Tonight was frumenty. It was bland and grainy, similar to thick pea soup, but Magdalen was getting used to the meatless meals. No doubt it resembled what her people were eating.

"What are these bits that are sometimes in our food?" Magdalen pointed at a small piece of something fatty on her spoon.

"Oh, that is bacon," Katrin said. "Have you never had it?"

She shook her head. "It tastes quite good in the evening stews. I'd like to have a bowl of only bacon someday."

Katrin laughed. "So would we all."

Magdalen tried to eat the rest of her food without attracting attention. She had found that one or two of the male servants could be aggressive in the way they asked her to accompany them somewhere in the evenings after their duties had been attended to.

The maidservant on Katrin's other side started talking to her, and Magdalen focused on finishing her meal. When she was almost done, Katrin turned to her and grabbed her arm.

"Maggie! I almost forgot to tell you. Brigitta says that Frau Clara said that the duke is getting married in a week. We shall have a share of the feast." Katrin's eyes were wide and bright.

Magdalen's stomach sank. Would the duke marry Agnes? Would Magdalen be doomed to tend geese for the rest of her life? And where was the man she had met in Thornbeck, the one who claimed to be the Duke of Wolfberg? Had this shepherd been masquerading as a duke, as Avelina had pretended to be an earl's daughter?

She stared down at her bowl and its contents. Life had become so confusing ever since she left Mallin. She'd been so glad to get away, to feel as though she was about to live a full life, the life of an adult, away from her mother and her cruel words, which often felt like a load of bricks falling on her shoulders. But at least she'd had food, her own bed, and her loving sisters in Mallin. There she had been Lady Magdalen, an important person everyone knew.

Now she felt as if the ground had given way beneath her and the world had tipped upside down.

She had to do something. She could not continue taking care of geese and pretending to be an uneducated servant girl. Tomorrow she would not be quite so tired. Tomorrow she would think in the manner of her brave friend Avelina, and Magdalen would come up with a plan of action.

Chapter Seven

Steffan clenched his fists as he neared the door on the back side of the castle. The door was locked, as always. He used the key, quickly opened the door, and put the key back in his pocket.

Time was running out. It was only a few days before Alexander would wed Lady Magdalen. Steffan made his way to the back stairs. He climbed the empty staircase to the third floor, to his own bedchamber. To keep up the farce, would Lord Hazen have given his son the duke's bedchamber?

Steffan walked straight to his own door and opened it. He stepped inside.

The room was completely dark. He strode to the window. If Alexander was here, Steffan welcomed the confrontation. He could hardly wait to demand Alexander admit to him what he and his father had plotted against him.

He could see by the moonlight coming through the window, but no one was in the chamber. It looked just as it had when he left it. He walked to the trunk against the wall and opened it. Steffan's clothing and belongings still lay inside. Nothing was out of place and nothing had been added to the room.

If Alexander was not sleeping here, then where was he sleeping?

Steffan left the room and looked up and down the hallway. He kept the hood over his head in case he ran into his uncle or his cousin.

He heard voices and footsteps.

Steffan ducked back into his bedchamber, leaving the door open just a crack.

The voices came closer. One was his cousin Alexander, he was sure of it. The other was a woman. They must have stopped before passing Steffan's hiding place. He could not make out what they were saying.

A third set of footsteps approached. "Ah, the two lovers await their forthcoming wedding," a voice boomed. His uncle, Lord Hazen. He'd know that loud, obnoxious voice anywhere.

"Father, don't embarrass Lady Magdalen."

Lady Magdalen. How could she be fooled into thinking his chicken-hearted cousin was him?

Lord Hazen blustered on. "I'm not embarrassing her. She is as ready to have the vows said as you are. Look at her grin!"

Did Lady Magdalen believe Alexander was the duke? Perhaps she was too afraid to try to escape him and Lord Hazen.

Steffan took the chance of opening the door a bit more and putting his head out so he could see.

The three of them were in the corridor several yards away, standing in front of a bedchamber door. He would wait until Alexander and his father were gone and then Steffan would slip into her room and assure her that she did not have to marry his cousin. He'd sneak her out of the castle and take her to safety, and then he'd figure a way to save both of them.

Soon Lord Hazen's voice tapered off. Steffan stuck his head out again and—Lady Magdalen was kissing Alexander!

His stomach roiled. What madness was this?

He had not thought she could be so easily duped by Alexander. How could she kiss such a whey-faced, long-necked, fox-nosed man like him?

He found himself disliking the girl. Even though he had not intended to marry Lady Magdalen—his uncle had no doubt forged his name and sealed the proposal letter with his signet ring—Steffan had found her interesting and lovely when they talked together at Lord Thornbeck's ball. They had read a lot of the same books, and she had a kind, compassionate manner. Indeed, he'd spent most of the ball at Thornbeck talking with her.

Finally, Alexander's shuffling footsteps passed right by where Steffan stood hidden behind his own bedchamber door. He longed to reach out, clap a hand over Alexander's mouth, drag him into the room, and threaten him with immediate death if he did not reveal his true identity.

Steffan could not kill Alexander after promising the priest he would only kill in self-defense. But his cousin did not have to know that.

He had to be wise, to wait until he had proof before making his claims known to the world.

His cousin continued to the stairs and soon was gone. Was he going to Steffan's father's bedchamber? Was Alexander sleeping in Steffan's dead father's bed? Heat rose to his forehead as he itched to chase after him and strangle him for his insolence.

He took a deep breath. It was not enough. He dragged in another and another. Finally, his breathing had calmed enough to allow him to proceed quietly down the hall to Lady Magdalen's chamber.

Attempting not to make a sound, he tried her door. The handle did not even creak as he turned it. Ever so slowly, he pushed the door open and stepped inside.

No one screamed. In fact, he did not see anyone in the room at all. Had he gotten the wrong door? But then he heard voices from an adjoining room. The door between the two rooms was partially open, enough for him to see and hear two women talking, probably Lady Magdalen and her maidservant.

He took a step toward them, intent on telling Lady Magdalen the truth and taking her away from here. But something made him stop. He shifted until he could see the two women better.

The servant was wearing the usual white kerchief and blue sleeveless overdress. She was brushing Lady Magdalen's hair while the lady sat on a stool. Lady Magdalen was instructing the servant on how she wanted her hair braided for her night's sleep.

"Yes, Lady Magdalen." The servant put down the brush and started to braid.

The woman's hair seemed somehow different from Lady Magdalen's, and when she turned her head to look at the maidservant . . . the eyes and the mouth were all wrong. Even the shape of her face was wrong.

That woman was not Lady Magdalen.

His mind raced as he took a step back. The two women had not seen him, so he kept moving backward as quietly as possible as he let himself back into the corridor.

He raised a hand to his head. "What is happening?" he whispered. He shook his head. There was no reason to save the lovely and interesting Lady Magdalen from his dim-witted cousin because this woman was not her.

"Ho, there," a guard called from the other end of the corridor. "What are you doing in front of Lady Magdalen's door?"

"Oh, I am looking for Lord Hazen." Steffan walked toward the guard. "He asked me to come and—" Steffan struck the back of the man's neck at the base of his skull, knocking him to the floor. Then he ran as fast as he could down the stairs, taking them three at a time, and leapt for the back door.

He ran outside, then locked the door with his key. He walked at a normal pace toward the menservants' barracks.

His heart was pounding, partially from his encounter with the guard and from running down all those stairs, but also because of his thoughts.

Who is that woman who was kissing Alexander, and where is Lady Magdalen?

Magdalen herded her gaggle of gray geese down the side of the hill to a large meadow Katrin had told her about. It was too late in the summer for flowers, but she imagined this green grass would be covered in wildflowers come spring.

She had devised a plan. She would send a letter to Avelina, the wife of the Margrave of Thornbeck, and ask for her help. Magdalen could make a pen out of a goose feather. But how would she find ink and paper?

She did not like asking for Lady Thornbeck's help. Avelina had just given birth to her first child, and she did not need to be bothered with Magdalen's problems. It would also be humiliating to admit what had happened. Not to mention that it was partially her own fault—Magdalen could not even inspire loyalty in her household servants.

And yet . . . she needed help. She had no power, no money, no friends or family who knew of her problem. Her mother would be outraged, but she hardly had a contingent of soldiers hanging about Mallin waiting to rescue Magdalen from her embarrassing situation.

The geese were ambling about the meadow, making their contented noises—little half honks that sounded like laughter—while they grazed in the tall grass.

They looked safe, so she covered her face with her hands. "Oh Lord God in heaven, I don't know what to do." Her voice was muffled and low, but God could hear everything. "I am afraid. I have no one to help me, except Lord and Lady Thornbeck, and I don't know how to ask them. They are so far away. I need Your help." What else could she say? "I might ask more specifically, God, for help, but I don't even know what to ask for. But I assume You know what to do. You are God, after all. So please help me."

Her way of praying to God was not the usual way, and perhaps it was not the prescribed way, but she had started praying as if she were speaking to her father when she was a child. She would never pray this way if anyone could hear her.

There seemed to be nothing else to do but write a letter to Lord and Lady Thornbeck. And she must write to her mother as well. As humiliating as it might be, they would send help and restore Magdalen to her rightful place.

Now she just needed to figure out how to get paper and ink—and messengers to take the letters.

The sounds of the geese broke into her thoughts. Being alone with them in this open field reminded her of the long walks she used to take. Sometimes she would sneak away so she wouldn't have to hear her mother's disapproving words about a baron's daughter "climbing up and down the rocks like a mountain goat." And when she went with her father to visit the mines, Mother would say nothing—until she came back.

"Disgraceful for a baron to take his oldest daughter to the mines around those rough peasants," she would say. "Your father wishes you were a boy."

"Father, do you wish I was a boy?" she asked him the next time he took her with him.

"No, of course not. You are perfect as a girl. Besides, what need have I of another boy? I already have one." Then he smiled and patted her on the shoulder, as he was wont to do. But her brother had died not long after her father. Would Father have wished she were a boy if he'd known his only son would die?

Father rarely ever spoke to Mother with affection, and Magdalen secretly believed Mother was jealous of her relationship with her father. Magdalen sometimes felt ashamed for thinking her mother could be guilty of being jealous of her. But Mother had sneered contemptuously at Magdalen too many times for her to believe her mother loved her.

When her father died of an attack of the heart, her sense that she was deeply loved had died with him. Emptiness and loss plagued her for many months afterward, and her grief had been assuaged only when she comforted her younger sisters.

She pulled her hands down from her face and stared at the geese. "What would Mother think if she could see me now, climbing up and down the Wolfberg Castle mount with a bunch of geese?"

"Pardon me."

Magdalen screamed and spun around. "You frightened me nearly to death." She could barely speak, she was breathing so hard.

The man she had seen in the dining hall, the new shepherd, stood gazing down at her.

Had he been listening to her prayer? He had certainly heard her speaking aloud.

"I thought I was alone." She stood and took a step away from him, as he was standing rather close, and picked up her stick.

His countenance changed as he stared at her face, his eyes wide and his mouth agape.

Steffan was staring at Lady Magdalen. But how could it be? Why would the baron's daughter be tending geese when she was supposed to be marrying the Duke of Wolfberg? But then again, he was tending the sheep.

"Do I know you?" she asked.

Was he ready to tell her that he was the duke she had met in Thornbeck? What if his eyes were playing tricks on him and she was not Lady Magdalen? He certainly wasn't ready to reveal to this servant girl that he was the duke.

"I don't know. Do you know me?"

"I don't know any *shepherds*."

If she was Lady Magdalen, should she not recognize him? Perhaps his disguise worked.

"You should have made your presence known," she went on, "instead of sneaking up on me."

"I did not consider myself sneaking. You are not very aware of your surroundings, are you?" He couldn't help staring at her while leaning on his shepherd's staff. Just as her delicate beauty had struck him when he'd met Lady Magdalen at Thornbeck, this goose girl's strawberry-blonde hair, green eyes, and perfect mouth and nose made it hard to look away.

Her eyes narrowed, as if she did not appreciate him speaking to her as if she were only a goose girl. "What is your name?"

"What is *your* name?" she countered.

"Steffan. But I asked you first."

"It is not my name, but you may call me Maggie."

What game was this? He might as well play along. He rubbed a hand over his bearded chin as he continued to study her. He had intended to speak a greeting to the girl and then herd his sheep away from her and her geese. He did not like geese, and one was wandering closer and closer to him.

Finally, he said, "Do you always graze your geese here?" If so, he would need to stay away from this meadow in the future.

She looked behind him and seemed to notice his sheep.

"I was told I might graze the geese here." She lifted her shoulders and looked him in the eye.

He wanted to stay and talk with her, possibly find out if she was truly Lady Magdalen. But geese were evil, and even Lady Magdalen herself could not convince him otherwise.

Chapter Eight

A worried wrinkle formed between the shepherd's eyes as he stared at her geese, and Magdalen had that sudden thrill of wondering, again, if he was the Duke of Wolfberg. But how could the duke allow himself to dress like this and take care of animals while someone else took his place?

He could ask her the same question.

"You do not speak like a peasant or a servant," he said.

"And who do I speak like?" She lifted a brow.

He had a rather large nose, and as she recalled, the Duke of Wolfberg also had a slightly larger-than-average nose. This man had a forehead much like the duke's. His hair was dark brown with a pleasant wave on top. And this man had the same brown eyes as the duke.

"I don't like geese," he said, the wrinkle in his forehead getting deeper, giving him the same vexed look he'd had when she saw him in the dining hall. "The sheep don't like them either."

She sighed as he spoke to her as if she were a fellow servant, just like everyone else. She had been foolish to think he could be the duke.

"I shall allow my geese to go where they like." She turned her back on him. "They want no part of you and your sheep."

She walked over to the nearest goose, sat down, and started stroking its back. It didn't even make a sound, just kept on eating.

"What are you doing? You shouldn't be touching that bird." His voice was different, high-pitched and nervous.

She turned to look at him. "There are only two or three ornery ones. I can attest to their bite." She showed him her forearm where the bite was still scabbed over and healing. She wasn't sure why she was speaking with him, except that she had been alone with no one to talk to every day for a week.

"Dastardly creatures!" The man scowled quite ferociously. "You should be careful that doesn't fester."

"Thank you for your concern. I shall."

It was perversely enjoyable to speak in such an impertinent and saucy way to a young man, to not worry about being polite or well spoken. She sat on the ground, keeping her back to the shepherd. Finally, she lay down and gazed at the trees farther down the side of the hill, listening to the strange roaring sound in the distance.

He had said his name was Steffan. Too bad she did not know the given name of the Duke of Wolfberg. She might come right out and ask him if he was the Duke of Wolfberg, at the risk of him laughing her to scorn, but how could a duke who was forced to watch sheep possibly help her regain her place as a baron's daughter?

"How close are we to the sea?" She turned in the direction where he sat, not even sure if he was still there.

He actually had a book in his lap, and she wished she had the courage to ask him where he got the book.

"The sea is just beyond those trees." He nodded below them. "Are you not from Wolfberg?"

"No." There didn't seem to be any reason not to tell him. "I am from Mallin."

His gaze grew sharper. "What brings you to Wolfberg?"

"That is a strange tale, and you would not believe me if I told you." She stood. "Will you watch the geese? Only for a few minutes? I want to see the ocean."

"Have you never seen it before?"

She shook her head.

He stood and tucked his book in a leather pouch. "I shall walk with you. There is a steep cliff just beyond the trees. If you aren't careful you can fall over the edge."

"Will the geese and the sheep be well if we leave them alone?"

"Truthfully, I know very little about sheep, and only slightly more about geese, besides the fact that they are fiendish creatures. But I can't imagine they will wander off if we are only gone a few minutes. But I would understand if you do not trust me enough to go with me where you have never been before." He bowed to her, a gallant and humble gesture.

"I have a gift for reading people's intentions." She looked him in the eye, searching his face. "And you, I believe, are an honest person without evil intentions." Truly, she did not know if she had a gift for reading people's intentions. But she wanted to say something equally magnanimous.

He bowed again. "You are safe with me, my lady."

His words made her mind race back to the ball at Thornbeck Castle. She looked askance at him, but he was glancing back at the sheep and geese.

"Let us go. We shall return before they can have moved far."

They walked down the hill and into the coolness of the thick stand of trees.

"The roaring sound is getting louder. I feel as though I might be walking to my doom."

"The sea is no danger to you if you do not plunge into it."

She had no intention of plunging into it, and she'd be sure to watch her step as they drew near to the edge of the wooded area. A bright patch of blue-and-white sky lay ahead, and something else quite blue. Was that the sea?

She walked carefully as they stepped on sticks and rocks under and among the leaves. Finally, they moved out of the trees onto a narrow strip of land.

"Oh." A bright expanse of water stretched out before her, and . . . it never ended. It seemed to meet the sky a long way out, as if there were nothing else on the earth except sky and water.

"Be careful." The shepherd extended his arm toward her. "The cliff is just ahead, as you can see, and it is a long way down."

Her eyes devoured everything in front of her, and yet they did not seem any closer to getting their fill.

"To the left you can see that the cliffs curve around, and they are white where they face the ocean," he said. "There is sand at the bottom, where it meets the water."

"It is perfectly miraculous. I never imagined it would look like this." She pressed her hand against her chest, as if to prevent her heart from beating too hard. "The water is so . . . beautiful."

Her life stretched out in front of her, just as this shimmering ocean did. She had left her childhood behind and was free of her mother's suffocating control for the first time. Magdalen's life could be used for so much more than trying to avoid her mother's anger. Life could be beautiful, surely, could be worthwhile and inspiring, and she could accomplish good things, for herself and for others.

Steffan was watching her, a slight smile on his face.

"Now I see what is making that roaring sound." She took another step toward the edge and looked down. "The waves crashing against the land."

He nodded. His face was expressionless as he stared out at the vast waters.

She let her gaze roam over the white cliff faces and the sand below. Together with the powerful ocean waves, she suddenly felt as if anything was possible. Though she was in an unexpected and difficult situation, God would empower her to do things she never imagined when she was living a small, insignificant life.

Steffan said, "I have been blessed to grow up in a place where I am surrounded by both forests and the sea."

"Mallin has only mountains and mines—empty copper mines. And we have lakes where the geese love to swim and live." Absently, she said, "The lake waters must make them feel safe from predators. Too bad the geese at Wolfberg have no lake to swim in."

"Speaking of geese, we should get back to our animals." He took one last look below, then turned and they headed back through the trees.

His face was difficult to read, especially with that beard and the way his brows drew together. She was just about to tell him how much she loved the ocean and the cliffs when they came out of the trees and into the open meadow. The geese and sheep were intermingling, grazing peacefully together.

Steffan the shepherd groaned. "Evil birds. What are they doing among my sheep?" He raised his arms. "Shoo, you cruel little beasties."

But instead of scaring the geese away from the sheep, his display seemed to spook the sheep who bleated and became even more commingled with the geese.

Steffan threw up his hands again, starting to walk away.

Magdalen laughed.

He turned wide eyes on her. "There is nothing funny about these vile creatures. What if they attack the sheep and send them running? They could all plunge off the cliff to their deaths."

"That isn't likely, is it?" Her stomach twisted at the thought. It was true, the geese could start flapping their wings and honking. They were rather frightening when they did that, and they could bite.

A grim look on his face, he stepped sideways, placing his body between the sheep and the trees and, ultimately, the cliff.

"Perhaps I can separate them." Magdalen took her long, thin stick and moved cautiously so as not to frighten the sheep. She urged one of the geese to move, a bit at a time, until she had herded it away from the sheep. But twenty-nine more geese still infiltrated the sheep flock.

Gradually, painstakingly, she managed to coax all the geese out from among the sheep and into their own side of the meadow. Meanwhile, Steffan talked to the sheep.

"Do not worry," he said in a soothing tone, "just keep eating your grass." He kept his body between them and—to judge by his expression—certain death. "Stay where you are. No running off, now. That's a good flock."

"How long have you been tending sheep?" she asked as she separated the last goose from the sheep.

"I am an inexperienced shepherd. Is that what you are trying to say?"

"Not at all." She shook her head, suppressing a smile. "It's only that I don't know much about sheep, but you seem to think them very timid creatures."

"They are timid. It's the geese you must watch out for. They are evil birds, bent on mayhem and cruelty."

"They only wish to eat and be safe. They're only birds, after all."

"How can *you* say so with that fresh wound on your forearm?"

"I'd hardly call it a serious injury. The bird was simply frightened of an unfamiliar person."

He grunted. "You should take care."

Magdalen studied his profile. He did not appear to be in jest. He seemed to genuinely hate the geese. But why? He seemed to like the sheep and treated them with gentleness.

For the rest of the day they grazed their animals, making sure they stayed separate, and talked occasionally. Near the end of the day, as the sun was getting low, he put away his book.

"Where did you get that book?"

"Oh, this? It was . . . in my bag." He obviously did not want to tell her.

"Well, if you have another in your bag, would you allow me to read it tomorrow?"

"You know how to read?" A suspicious light flickered in his eyes.

"Of course. I mean, I learned . . . when I was . . . younger." A servant, especially one as lowly as a goose girl, should not know how to read. But then, neither should a shepherd.

"I see." He shuttered his eyes, half closing them and turning away slightly. "I shall bring you something to read tomorrow."

"Thank you. Do you happen to have paper and ink as well?"

He turned back toward her. "I do."

"Would you bring me some?"

"In exchange . . ."

"Exchange for what?"

"For you telling me your name."

"Very well. Tomorrow when you bring the paper and ink, I will tell you my name."

Chapter Nine

As Steffan herded his sheep up the hill beside the comely servant girl and her easy smile, he was convinced this goose girl was Lady Magdalen of Mallin. But until he had proof in his possession of his own identity, he did not want to confide in her. She might think he had sent her the letter proposing marriage. But she was only a poor baron's daughter, and his grandmother had warned him not to marry beneath his station. Dukes did not marry for love. Marrying for love was foolish, and it led to heartbreak and sorrow.

Besides that, with his region's wealth and his title, he could expect to marry very well indeed.

His parents had married for love, and when his mother died suddenly, his father had been so heartbroken, he stopped caring about anything or anyone. He followed his wife to the grave less than a year after she died. Steffan had vowed never to fall in love like that, never to care so much for someone that he would grieve himself to death. And the only way to ensure that was to marry for practical reasons and not for love.

But why in the world would his uncle ask Lady Magdalen, a poor baron's daughter, to marry his son, then throw her out to watch the geese and instead marry him to an imposter? None of it made sense.

As they drew nearer the castle, a man was running and looking behind him as he ran. The goose girl noticed him, then hurried toward him. He was twice her size, and he was heading straight for her, his face twisted in a strange expression.

Steffan broke into a run, ready to defend her. But when the man saw her, he stopped.

"Oh, Lenhart!" the goose girl cried. "What has happened to you? You poor thing."

A line of blood ran down the side of the young man's face. And on getting a closer look, he seemed less of a man and more an overgrown boy of fifteen years.

She took a cloth out of her bag and dabbed at his face. "Who did this to you?"

He only shook his head.

"Come." She touched his arm. "I have to put these geese in their pen. As soon as I do, I want you to show me who hurt you."

"Do you need help?" Steffan asked.

"I might. Will you return after you put away your sheep?"

"I shall." He herded the animals to the barn—they could walk quickly when they were forced to—and ran back to where he had left the goose girl and the large young man.

She stood talking softly to him, dabbing at the blood on his temple and cheek.

"What happened?"

She turned to look at Steffan. "I don't know. Lenhart, show us who did this to you."

But the boy only shook his head, then pointed to the girl and shook his head again.

"Why does he not speak?"

"Lenhart does not speak with his voice." Then she looked into the boy's eyes. "Did Erlich do this to you?"

He hung his head.

"He did, didn't he? It's time to confront him."

Lenhart shook his head with vehemence, but the goose girl had already started off across the bailey. The boy went after her, and Steffan ran after both of them.

They headed toward the stables, and when they reached them, a man was dumping out a water trough and adding more water from a bucket.

"Where is Erlich?"

The man put down the bucket and stood to his full height.

"Run along, maiden. Everyone has a place here, and this is not yours."

Steffan stepped forward, but she was already speaking again, her voice icy. "Do you not know that this boy's angel is always in heaven beholding the very face of God? Erlich may be bold enough to mistreat him, but you and the other men should defend him if you have any fear of the Almighty."

"I asked him a question and he didn't answer me." A note of complaint entered the man's voice.

"He cannot speak." She looked at him as if he must be daft.

"If he can hear me, why can he not speak?"

"He cannot speak because his throat was injured. Nothing is wrong with his ears. And even if he could speak but did not answer you, that is no reason to stand by and do nothing when someone else strikes him and bloodies his face. God will not look favorably upon people who strike those who—" The goose girl took a step back as a man Steffan did not recognize emerged from the stable.

This man, who looked to be around forty years old and had long hair and squinty eyes, glared at her as he approached. She took another step back, then stopped.

"You are not to hit Lenhart again"—she looked him in the eye—"or he and I will speak to Lord Hazen about you."

"You will not, because you will be dead." The man lunged at her, grabbing her around the neck. He was strangling her.

Steffan ran forward as Lenhart leapt at the man, as did the other stable worker. The three of them reached him at about the same time and pulled him off of her.

Steffan clenched his fists. "How dare you attack this young maiden?"

But the man curled his lip and pointed at her while she held her hands at her throat and coughed.

"If she wants to live, and wants her friend to live, she had best stay with her geese."

Lenhart and the maiden both glared back at him, but he suddenly smiled, then laughed. "You cannot win against me. I am the stable master here, and I will do as I see fit. Lord Hazen listens to me, not some little goose girl and a mute puppy. You two." He pointed at Lenhart and the other stable worker, whose eyes were cautious. "Get to work."

"People in Wolfberg are expected to treat others with mercy and respect," Steffan called after the man, but he did not even acknowledge Steffan's words. What kind of fiends had his uncle hired to work in place of their old loyal workers?

He turned to the goose girl. "Are you all right?"

She nodded, still rubbing her neck gingerly, while Lenhart hovered next to her.

"Let me see." He eased her hand away. Two red thumbprints

marked the front of her pale throat. "I should have that man thrashed for what he did to you." And he would, if he were still the Duke of Wolfberg and the ruler of this castle and town.

She looked at him curiously. Did she know he was the duke? Did she recognize him? Could it be that they were both in the same predicament?

But her gaze was drawn to the boy. "Lenhart, are you in danger? Do you think he would . . . kill you?"

Lenhart took a breath and let it out slowly. Then he shook his head.

"Perhaps you should run away, back to Mallin."

An uncomfortable look crossed his face, then he shook his head. Lenhart bent down and started writing in the dirt. *I want to stay with you. But I will go back to get help if you want me to.*

How did this mute servant boy learn to read and write? But he held the question for later.

The maiden seemed to think for a moment, then finally said, "No, it would be dangerous for you. It would take at least three days, especially if you had no horse, for you to make it back to Mallin, and anything could happen to you on the road. You might even get lost."

He brushed the dirt with his hand, erasing his words, and wrote, *Erlich said if I ran away, he would track me down, chop off my head, and hang it over the stable door.*

She suddenly threw her arms around him. "I'll find a way to save us," she mumbled against his shoulder as they squatted in the stable yard.

His heart gave a squeeze at their affection. He shoved that feeling away.

She let go of Lenhart and stood. "You know where I am if you need me?"

He nodded, then gave her a wave. She waved back and turned away.

"Who is that insane man who tried to strangle you?" Steffan said as they walked back through the bailey toward the servants' barracks.

"He is the stable master now. He . . . does not like me or Lenhart."

"And how do you know Lenhart?"

"I have known him for a long time. My father discovered his own father was beating him, so Father brought him to live with us. He is a good boy but can be stubborn with men who remind him of his father. It makes me furious to think of someone striking him."

"I can see that." He felt a strange warmth as he remembered the way she had stood up for the boy, the way she clenched her fists and raised her voice and demanded respect for a poor mute servant.

"So, you both arrived here from Mallin recently?"

"Yes."

"You taught him to read and write, didn't you?"

"I enjoy teaching others." She did not glance his way as she brushed some dirt from her skirt.

He waited, but she wasn't going to give him any more information. "I'll walk you back."

Her green eyes were quite beautiful, whether she was giving a death glare to a man twice her size or giving Steffan a suspicious side glance.

He should not be—but he was—looking forward to taking his sheep out to graze tomorrow.

Magdalen could hardly wait to see the duke's look-alike shepherd so she could get the paper and ink from him that he had promised. She arose early, got dressed, and sat on the edge of her bed.

If she could only write those letters and find someone to deliver them to Thornbeck and Mallin, she would feel she was finally making progress toward getting her identity back—and discovering what had happened to *her* duke.

Katrin rolled over and blinked. Her eyes focused on Magdalen and she sat up. "Why are you up so early?"

"Oh, I'm hungry, and . . . I was tired of lying in bed." Both of which were true. She had awoken before anyone else and could not stop thinking about her situation, trying to think of what to say in her letters, writing them over and over in her head.

Her mind also kept going back to the shepherd, Steffan. Where would he get paper and ink? What if he was lying to her? She might not even see him again if he did not graze his sheep in the same meadow.

When Katrin finished dressing, they went together to the privy, to the well to get water to wash their hands and faces, and then to the servants' dining hall. They were almost the first to arrive, and Steffan was not there.

The breakfast was the usual porridge, but today it had a scorched taste.

Katrin looked disgusted. "Can they at least not burn the tasteless food?"

"It isn't tasteless. Now it tastes like coal."

"Or half-burned peat."

Magdalen put another bite in her mouth. She would have to wait several more hours before eating again, so she chewed the bits of oats in the porridge and swallowed. Katrin held her nose while shoveling it in. "It's easier to eat it if you can't smell it."

Magdalen ate another bite, also holding her nose. But after three more bites, her stomach began to protest. Since she didn't want it coming back up, she put her spoon down and took a deep breath.

She took notice of every face around the room and each person who came in the door. Steffan had not shown up. She let out a deep sigh. How would she get her paper and ink now? But she still hoped she would see him in the meadow. The hours went by so much faster the day before, and it must have been because she'd had Steffan to talk to.

Magdalen fetched the geese, letting them follow her down the castle mount and to the meadow where they'd grazed the day before. Steffan was not there either. She let out the breath she hadn't realized she'd been holding when she saw that she and the geese were the only ones there.

Ah, well. She didn't need Steffan. Perhaps God wanted to teach her that she did not need to depend on this man's help. God wanted to show her He could provide the paper and ink—and fend off the dullness of a long day—another way.

She sat beside one of the friendly geese, whom she had named *Flaumig*, and stroked her back while she fed on the tender green grass and clover.

Suddenly she heard the gentle bleating sounds of a flock of sheep coming her way. She watched the narrow pathway from the other end of the meadow, her heart beating just a bit faster when Steffan appeared, leading his sheep.

His whole face was scrunched as he caught sight of her. "You will not believe what has happened. I am beginning to think Wolfberg the most lawless, evil place I've ever been to."

"What? What happened?"

"The paper and ink you wanted? I had them. I had them in my small trunk, which I kept under my bed, and some scoundrel has stolen them. Stolen everything!" He threw his arms out wide as though the statement was inconceivable.

"Nothing truly valuable was in the trunk," he went on. "No gold or silver or copper coins. I was not foolish enough to leave such things in plain sight. But some people will steal anything. The only things they did not steal were my books."

He looked like he had the first time she'd seen him in the dining hall, with his brows drawn down in a scowl. How could a shepherd—one of the lowliest of the servant positions—be so appalled that someone would steal his things? And how did a shepherd know how to read or have the money to possess books and paper and ink?

He squatted next to his sheep and pounded his fist into the ground.

She would have felt more pity for him if he had not lost the paper and ink she so desperately needed. "How did you get paper and ink? Perhaps you could go acquire some more."

"I . . . brought it with me."

"You are not from Wolfberg?"

He heaved a sigh. "Do you want to hear all about my life . . . now?" He ran his hand through his hair. "You haven't even told me your real name."

"You did not bring me any paper or ink."

"As I just explained to you, they were stolen."

"You did not uphold your end of our agreement, but if you

cannot get any paper and ink . . ." She did not want to be cruel, but she needed those materials.

He closed his eyes while raising his brows in that imperious way of his. "Very well. If you will watch my sheep for me, I shall retrieve the items for you."

"Where are you going?"

"Into town to purchase some paper and ink."

"Do you want to know my name that badly?"

"Nearly. I also want to know why you want paper and ink."

"How do you know I will tell you?"

"Because if you do, I shall buy you something to eat besides that burned porridge I heard about."

The thought of edible food—some roast pheasant or wheat bread with a thick slice of butter—made her mouth water. She had been hungry since arriving in Wolfberg. But did she dare tell him why she needed the paper and ink? Perhaps she could get away with being vague.

"Decide quickly, for I am going to buy myself something, regardless."

"Are you always so curious about your fellow servants?"

He looked up at the sky as if he was thinking. Finally, he looked back at her. *"Nein."*

"Very well. I am so hungry I could eat three breakfasts."

He stood and bowed to her. "I shall return as soon as I can."

"I cannot pay you for the food."

He gave her a tiny smile. "I may not be a knight, but I am too chivalrous to allow you to pay me for food." And with that he loped away on his long legs.

Magdalen had a strange feeling in her stomach, which she was vaguely aware that she had felt before. Where had she felt this? Oh yes. At the ball at Thornbeck when she danced with the Duke of Wolfberg. If this shepherd was not the duke . . . he made her feel the same way he had.

How strange.

She must have waited at least an hour before Steffan appeared at the end of the path at a fast walk. He carried a large pouch under his arm. Her blood seemed to quicken as she sat on the grass with the peaceful sheep on one side and the noisy geese on the other side, grazing and barely noticing the tall shepherd approaching. But she was only excited about writing a letter to Avelina.

He strode toward her and pulled out a cloth bundle from the leather bag. He squatted beside her and unwrapped the cloth, then held it out to her. Inside were four bread rolls.

She accepted one. It was still warm. "What is it?"

"A stuffed roll." He picked one up and took a bite.

She did not want to be rude, so she didn't ask what was inside. She was too hungry to care much anyway and bit into the soft bread.

Inside was some kind of meat, minced potato, and something sour. She closed her eyes, savoring the wonderful taste and smell. When she opened her eyes, she said, "Is that bacon?"

He smiled. "I think so. Bacon, potato, and sauerkraut. Do you like it?"

"Very much. But what is sauerkraut?"

"You've never had sauerkraut?"

She shook her head.

"Fermented cabbage."

That didn't sound very appetizing, but the flavors mixed together pleasantly in her mouth. Soon she had eaten the entire roll. "Thank you. That was delicious."

"Have another one."

"Are you sure?"

"I bought three for you. You said you were hungry enough to eat three breakfasts."

"I would look like a pig if I ate more than you."

"I've already eaten two."

She laughed and took another roll, again closing her eyes at how good it tasted. Her family's cooks at Mallin had never made anything like this. Bacon was not considered elegant enough for a baron's family, and neither were these stuffed rolls, no doubt, but from now on—if she was ever restored to her rightful place—she would ask for bacon, potato, and sauerkraut rolls every day. And bacon. Copious amounts of bacon.

When she had eaten half of the second roll, she suddenly felt guilty. Here she was eating this wonderful food when Katrin and the other servants were undoubtedly still hungry. She took out a cloth from the bag at her belt, wrapped up the half-eaten roll, and tucked it away so she might give it to Katrin when she saw her tonight.

"You know." Steffan stared at the ground as he used a stick to stab at the dirt. "Wolfberg did not always treat its servants so poorly."

She waited for him to go on, admiring the soft waves in his dark-brown hair.

"They had better food, at least." He ceased stabbing the ground and just stared across the meadow. Then he threw down his stick and reached into his big leather bag. He pulled out a thin wooden board and some paper.

"Here is your paper. I only bought three rectangular sheets. I hope that's enough."

She took the paper from his hand.

"And here is the ink."

It was in a tiny glass pot with a cork stopper. Where did a shepherd get enough money to buy paper and ink? Wherever he got it, she had a funny feeling in her chest as she stared down at the paper in her lap. How humbling that someone would go to so much trouble to bring her paper and ink and even food, a man who hardly knew her. If she thought about it much longer, tears would sting her eyes.

He could have demanded that she give him the information he wanted before he gave her the food. Would he not force her to tell him her name after all? But she had promised him.

"Now for my end of the bargain." Magdalen cleared her throat.

"Yes. You will tell me your name and what you plan to do with the ink and paper."

She smiled to cover her uncertainty. How much should she tell him? How much could she get away with concealing?

Chapter Ten

Steffan watched her. She stared down at her lap, then away at a goose that had separated itself from the rest of the mean-spirited creatures.

"Everyone here calls me Maggie—well, only a few people speak to me at all, but they call me Maggie."

Why was she so nervous?

"But you said that was not your name. Is it short for something?"

"Short for Magdalen, actually." She finally looked him in the eye.

Of course it is, because you are Lady Magdalen, the daughter of the Baron of Mallin. But why was she working as a goose girl? It made no sense, unless someone was forcing her out of her place. But who? And for what purpose?

Until he figured it out, he'd better not tell her who he was. He couldn't prove he was the Duke of Wolfberg yet anyway, and she obviously didn't recognize him with the beard and shepherd's clothing.

"You were also going to tell me why you need the paper and ink."

"I need them to write a letter. Two letters."

"Letters to whom?"

"Letters to my mother and to a friend." She looked away from him again, signaling that she was either lying or holding something back.

"How did a goose girl learn to read and write?"

"Is that what you think of me? That I am just a goose girl who shouldn't know how to read?" Her back was suddenly as straight as any tree, her chin lifted high. But there was also a slight smile on her lips and a sparkle in her eye.

"So you were not a goose girl in Mallin?"

"As a matter of fact, I was not."

"What were you?" He held his breath while he waited for her to answer.

"I was a daughter and a sister." Her voice was soft as she looked at her lap again. "And I not only learned to read and write in Mallin, I taught my sisters and many of the servants, including Lenhart. And how did you, a shepherd boy, learn to read and write?"

"You think me only a boy? I am older than you are."

"How old are you?"

"I am twenty-one. Not a boy."

"A bit older than a boy, I suppose." She smiled.

"And how old are you?"

"I am nineteen."

"Most young women your age are already married. Why are you not?" He watched her face closely.

"Oh, I suppose because . . . there was no one in Mallin I wanted to marry."

"But you are not in Mallin anymore."

"No, not anymore. And what about you? Why is a twenty-one-year-old man such as you still unmarried?"

"Such as me? Do you think I'm handsome?"

"I might, if I could see your face through all that hair." She laughed.

"You don't like my beard?" He rubbed his facial hair and shook his head. "The truth is I'm not ready for marriage."

"Oh? Why not? Do you not wish to be in love and have children?"

"I don't believe in marrying for love. People should marry for better reasons than love."

Magdalen raised her brows, her mouth hanging open, then she made a sound like, "Uh!" and shook her head.

"Besides, I have other plans, for now. Perhaps I shall marry when I'm thirty."

"What plans do you have? Do you need to study how to be a better shepherd?"

"Something like that."

She looked askance at him. "I never know whether to believe you."

"Why would you say that?"

"Something about your eyes. I do not think you are a bad person. But there are some things you aren't telling me. You are hiding something."

"That is very strange, because I get the same feeling about you."

She nodded once, then looked away from him, as if searching the ground. "I cannot very well write a letter without a pen."

She walked toward her gaggle of geese and picked up a feather off the ground. "This looks like it will make an excellent pen."

"I'll make it for you." He accepted the feather from her and took his knife from the little sheath that hung from his belt. To her questioning look, he said, "I am very good at making pens."

Steffan cut the hard end of the feather in half lengthwise for about two inches, carefully cutting and whittling to make the best point. When he was satisfied it was perfect, he handed it back to her.

She examined it closely. "Not a bad job. For a shepherd."

"Were you this impertinent when you lived in Mallin?"

"It's easy to hone your impertinence skills when you have a lot of sisters. Don't you have any sisters?"

Just behind her, a goose toddled toward them. No, it passed right by her and headed directly to him. Steffan began backing away.

"What is it?"

"The beast . . . What does it want? Get away." He waved his arms at it, but it kept coming.

"Are you afraid of a little goose?"

"Magdalen . . . take care not to get too close. Will it listen to you? Don't let it bite you." He could feel the blood draining from his face.

She actually laughed as she got in front of the goose and shooed it back toward the others.

He cleared his throat. "I don't know what is so amusing. Those birds are vicious."

"What happened to make you so afraid of geese?"

"I am not afraid. I simply do not like them."

"No, it's more than just not liking them. What is it?"

A prickly feeling snaked up his spine. He opened his mouth to tell her that she did not know what she was talking about, but his mind flashed back to when he was a little boy. The cold, blinding fear came over him, just as it had that day. His hands started to shake. He was falling, falling . . .

"What? What happened?" Her voice was soft and her eyes were kind as she stepped closer to him.

"I . . . I was just remembering . . . something."

"Won't you tell me?"

"It is nothing. Only, when I was a child a goose chased me and I fell down an old abandoned well."

"Oh no!" Her brows rose.

He stared at the ground, trying to shake off the feeling that had overtaken him, and concentrated on breathing normally. He was a child again as the memories flooded his mind.

"Were you hurt?"

"I got stuck on some debris before I reached the water. It was daytime when I fell in, but it was dark when they pulled me out." A shiver skittered through him, the same feeling of being in the cold, dank well, everything covered over in green slime and black mold.

"Then what happened?"

His stomach sank as he relived what had happened after he was freed. He shook his head and turned his back on her.

The worst thing that could happen to a child . . . that was what happened.

Not waiting for him to answer her previous question, she asked, "How old were you?"

He swallowed. "I was five. I haven't thought about it in a long time."

Something touched him. He spun around and found Magdalen standing beside him, her hand on his arm, looking up at him with those sympathetic eyes.

"What an awful thing to happen to a child. It must have been terrifying, being stuck in a deep, dark well."

He could still hear his own screams, his throat aching and raw from so much shouting for help and crying. When they finally found him, it seemed to take forever for them to reach him. They lowered one of the house servants, a small young man, down on a rope. He'd been terrified the man would fall on top of him and send them both down into the black water below. But he hadn't fallen, and he held Steffan in his arms as several men hauled them to the top.

"If that happened to me, my mother would have been yelling at everyone, including me. What happened when they pulled you out? Did you tell them it was the goose's fault?"

He might as well tell her the whole tale so she would stop asking questions. "I was crying and begging to see my mother. But . . . her time had come to give birth to my younger sibling. She died while they were bathing the stench and slime of the well off me. Both she and the baby died." His father had been so distraught . . . too distraught to pay any attention to a sobbing little boy. Even his nurse was not very attentive.

"Oh. I'm so sorry." Her voice was breathy and her face even softer. "Just when you needed your mother to comfort you."

She fell silent, and he tried to swallow past the constriction in his throat. The compassion in her face and her tone made it harder to push the feelings away.

Finally, she squeezed his arm and let go. "I can see why you hate geese. They make you think of that terrible day. I should take the geese to graze somewhere else so you won't have to see them."

"I don't wish you to do that. I like talking with you."

"I like talking with you too."

"Then tell me about your family." Anything to take their minds off the worst day of his life.

Magdalen sighed, still feeling pity for the poor shepherd's terrible experience. But he obviously wanted her to talk now.

"I have a sister named Jonatha. She is closest to me and sleeps in my bed. My other sisters are sweet too. There's Hildegard, Britta, and Anna. I had a brother, Wilhelm, but he died." Her voice hitched and she had to take a deep breath to drive away the sorrow. "A year and a half ago. He was always sickly."

"I'm very sorry." And he sounded as if he was.

"It was very sad. But what about you? Do you have sisters or brothers?"

"I have one sister."

Was his sister named Gertrudt, like the Duke of Wolfberg's?

"She married and I have not seen her since the wedding. We are good friends, as much as a brother and sister can be, I imagine, she being only one year older. I told you about my parents dying when I was very young. Tell me about your parents."

"My father died three years ago. And my mother . . . she doesn't care for me very much."

"Doesn't care for you?" He sounded surprised.

"It's difficult to discuss." Perhaps she should not have told him. She fingered the paper he had given her.

"It must be painful to feel your mother doesn't care for you."

"She once told me that I was selfish for wanting to see my father when he was sick. She said he just wanted to rest and not be bothered with me. But I sneaked in after she left, and he said my presence made him feel better. I think she was jealous of me." She made this last statement more quietly. "You don't want to hear my sad stories about my family."

"No, I do. Please, go on."

She hesitated, then said, "My mother yelled at my father a lot. She often accused him of ignoring her and paying more attention to his children than to her. And it was true. He did." She didn't say anything for a few moments. "That was wrong of him, I suppose, but she was always so angry, always yelling. And I was so grateful for his love. And I tried to make up for my mother's coldness by doting on my younger sisters. I didn't want them to feel unloved. I hope they are being affectionate to each other while I'm gone."

"Your mother's coldness was not your fault. She must have been an addled and sad person not to love a sweet girl like you."

His words caused a dryness in her throat, and she found herself unable to speak. It was as if he knew the exact words she needed to hear. At least a part of her had always believed her mother's cruel criticism and blame to be true, that it was Magdalen's fault her mother was always so angry with her. The first time she'd ever seemed close to being pleased with her was when she thought Magdalen was going to marry the Duke of Wolfberg.

She swallowed twice before she was able to say, "That is kind of you."

"It is the truth. Any mother would be proud to have a daughter such as you—clever, brave, kind, and generous."

Her foolish heart fluttered, but it was strangely pleasant to be so complimented by a handsome shepherd who thought she was only a goose girl.

Steffan should not say such complimentary things to Lady Magdalen. At least she still thought him only a lowly shepherd.

"Give me one of those sheets of paper. You only need two, after all." He reached toward the paper she was holding in her hand.

She gave him one. He pulled out a piece of drawing charcoal from his bag and sat down. Drawing always helped him forget things he'd rather not think about.

"What are you doing there?" She came and looked over his shoulder.

"Should you not be writing your letters?"

"I will, but I want to see."

"You can see when I'm finished." He motioned with his hand for her to go away. The lump that had formed in his chest began to fade somewhat as he traced the outlines and contours of Magdalen's face on his paper. He sketched in her hair and gradually brought out her eyes and nose and mouth.

Meanwhile she was hunched over her paper, the ink pot by her side, as she wrote her letter. She was quite lovely, with her small nose and delicate eyebrows that were browner and darker than her reddish-blonde hair. She also had a cute little chin that jutted slightly forward. Yes, he remembered that chin from the last time he had sketched her portrait—two years ago at Thornbeck, though she had not known it then.

She paused and looked up at him, a furrow wrinkling her forehead. "I don't know how I will get these letters to their destinations."

"I suppose you'll have to pay a courier. Do you know someone you trust?"

Her sad eyes stared across the field. "No."

His first impulse was to tell her he would take care of it for her. But what if the letters brought important people here, like the Margrave of Thornbeck, before he had proof of his own identity? He needed proof that would help him defeat his uncle and cousin at their nefarious game.

"Let me find someone to deliver your letters for you."

"But I don't have any money, or anything else, to give them."

"I shall take care of that for you." He would take care of it, but he would also hold the letters for a while first.

A pang shot through his chest. He was deceiving her, but he would make sure she eventually got back her place as the daughter of the Baroness of Mallin. The girl who would champion a mute boy at risk to herself deserved a champion of her own. He would help her. But perhaps not in the way she was expecting just now.

"You would find two trustworthy couriers and pay them to take my letters to Mallin and to Thornbeck?"

"I cannot make any promises. A courier with a dependable horse who is available for hire is not that easy to find."

"But you will try to find two, one for each letter? I would be so grateful, and I would pay you back whatever money you give them, once I—once my letters find their way to their destinations and I receive . . . what I'm expecting."

He could not look her in the eye as he grunted, then nodded.

He spent most of the rest of the day finishing his drawing of her face. Later, when he showed it to her, she gasped.

"You are very talented at drawing."

"Thank you."

She was still studying the drawing, but he took it away from her and tucked it into his bag, afraid she might ask to keep it.

As he had been sketching her, his mind was busy planning

how to get back into the castle and find his portrait. He prayed it had not been destroyed. Fury rose inside him for the thousandth time at what his uncle had done to him. Steffan had been forced to kill two men because of his uncle. Locked out of his own home, he felt helpless, but when he finally captured his uncle, then *he* would know what helplessness felt like.

When his grandmother had come to live at Wolfberg Castle, Steffan was a fatherless, motherless heir. If his grandmother had not had some powerful friends, his uncle would have forced her from Wolfberg and become Steffan's guardian himself. So when *Oma* died, Hazen wasted no time moving in and trying to influence Steffan.

Steffan had been grieving his grandmother—and his parents' deaths had come back to haunt him—and he had not been thinking prudently. If he had been, he might have been able to discern his uncle's evil intentions.

Magdalen spent most of the rest of the day writing her letters. She must feel as angry and helpless as he did, but she still managed to smile and speak with kindness. He couldn't help but admire her. He also felt guilty for not admitting his own identity— and the fact that he knew hers.

"I finished my letters," Lady Magdalen said. "I have no way to seal them, so folding them is the best I can do."

He took the letters from her, his fingers accidentally brushing hers. She had written *Baroness Helena of Mallin, Mallin Park House* on the outside of one letter and *Lady Thornbeck, Thornbeck Castle* on the other.

Lady Magdalen and the woman who ended up marrying the Margrave of Thornbeck had been inseparable at the ball and party at Thornbeck Castle. Of course Lady Magdalen would ask them for help. But Steffan needed to find that portrait. If his uncle were to destroy all proof of Steffan's identity, then, rather than ensuring his salvation, the margrave could side with his uncle and cousin, which would bring about Steffan's ruin.

Chapter Eleven

The day of the big wedding had finally come. Magdalen's heart felt heavy even as energy flowed through her to do something.

She led her geese toward the little spring pool in the trees. She wanted to get them watered and then take them to the largest pasture where they could graze while she sneaked off to the wedding.

She simply *had* to see who Agnes was marrying today. If the wedding was like most, she'd be able to watch them walk from the castle to the cathedral in town. Hopefully she'd be able to get a look at the "duke" and see once and for all if he was the man she had met two years ago.

But truly, did it matter if he was the man she met? She hardly knew that man, and she had come to Wolfberg to marry a duke. Her mother expected her to marry a duke. The people of Mallin expected her to marry a duke to provide some kind of work for them. Her sisters expected her to marry a duke so they would be able to make better matches. But now someone else was marrying her duke.

She couldn't stop the wedding. If she so much as showed her face there, Agnes's father would kill her.

She could not let her mind go to hopeless places. She had to think wisely, and she couldn't do that if her mind was full of gloom.

Would the geese be all right if she left them here? Surely no wild animals hunted geese on the castle mount. Hungry animals or not, she had to go and at least try to find out who was wedding Agnes.

She threw her long herding stick on the ground and dashed up the hill.

She ran all the way to the front of the castle. Her breath was coming in great gulps and gasps, but no one was there. Had they not left the castle yet? Or had they already made their way down the castle mount to the town below? Since no one was around, she guessed they had already gone.

She rushed through the front gate and started down the hill. She was less than halfway down when she saw a great crowd of people just as they reached the bottom and started along the main street toward the cathedral. Several young women and children were skipping and dancing and waving brightly colored scarves and ribbons on sticks. It was a typical wedding-day procession to the church.

Her heart in her throat, Magdalen ran down the hill. Would she reach them before the vows were spoken?

She hurried along the street to join the rest of the town as they gathered in front of the church steps, where the priest would lead them in their wedding vows.

Magdalen caught a side view of Agnes's face. She was grinning, her usual smirk. Magdalen maneuvered her way to the other side of the crowd. But even before she saw the groom's face, she knew he was the man she had seen in the Great Hall with Agnes.

When she got far enough to see him from the side, his face shining in the bright, late-morning sunlight, she noted his countenance. The Duke of Wolfberg would never have such a lax, timid look on his face. This man might have similar features to the man she danced with at Thornbeck, but he did not have the same expressions. He almost looked afraid.

"As well he should, since he's marrying Agnes," she muttered under her breath. But was this man the duke?

The priest asked if anyone knew a reason why these two should not be wed. Magdalen could speak up. She could shout that these two people were not who they said they were. She could accuse Agnes of taking her place as Lady Magdalen of Mallin. But who would believe her?

Just then Erlich turned in her direction as he stood near the front of the crowd. If Agnes's father were to see her . . .

She backed away, keeping her head down, slipping through the crowd again and heading back toward the castle mount.

She trudged up the hill. Climbing up was much harder than going down. By the time she made it to the little trail where she and the geese walked every morning and every evening to and from their little shed, her legs were burning. Her knees were weak, and her hands were shaking.

She had written a letter to Avelina at Thornbeck Castle. Steffan had promised to find couriers to take her letters to Mallin and Thornbeck, but he had admitted the day before that he had not yet found any couriers.

What hope did she possibly have unless this shepherd was able to hire those couriers?

She had been summoned here expecting to marry a duke, a duke with kind eyes and a friendly smile, and she had been stripped of her belongings and her identity and forced to tend to a gaggle of geese in exchange for bad food and a tiny bed in the servants' barracks. No one knew who she was, and no one who cared about her had any idea that she had been forced to change places with a vindictive maidservant.

She walked down the little trail and finally came to the large meadow where she had left the geese. But . . . they were nowhere to be seen.

Magdalen found her stick where she had thrown it. Where had the geese gone? Had a bear or a pack of wolves killed them all and dragged them away? What would Frau Clara do to her for losing all the geese?

She should go look for them, but which way should she go? Her legs were shaking so much, the thought of running all over the side of this giant hill, seeing Agnes looking so smug, marrying the man who might very well be her intended husband . . .

Tears welled up and she sat in the grass. She dropped her stick, then she put her face in her hands and sobbed.

Crying was a foolish thing to do. It would only make her feel more tired. She wiped her eyes, but the tears just kept coming. She dabbed at her face and nose with the cloth she now carried everywhere with her in the small bag that hung at her belt.

"God, why?" she whispered into her cloth. "Why did You send me here only to snatch away everything I've ever known? Everything I've ever counted on is gone." She let out another sob and pressed the cloth to her eyes.

"I don't know what to do. I don't want to go back home. What will Mother say? She always criticizes me and speaks to me as if I'm nobody, then lectures me on demanding respect. I told Avelina she should demand respect, but I have always been too afraid of my mother's cruel tongue to stand up to her. I thought I could get married and I wouldn't feel crushed, the way I do when Mother says her cruel things to me. And now . . . my chance for marriage to someone I could care for is gone. I'll have to go back to my mother." Another sob shook her body, and she bent forward and gave in to it.

A sound of sheep bleating made her lift her head. Steffan was hurrying toward her.

Her sobs shuddered to a halt. She wiped her eyes and nose with the cloth, keeping her face averted from Steffan. She was too embarrassed to blow her nose, so she just kept wiping.

"Magdalen." Steffan knelt beside her, leaning toward her. "Are you well?"

How humiliating to have this shepherd see her tears! She could almost hear her mother say, "For shame! Behaving the same as a common peasant."

She jumped to her feet, trying to hide the cloth in the folds of her skirt. She lifted her head and shoulders to regain her dignity. "I am very well, but I'd rather you did not say my name where anyone might hear. You may call me Maggie as everyone else does." She sniffed before she could stop herself. "My name is something I only tell people to whom . . ." She gazed up into his eyes for the first time. A look of concern shone in his brown eyes.

"Why were you crying?"

"It is not important." She broke her gaze away from his intense brown eyes and stared down at the cloth still clutched in her hand.

"If it made you cry, it must be important."

Her heart fluttered strangely. Even though she had been rather rude to him, he still spoke with kindness to her.

"I didn't know what had happened to you," he said. "I took the geese with me when I didn't see you. Believe me, I did not want to."

He raised his brows. "But I hope you were not crying because you thought you lost the geese." He stepped aside, revealing the entire gaggle of geese waddling behind him in the middle of the flock of sheep.

"Oh, thank you." Magdalen covered her heart with her hand at seeing the big gray birds. "I cannot believe you took care of the geese. I know how much you hate them." Her bottom lip trembled, and she bit it to keep it still.

"Please forgive me. I didn't mean to cause you so much distress."

"Oh, I wasn't . . . wasn't crying about the geese." He had such beautiful eyes.

"Why were you crying, then?"

He seemed pleased as he leaned down from his great height.

"I was crying because I . . . I wished to marry someone, and he . . . I think he married someone else."

"Did this man know you wanted to marry him?"

"Why, yes. He asked for my hand, and my mother granted him permission to marry me."

"You were in love with this man, then?"

"Oh . . . I don't think I knew him well enough to be in love with him."

"Then why did you want to marry him?" He seemed to be searching her face.

"I enjoyed talking to him. He seemed very kind and friendly. Except that . . . I'm not even sure if I ever met him." She waved her hand and shook her head. "I know that makes no sense."

Steffan let loose a heavy sigh. "Won't you please come and sit down? I have something to tell you."

"Let me go round up these geese that are wandering off."

They both herded their respective animals in closer, then sat on a felled tree at the edge of the meadow.

Magdalen waited for Steffan to speak. His face was a bit crestfallen as he seemed to be staring at the half ring of mushrooms on the ground in front of them. He sighed again.

"What is it?" An uneasy feeling crept through her limbs.

"I have a confession to make. I know who you are. And"—he suddenly sat up straighter and looked her in the eye—"I am a little insulted that you don't know who I am."

"What?" Her breath hitched. "Do you mean . . . ?"

"You are Lady Magdalen, daughter of the Baroness of Mallin, and I am the Duke of Wolfberg—Steffan is my given name. I met you in Thornbeck almost two years ago. How do you not remember me?"

"Oh, I am so glad!" She laughed and nearly threw her arms around him but controlled herself. "I am so glad it is you, so glad to finally find someone who knows who I am. But why are you a shepherd? Please explain to me what is happening here."

Was this the man she would marry? Her stomach fluttered again. He was handsome, and he possessed an appealingly confident way of walking and talking.

"I could ask you the same thing," he said. "Why is a baron's daughter herding geese?"

"No, I asked you first. Please."

"I suppose you saw who was getting married at the cathedral, and it was not you and me. I can only tell you who the groom was, because I do not know the bride. The groom is none other than my cousin Alexander van Verden."

"But how can anyone think he is you? He looks somewhat similar, but it is still easy to tell the difference."

"I thank you for those words, my lady." He gave her a slight bow. "It seems while I was away at the university in Prague trying to learn things that might help my people to prosper, my uncle, Lord Hazen, got rid of the house servants who would be most likely to recognize me and replaced them with people from Arnsbaden who either didn't know Alexander or were loyal to them. Then he brought his son in and began saying he was the Duke of Wolfberg."

"Oh my." Magdalen shook her head.

"He sent some men to kill me on the way home."

"Oh!" She covered her mouth. Poor Steffan! To be so betrayed by his own family!

"But with God's help, I managed to defeat them. I grew a beard to disguise myself and got hired as a shepherd. I plan to sneak into the castle and find proof that I am the Duke of Wolfberg."

"That's even worse than what happened to me." But at least the real duke didn't marry Agnes!

"And what did happen to you?"

She felt herself start to blush as she said, "I was on my way here to Wolfberg to marry you." She paused a moment, but he said nothing, and her face burned. "On the last day of our journey, my maidservant and her father, who had accompanied us, forced me to change places with her. They took my clothes and all my things and gave me hers, and when we arrived in Wolfberg, everyone at the castle simply believed she was Lady Magdalen. I could not have fought back, even if I had a weapon, because they threatened to kill poor Lenhart if I told anyone who I was. And now he and I are here, working as servants."

He did still plan to marry her, didn't he? Perhaps he was feeling as shy as she was, thinking that they would be married soon, as soon as they were able to get their places back from their usurpers.

"I'm sorry I did not recognize you," she said. "The first time I saw you, and many times after that, I thought you looked like the Duke of Wolfberg, but I wasn't sure. After all, you were a servant."

"I do not blame you." But he kept his head down, as if staring down at his clenched fists.

A coldness settled in her middle at his awkward silence. Then a thought struck her. "You did not send me the letter asking me to marry you, did you?" She suddenly went numb all over.

"No," he said quietly.

"Then who sent it?"

"My uncle. And I don't know why."

Magdalen's cheeks burned even hotter, and she felt as if he had punched her with one of his clenched fists.

Chapter Twelve

Magdalen had imagined that Steffan often thought about her after the dance at Thornbeck. She had thought the duke had fallen at least a little in love with her, that he wanted her. She had been pleased to marry him, to leave her home for his.

She felt sick, her stomach rising into her throat. He must think her a lack-wit.

Meanwhile, he said nothing. What could he say? He did not want to marry her, had never intended to marry her. Truly, she should not feel angry at him. It was all his uncle's fault and he had nothing to do with it, but in spite of this, she suddenly hated his calm demeanor and silence.

"How daft you must think me." The words slipped out before she could halt them. She turned away as her lips trembled with impending tears. *Stop!* How she hated herself for those tears, for trembling lips!

"I don't think you're daft," he said, a groan in his voice.

And she hated his groan! He did think she was daft. And pitiable. If only she could disappear. But she couldn't run away. She had to stay with the geese.

"I'm so sorry, Lady Magdalen." A hand touched her shoulder.

"Don't." She should pull away from him, refuse his pity. But his hand was warm and, unfortunately, she wanted his comfort. "It isn't your fault anyway. I suppose your uncle meant for me to marry his son."

Her words were steady, thankfully, but they made the tears spill from her eyes down her cheeks. At least he couldn't see them. She had her back to him.

"And now he's gone and married your treacherous maid-servant. Serves him right."

Bitterness permeated his voice. He'd already forgotten about her. Good. Magdalen hoped she could get these tears under control before he realized she was crying.

She did her best to surreptitiously wipe the tears from her cheeks.

"I'm sorry for all that has happened to you, Lady Magdalen." He patted her shoulder as someone might pat a sister.

The tears she wiped away were quickly replaced with more.

"I'm going to get a drink." She practically ran to the little spring at the edge of the trees. She fell to her knees beside it, bent, gathering the cold water in her hands, and splashed it on her face. And still the hot tears squeezed from her eyes onto her cold cheeks.

She took deep breaths. Thoughts flitted through her mind.

Mother will be so angry that I'm not marrying a duke after all.

I was a fool to think a duke would marry me.

The handsome shepherd, who's also the handsome duke I met years ago, doesn't want me, isn't even willing to do the honorable thing and promise to marry me.

Her heart ached, but her pride was injured the most. Foolish pride.

Why should I care if he doesn't want me? I have to focus on getting back to Mallin.

But her mother would be furious and blame Magdalen. Somehow everything was always her fault. Such as the time when her mother's favorite dress had become entangled in a thornbush after she alighted from her horse.

This is your fault, she had screamed after looking down at her ripped dress. *You love these ridiculous bushes with their berries and flowers. Now look at my dress—it's ruined!*

Mother could not accept that anything was her own fault. So her dress had ripped because Magdalen loved the flowers of the thornbush that ripped it.

And now, whether Steffan was able to take back his rightful place as the Duke of Wolfberg or not, it would be Magdalen's fault that he didn't marry her. She would face the humiliation of having thought she was to marry a duke, as well as her mother's many recriminations for allowing it to happen. Magdalen might as well face it and go home forthwith, even though she would have to walk the entire way.

And the Duke of Wolfberg would just have to solve his own problems.

These empowering thoughts completely stopped her tears. She took out her cloth and dried her face, taking more deep breaths as she reclaimed her dignity and stood up straight and tall, squaring her shoulders and lifting her chin. Without even a glance behind her, she turned and started walking toward the servants' quarters.

"Where are you going?" the duke asked, much closer than she might have expected. He must have followed her to the spring.

"Home." She flung the word over her shoulder and kept moving at a brisk pace.

"What do you mean?"

She didn't answer. Let him figure it out.

"You cannot go. Not yet."

"Why not?" She should have had the self-control not to ask him that, because she truly should not care. She quickened her pace as he caught up with her.

"I may need you to help me prove who I am. You are a witness."

"But no one believes I am Lady Magdalen, so I am useless to you."

They were climbing the path up the castle mount and would soon be in the bailey and among other servants.

"But I need you not to tell anyone what is happening here, not until I can prove my identity."

"You had better hurry up and prove it, then. Because as soon as my mother finds out what has happened, she will demand justice, spreading the news from one corner of the civilized world to the other." She was not at all sure that was what her mother would do, but it sounded good.

"I cannot allow that." Panic was in his voice now.

She rather enjoyed his distress. It lifted her shoulders.

"Please, Magdalen. For the sake of our friendship."

"Friendship?" She halted just short of the top of the hill and faced him. "Friends don't go two years without writing." Now he would know that she was angry he had not written to her, that she had expected him to after their time at Thornbeck.

"Well . . ." He seemed at a loss for what to say to that. "Some friends don't write. Some friends stay friends even though they haven't seen each other or spoken for two years, or many more years than that. Some friends, like us, recognize each other even after two years have passed and one has grown a beard and the other has become a goose girl."

Magdalen clenched her teeth to hold in the growl of contempt in her throat. "I would be a fool to stay here now that I know you never wished to marry me. I came here to marry a duke, and now I am going home. Do you hear me? Home. Where people respect me and care about me and have my—*my*—welfare in mind." Not her mother, perhaps, but she would not tell him that.

"Lower your voice." Steffan glanced around. "Someone might hear you."

"Is that all you can say to me?" She spun around and marched straight to the servants' quarters.

"You cannot leave now. Wait until tomorrow." He followed her across the open yard.

She suddenly realized something else and spun around so swiftly, he had to bring himself up short to keep from running into her.

"You were never planning to send my letters, were you?"

The guilty look in his eyes and the way his mouth hung open gave her the answer.

"Give them back to me." She thrust out her hand. "Immediately. I demand you give me back my letters." She stared pointedly at the big leather pouch hanging by his side.

He put his hand protectively on the bag.

How dare he keep her letters from her? She lunged at the bag. He held on to it, holding the flap closed. She tried to rip it out of his hands, but he was too strong.

"Stop. I will give you your letters, if you are so determined to have them."

She let go and he reached in, pulled out her two letters, and held them out to her. She snatched them from his hand and marched to the servants' quarters.

Just as she reached the door, a voice called out, "Agnes!"

The voice was so familiar, Magdalen turned her head.

The real Agnes was walking toward her with one of the guards from the castle. But she was not smirking. Her eyes were wide and she looked almost . . . afraid.

"Where are you going?" She tried to smile. "I thought you were taking care of the geese."

"I . . . I was . . . looking for something in my room."

"What is that in your hand?"

Magdalen's stomach sank like a stone.

"Nothing. Just some paper."

"Magdalen, I want you to work in the castle, close to me. Come. Get your things and I shall make you an indoor servant. You would like that better than being a goose girl, would you not?"

Her mind was racing. Why would Agnes want her working in the castle where the duke—Alexander—might see her? Did Agnes know he was not the real duke? Or was she planning to lure Magdalen into the castle and then lock her in the dungeon? Either way, this would ruin everything. She had to run away, to get back to Mallin, and she could not if Agnes held her captive in the castle.

She glanced back at Steffan, but she could not ask for help from him. He was supposed to be dead—or he would be if Agnes's husband and Lord Hazen discovered he was still alive.

With the guard standing there, she had little choice but to go inside the servants' barracks, gather her things—the things Agnes had allowed her to have—and head back out to where Agnes and the guard were waiting for her.

Steffan stood not far away, watching, but she ignored him.

But as she passed him, he asked, "Should I watch the geese for you?"

"Oh, Ag—I mean, Lady Magdalen, won't you find someone to watch the geese? This shepherd will not be able to watch both the sheep and the geese."

"Of course." Agnes looked down her lashes and said, "I shall have someone take care of finding a new goose girl."

Magdalen was following behind Agnes, with the guard just beside her, when Steffan touched her arm and whispered, "Are you in danger?"

She shook her head, even though she was not certain, and whispered, "You should go." And she handed him the two letters.

He stuffed them in his bag.

"What was that?" Agnes turned around.

"The shepherd was bidding me farewell. Farewell!" Magdalen called, waving her whole arm in the air as Steffan hurried off. "Take good care of those animals." She turned back to Agnes. "He is very good with sheep, but he is not so good with geese."

"As I said, I shall send someone to help with the geese," Agnes said with the kind of tone one might use with a child.

Out of the corner of her eye, Magdalen could see Steffan gazing over his shoulder at her. She refused to look in his direction.

They went inside the castle, up two flights of stairs, and then down a corridor. Agnes paused in front of a door and told the guard, "You may stand guard here."

The guard bowed, and she led Magdalen inside and shut the door behind them. Did Agnes plan to murder her here in the castle? Magdalen was determined to fight to the death. She glanced around, looking for a weapon.

Chapter Thirteen

Now, don't try to attack me." Agnes held up her hands. "All I have to do is scream and that guard will come and defend me. He will not hesitate to kill you."

"I have no wish to attack you, Agnes. I simply want you to tell the truth about who you and I are."

"I cannot very well do that. I am married now to the Duke of Wolfberg."

Should Magdalen tell Agnes that her husband was not the real Duke of Wolfberg? She decided to keep this information to herself for now. "And where is Wolfie? I don't see your doting husband anywhere."

"You will be respectful, or I shall have you thrown in the dungeon."

"Why did you bring me in here, Agnes?"

"I want to keep an eye on you. I can't have you running back to Mallin, can I?"

"Are you not afraid your husband will recognize me and realize what a terrible mistake he has made?"

"Not very much." Agnes aimed her nose at the ceiling. "He

admitted to me that he barely spoke to Lady Magdalen at the Thornbeck party. He doesn't even remember what you look like."

Was that what he told her? No wonder she wasn't afraid he would recognize Magdalen.

"Here is your new clothing." Agnes moved to take some clothes from a table.

"Why keep me here? Why not just kill me?"

Agnes shrugged. "I imagine my father plans to do just that. To be honest, I don't want that on my conscience."

"You have a conscience?" Perhaps she shouldn't antagonize Agnes, but the bitterness just flew out of her mouth on its own.

Agnes pursed her lips and narrowed her eyes. "If you stay close to me, I can protect you from my father. But if he suspects you are trying to tell someone about what we have done, he will not hesitate to stop you, in whatever way he deems necessary."

If I wish to survive, I must go along with her. "I understand."

"Good. Now, here is what every house servant wears at Wolfberg Castle. I will expect you to attend me at all times during the day, but at night you may sleep with the other house servants at the top of the stairs."

Magdalen looked down at the clothes, the same color and style as those she had stolen and were now stuffed under her bed at the servants' barracks.

Agnes put one hand on her hip and gestured with the other. "Now I want you, *Agnes*, to put on these clothes and clean my rooms while I go downstairs and join my husband. He is in the Great Hall waiting for me, and we have a wedding feast to attend."

Magdalen's blood boiled. *She will get what she deserves when everyone finds out what she's done.* When Steffan revealed the truth, she would discover that she wasn't married to the Duke of Wolfberg at all, but his cousin, and Agnes and her pretend husband would be executed for their actions. People had been hanged for far less.

Agnes spoke muffled words to the guard on the other side of the door. Magdalen was left alone in the silent room.

Trapped. If only she had left as soon as she saw the man Agnes was marrying. But it was dangerous for a woman to travel alone. And she had not looked forward to going home and facing her mother.

This deception Lord Hazen had played on the people of Wolfberg and the true Duke of Wolfberg would have been chiefly perpetrated against Mother. His actions would have caused her by far the most injury. And Agnes . . . Mother would be convinced that Agnes had forced Magdalen to switch places with her to get back at Mother for some unjust reason. And Magdalen's suffering at Agnes's hands would be nothing compared to Mother's disappointment, Mother's humiliation, Mother's suffering.

Father had always been quick to ask himself how someone else might feel in any situation. He seemed to know, instinctively, what other people were thinking and feeling. He was sympathetic, gentle, and kind. At least she'd had his example.

Magdalen sighed. Perhaps Lenhart could go home with her, minimizing the dangers.

Poor Lenhart. He was not accustomed to working in a stable any more than Magdalen was used to cleaning up after the woman who was once her own servant.

"This is unfair, God," Magdalen whispered. "I never mistreated Agnes in any way. Please come to my rescue. Defend me and restore to me my fortunes."

It was the people's plight that filled Magdalen with guilt and regret. They were depending on her to marry someone wealthy who could help them improve their lives and provide a better way of sustaining themselves than trying to live off crops grown in their rocky soil.

She tried not to dwell on these painful thoughts as she tidied up Agnes's room, putting away her discarded clothing.

Shouting erupted from the corridor outside the bedchamber door. Magdalen stood still and listened. Was that Steffan's voice?

She ran to the door and opened it, just in time to see the guard slam the hilt of his sword into Steffan's forehead, then punch him in the stomach.

He crumpled to his knees. The guard grabbed him under one arm and raised his sword.

"Stop!" Magdalen lunged forward and threw herself between the guard and Steffan. "What are you doing to this poor shepherd?" She glared up at the guard, then remembered that she was not the daughter of a baron now. The guard could knock her out of the way and no one would blame him.

"He does not belong here," the guard growled. "Get back in Lady Magdalen's chamber where *you* belong."

If she obeyed, he would surely continue to pummel Steffan. Her limbs went weak at the thought.

"Please, please do not harm this man. He . . . he did not know where he was. He was looking for me." Her mind was spinning, trying to think of the most plausible thing that might convince him to stop beating Steffan.

"Looking for you?"

"Yes, he . . . he is very simpleminded and has attached himself to me." She clasped her hands together in what she hoped was a meek and humble posture. "Please, he is quite harmless. Do not beat him anymore. In your great strength you will surely kill him."

The guard stepped back and his face lost some of its scowl. "Simple? Do you mean he is daft?"

"Yes, now please, help me get him up. He is bleeding all over the floor."

The guard didn't move for a moment, then he sheathed his sword and placed a hand under Steffan's arm, lifting him up.

Magdalen put his other arm over her shoulders and walked him through the open doorway of Agnes's bedchamber.

The guard growled, "If you get blood on Lady Magdalen's chamber floor—"

"I'll clean it up. Please don't trouble yourself."

He guided Steffan to a bench by the wall, where Steffan plopped down, his head still lowered. That was when Magdalen noticed the blood dripping on the floor.

"Clean his face," the guard said, "then send him out before Lady Magdalen gets back. Tell him he's not to be in the castle. His place is with the sheep."

"*Ja*, of course." Magdalen ran to the water pitcher while the guard shuffled out the door. She grabbed two cloths and poured water into the bowl, splashing it on the floor in her haste. She carried the bowl and cloth back to Steffan, then set it on the bench beside him.

"Hold your head up. Let me see." She pushed on his shoulder to make him sit up straighter and knelt in front of him. The blood flowed from a cut above his eye. She pressed a cloth over it.

"Hold this here." She put his hand over the cloth. "Press it firmly to stop the bleeding."

His lip was also bloody. She dipped the other cloth in the bowl of water and squeezed it out. "Are you in much pain? Say something." She wiped the blood that had run down his cheek.

"I will live."

She started dabbing at the blood on his lip just as he started speaking.

"What did you say?"

He touched her wrist and pushed her hand away. "I said, why did you tell him I was daft?" His voice was strained, as if it hurt to talk.

"I was trying to save your life. And it worked. If I had not said that, he would have beaten you senseless and dragged you down to the dungeon."

"I suppose that's true."

His hand was still holding her wrist, and her stomach did a strange flip-flop, partly in sympathy for the pained look on his battered face and partly because his hand felt warm and gentle on her wrist.

But neither of them were safe at the moment. She needed to keep her mind clear.

"Here. Let me see." She pulled his hand away from the wound. "It's still bleeding. Keep holding it." She pressed the cloth back to the cut above his eye. "What were you doing coming into the castle, drawing attention to yourself? You know it's dangerous for you. What if Lord Hazen or your cousin were to see you?"

"They'd have me killed."

"Yes! Why did you do it?"

"I thought that woman might try to murder you."

Her heart clenched at his bloody face, wounds he acquired while trying to protect her. He didn't meet her gaze. But she knew already that he did not care for her, not any more than he would care for any other lady. She needed to hold on to that anger because he took her letters but did not intend to send them. He lied to her. She should remember that.

"Does that woman not plan to kill you?"

"I don't think she has the courage to kill me, but that man at the stable who tried to choke me, he is her father and he would kill me. She wants me close so I don't run away to Mallin. She thinks she can keep my identity a secret forever, I suppose. Thinks she can prevent me from exposing her."

Magdalen had always disliked beards, but his was dark brown and short enough to show the contours of his face. It made him look quite rugged. No wonder she had not recognized him from the refined, young, kind face she remembered from before. At this moment, however, his warm brown eyes were soft and vulnerable, just as they had been when she'd danced with him at Thornbeck Castle.

"You still have some blood in your beard." Her voice sounded a bit harsh as she tried to make sure he did not guess her thoughts.

She dipped her cloth in the water bowl and squeezed it out. She lifted the cloth to his face and rubbed his beard, cleaning the drying blood. This time his gaze was on her, watching her.

"Thank you," he said.

She couldn't meet his eyes. She looked down, threw the cloth in the bowl, and carried it back to the table. She would put a bandage on his wound, send him back out of the castle . . . and then what? Somehow she had to come up with a plan of escape—without getting them both killed.

Chapter Fourteen

Steffan held his breath as Magdalen wiped the blood from his beard, the wet cloth cooling his heated face. She was quite near. Even through his haze of pain, he noticed the reddish color of her hair and the pleasant perfection of her pale skin and lips. She was so close he could see the tiny flecks of gold in her green eyes.

She abruptly stood and carried the water bowl away. She opened the window casement and threw out the bloody water. "I'll need to find something to bandage that wound over your eye."

He should probably tell her it didn't need a bandage, pretend it did not send bolts of pain through his skull. But he actually hoped she'd come back and bandage it, just so he could feel her gentle touch.

Foolish thoughts. He had far too many things to worry about at the moment.

"It is well, I'm sure." He took away the cloth he'd been holding to the wound and looked down at it.

"Wait. Let me see." She hurried over and examined the small gash. "It's ceased bleeding, but you need a bandage to protect it."

"Should you sew it up?"

"Perhaps. Forgive me, but you'll have to find someone else

to perform that task. The thought of piercing your flesh with a needle makes me feel like I might lose the food in my stomach."

"What every duke wants—a scar on his face."

"Well, you shouldn't have run in here, knowing you were putting yourself in danger." She walked away and returned with some cloth bandages.

"My chivalrous actions were not appreciated, I can conclude."

"I did not say I didn't appreciate it, but . . . I did not need your help, and, well, I was surprised you would rush in here to rescue me."

"You think me selfish and unfeeling, then? That I cannot be concerned about a lady in danger and in need of a protector?"

"I am glad to see how unselfish and self-sacrificing you are, that you are willing to risk your life for mine."

She was making a jest from the smirk on her lips. He grunted. Truly, it had been foolish. She had not even needed his help, and even if she had, he could not have helped her. He was too busy getting thrashed by the guard's fists and sword hilt.

His pride had taken an even worse beating. If only he'd had a sword.

She was taking a long time with the bandage as she folded the cloth into a rectangle and finally pressed it against his wound.

He sucked in a breath between his teeth, creating a hissing sound.

"I'm sorry." She lessened the pressure, then she wrapped another cloth around his head and tied it in place.

Her hands were gentle and soothing.

"There." She stepped back. "You look as if you've just returned from battle, a warrior who won, but only just."

She was smiling. Her teeth were perfect except for two that

overlapped each other a bit. But that tiny flaw somehow made her more endearing.

The blows had addled his brain, apparently. But she was pretty. He had always thought so. Still, she didn't seem to like him very much, and he had no time for errors in judgment. One had already cost him a beating. And admiring her beauty was only one step away from the most unwise and costly mistake he could make—falling in love.

"Thank you for the bandage." He could at least be courteous. Magdalen might be his only ally, and now that she was in the castle, she could be an even bigger help to him.

Why had he not thought of that before?

Magdalen was starting to clean up the blood from the floor.

"Listen. I need your help. Now that you're in the castle, you can help me prove that I am the duke."

"What do you mean?"

"Something is hidden in the castle that will prove my identity. If I can recover it—" But the thought of asking her to risk her life for him . . . Perhaps there was another way, so she was not putting herself in danger looking for the things he needed.

"Do you think you could help me get a job working inside the castle?"

"Do you not think that is dangerous? If your cousin or your uncle should see you—"

"With my beard, I don't think they will recognize me. Besides, I will keep my head down when they are around, and they rarely pay attention to servants."

It was a huge risk, but she did not have to know that.

"Very well. I will do what I can."

He stood, thinking to help her clean the floor, but the room started spinning, and the pain in his ribs made him gasp and bend over.

"Oh dear." She grabbed him by the arm. "You should sit."

He was already doing so, as the room continued to tilt and turn. He put his head in his hands and closed his eyes. When he opened them again, perhaps he'd have his balance back.

"I hope you will be well. I'm so sorry."

"It is not your fault."

"Thank you for attempting to save me. It was very chivalrous of you."

He could hear her wiping up the floor. Most ladies in her position—wrongly forced to act as a servant after being served all her life—would not have taken it as well as she had. Most would have either dissolved in self-pity or become enraged and lashed out. The first behavior would have gotten her scorned by the evildoers, and the latter would have gotten her killed.

She moved away from him and seemed to be cleaning up the room, as he heard the swish of her skirts on the flagstone floor.

The door to the room suddenly opened. Steffan lifted his head.

"What has happened here?"

Magdalen's usurper entered the chamber, her gaze coming to rest on Steffan.

Before he could speak, Magdalen hurried forward. "Forgive me, my lady."

She was good at pretending to be the humble servant.

"What is this man doing in my chamber?"

"This is but a lowly shepherd who wandered into the castle in search of me." She spoke quickly, as if expecting the woman to interrupt her at any moment. "He had attached himself to me when we were both in the fields tending our animals. He is very simpleminded, but he is a hard worker. Perhaps you could allow him to work in the castle so he will not be so anxious for me."

She made him sound like a lovesick imbecile. Again he felt a stab to his pride, but he could not afford pride, not until he had his identity back. Neither of them could.

She curled her lip as she stared at him. "Why should I? We don't want a daft man in the castle."

A man's voice sounded just outside. *"Liebling?"*

Alexander's face appeared in the doorway.

Steffan ducked his head, covered his face with his hand, and prayed, *God, don't let him recognize me.*

"Oh, please, Your Grace."

He peeked out from between his fingers. Magdalen had fallen at Alexander's feet, onto her knees, in fact, and was pleading with clasped hands.

"Your Grace, please do not have this poor man beaten any more. He is a simple but good soul. He only wants to be near me, and if you allow him to work in the castle, I promise he will work hard and I can watch over him."

"Liebling, what is this?" Alexander looked at his new bride. "I do not think it can hurt to allow the man to work in the castle. Do you know anything about him?"

"N-no," Agnes stuttered.

"Is this your new maidservant?" He looked down at Magdalen.

"Yes, my *liebchen.*"

"I promise he will be no trouble to you," Magdalen added.

"Is he your sweetheart? Is that why you want him working in the castle?"

"Oh no, Your Grace. He is but a poor, simpleminded shepherd who has formed an attachment to me because I look after him sometimes. Please have mercy on him. I fear for what will become of him if he is forced to work outside. Those servants are sometimes cruel to him. If you send him back outside, he may do harm to himself. In the name of all that is merciful and holy, please allow him to stay."

She was better than the traveling mummers who put on miracle and passion plays at Easter.

Alexander turned his gaze on Steffan. He quickly ducked his head again.

"I do not like to think of a simpleminded person suffering cruelty." Alexander always was easily swayed. Thankfully. "What do you think, my dear?"

"Oh, of course, *liebchen*. I would not want him to come to harm either. I am ever compassionate to unfortunate souls like him."

Now he just had to figure out a way to get past Alexander without being recognized.

Magdalen stared openmouthed at Agnes. She wanted her husband to think she was compassionate. Surely she was too coldhearted to be in love with him.

Agnes was smiling at Steffan's cousin. It would be fitting and just if she worried that he would find out what a mean-spirited, selfish person she was, but it was too difficult to fathom that she could be genuinely in love with him.

"And if he cannot do the work or causes problems, we can give him some other job."

Magdalen couldn't help glancing back at Steffan. *Dear God, don't let his cousin recognize him.*

"I will speak to Frau Clara. But I would like him to leave now." Agnes's gaze darted around the room, not focusing on anyone, and she fidgeted with her hands and her dress—one of Magdalen's best and most expensive dresses. In fact, it was Magdalen's favorite.

"Of course. St-Stoffel," Magdalen's heart thumped at her nearly calling him Steffan. "Come, Stoffel. No one is going to beat you anymore. We will find you some work to do in the castle."

So many deceptions existed in this one room. Alexander did not know his wife was a servant from the household of the real Lady Magdalen. Agnes did not know that her husband was the cousin of the real Duke of Wolfberg. And indeed, since they both used false names, they were not married in the eyes of the law, nor in the eyes of the Church authorities.

And neither of them realized that the real Duke of Wolfberg was in the room, pretending to be a simpleminded shepherd.

Steffan got up and shuffled toward her, his shoulders slumped and his head down. She took his arm and led him out the door.

"Darling," Agnes said with a tremulous smile. "I shall return in a moment. I need to speak with my servant and with Frau Clara."

"Of course, my darling." He stood in the middle of the room while she shut the door.

Agnes's smile vanished. She gave Magdalen a sharp look. "Come with me, both of you."

They went down the stairs. Magdalen dared a few quick glances at Steffan. He was pale, and he peeked at her in return, but neither of them attempted to speak as they followed Agnes.

Soon they found Frau Clara instructing a servant on how to clean the wall sconces.

"Frau Clara," Agnes said, "can you find some indoor work for this young man? He is said to be a hard worker but simpleminded."

With a scowl on her face, Frau Clara looked him up and down. Then she reached out and squeezed his upper arm. "He seems strong. He can attend the kitchen fires and fetch and carry firewood and water. Is he injured?" She pointed to the bandage on his head. "Is he able to work today?"

"He was beaten by one of the guards," Agnes said.

"Is he violent? A troublemaker?"

"Oh no," Magdalen said. "If you please, Frau Clara, he is a very gentle soul." She dug her fingernails into her palm and prayed he would live up to what she was saying about him. "He has an attachment to me, you see, and the guard misunderstood his desire to see me for some kind of mischief. But as long as he thinks I am safe and well, he will be quite calm and hardworking. Isn't that right, Stoffel?"

Steffan grunted and nodded without making eye contact with anyone.

"Very well," Frau Clara said in a resigned tone. "If it is what Lady Magdalen wants." She looked to Agnes.

"Yes, thank you, Clara," Agnes said, without the title of respect everyone else used when speaking to Frau Clara, who didn't seem to notice or mind.

Magdalen touched Steffan's arm. "This is Frau Clara. You will do everything she tells you, *ja*?"

Again, he grunted and nodded.

"I will try to see you tonight at the evening meal," she said softly.

"Come, Agnes," Agnes said.

As Magdalen was watching Steffan shuffle away, she realized Agnes was talking to her.

They went back toward the stairs, and as they climbed halfway up the first flight, Agnes turned to her and whispered, "I expect you to behave as a servant should. And if you say anything you should not to the duke, I shall not only let my father do what he wanted to do from the beginning, which is to get rid of you, but I shall also make sure he kills the mute boy your family is so fond of—and this new daft man you have collected. Truly, your taste in companions has not changed." Agnes rolled her eyes. Her top lip curled in disgust.

"Do not worry, Agnes—"

Agnes pinched her arm, hard. "Don't ever call me that. I am Lady Magdalen."

"Lady Magdalen." She let her own lip curl as she resisted the urge to rub her arm. "I will not say a word to your husband."

"Good."

"But I truly do not know how you expect to keep this a secret forever. At some point my mother will come to visit me, and so—" She almost said, "And so will the duke's sister." But of course, Agnes did not know her husband's similar secret.

"My father has some plans for when your mother and sisters visit."

"Does he plan to kill them?" Her heart rose into her throat.

"Be quiet. Not another word."

They continued up the stairs in silence. When they reached the third level, where Agnes's rooms were located, Agnes hissed, "You will leave my chamber any time you see my husband enter. You are also not to sleep on the servant's cot in the adjoining room. When I have released you every evening, you are to go up to the next level where the other indoor servants sleep. And if I find you have spoken to any of them about our little secret, I will have my father kill them and you."

Agnes looked into her eyes, but it was as if she was not seeing Magdalen. Agnes's eyes were dark, but something besides hatred and murder suffused them. If Magdalen did not know better, she'd say fear was in the pinched expression on Agnes's face.

"Why are you not taking yourself upstairs to the servants' quarters?" Agnes whispered. "My husband is waiting in my room, so go."

Magdalen hurried up the stairs, praying for herself and for Steffan.

Hazen eyed the snippet of a girl who had married his son as she nervously glanced at the cloth across her lap. She seemed quite unaccustomed to cleaning her hands on it, as she hesitantly touched it after eating her pheasant with her fingers. She kept leaning over to say something in Alexander's ear, as if she was afraid he would stop thinking about her if she did not speak to him nearly every moment. Her gaze kept darting to his face. She was even more unsure of herself than his spineless son, though she tried to hide the fact with haughty looks.

When the meal was over, Hazen said, "Your Grace, I have a small matter of business I'd like to speak with you about. Will you accompany me to the library?"

"Yes, of course." He turned to his wife. "I shall come to your chamber."

She accepted the squeeze of his hand before she departed.

He and Alexander walked to the room where Hazen wrote his letters. "Please be seated." He indicated a chair and then sat behind the desk.

"Is everything well?" Alexander asked.

"I wanted to ask you the same question. Is marriage to your liking? What do you think of your new wife?"

"It . . . it is good. We are well suited to one another, and she is . . . a good wife. All is well. W-why do you ask?"

Hazen clenched his jaw at the timid way his son answered him, stammering and stumbling because he was afraid of saying something that would displease him. His son's behavior was a disgrace to the Hazen title. He should not have entrusted the boy's care to nurses and servants and the boy's mother. He should have taken him in hand much sooner. Or perhaps the boy was just too much like his mother—frightened and unable to support an independent or ambitious thought. Ambition was everything. How many times had he told his son that?

"You are aware that I have asked all the servants to report anything suspicious to me, especially of anyone disloyal to you or me."

"Yes, Father."

He gave his son a withering look.

"Oh, I meant to say, Uncle Hazen."

"It has come to my attention that there is a servant girl who came here from Mallin at the same time as your wife, and this girl's name is Maggie."

Alexander stared back with a blank look.

"Must I explain everything to you?" He glared at his son. "Has it never occurred to you that Lady Magdalen, your wife, does not possess the manners of a baron's daughter? Is there not something a bit coarse about her?"

"Are you saying . . . ? Fa—" He checked himself. "Just because we are perpetrating a deception does not mean Lady Magdalen is as well. Perhaps it is your guilty conscience causing you to think such a thing."

Hazen burst out laughing. His son's face turned pink. He was almost showing a backbone finally. Almost.

"What makes you think I feel guilty about anything I've done? The wealth of the world belongs to the strong, and that is how it should be." Hazen eyed his son and shook his head. "I am only saying you should keep an open ear and eye for discrepancies in her story, evidence that she may not be who she says she is."

"And what will you do if you discover she is an imposter?"

"I shall find out how she might be helpful to us, and when her usefulness is exhausted, she must die. A deceptive person who is not loyal to me is not someone I wish to keep around."

Alexander's already pale face turned ashen. "She is not an imposter," he said, his voice raspy. "She is not."

"We shall see."

With Wolfberg's nearby harbor and lucrative shipping trade with its neighbors, not to mention its fishing revenues, Hazen would have found another way to take over Wolfberg had he not chosen to have his son impersonate the duke. But it amused him to do it this way. And if Alexander proved himself unequal to the task, he would simply have to kill him. With no duke to steward this busy and wealthy area, and with Hazen already entrenched at the castle, the king would no doubt grant his petition to take over.

Chapter Fifteen

Steffan's head still pounded, but Frau Clara was allowing him to follow around the young man who was currently in charge of starting the fires and fetching and carrying firewood. The kitchen maids were quick to instruct him on where things were kept and what he would be expected to do.

Katrin, Magdalen's friend, hurried toward him with a big smile after he watched the other fetch-and-carry boy stoke the kitchen fire.

The cook said, "Katrin, why don't you show him where the extra buckets are kept for drawing water."

The smile stretched wider. "Of course. Come with me, Steffan."

He cringed, but no one seemed to notice that she called him a different name.

As she led him outside to the small storage room, she said, "What happened to your head?"

"A guard hit me with his sword hilt."

"What were you doing in the castle?"

"Looking for Maggie."

"Here are the extra buckets. You will need several of these on wash days, when we have to clean all the linens and—"

"Katrin, I need you not to call me Steffan. For now, my name is Stoffel."

"I noticed they called you Stoffel, but I thought your name was—"

"In order for me to get this indoor job, I needed them to think my name was Stoffel. I also got this job because they think I am addled and simpleminded. You mustn't ruin my disguise or bad things could happen to me."

"Oh."

"I know it doesn't make sense." He lowered his voice as a guard walked by where they were standing outside the kitchen. "But I thank you for your help."

"So, I am to call you Stoffel and pretend you are daft?"

"Yes."

Her smile had vanished. "Very well. Does Maggie know about this?"

"Yes. She is also helping me keep my disguise so I can keep this job."

"Oh." She nodded, but she looked confused.

"Maggie is also working inside the castle now."

"Already? It took me months just to get a job in the kitchen!"

"It is a special circumstance. But one day she will explain it all to you, and she might even be in a position to help you get a much better job."

"As an upstairs servant?"

"Yes."

"Very well. I shall help you and not breathe a word to anyone."

"*Danke schön*, Katrin."

"You're very welcome." She smiled and winked, then turned to go back into the kitchen.

He sighed. He was a duke. He should feel humiliated at what he was being reduced to—first a shepherd, then a fetch-and-carry boy pretending to be simpleminded and unable to control his attachment to a fellow servant. But perhaps this was God's way of humbling him, of making him more grateful and mindful of his people.

The tale of David from the Bible came to mind, when he was trying to get away from King Saul and he pretended to the Philistine king he was insane, marking on doors and letting saliva run down his beard. David, God's own anointed, was afraid for his life, not so unlike Steffan and his present situation. And just as King David had been forced to leave his home by his son, Absalom, Steffan had been forced to leave his place as the Duke of Wolfberg. People cursed David and pelted him with stones as he left Jerusalem. But David would not even allow his guards to stop one old man from taunting him, but told his guard, "Let him curse . . . It may be that the Lord will look upon my misery and restore to me his covenant blessing."

As Steffan went back into the kitchen with Katrin, he prayed, *Lord God, I may be cursed and mistreated for the moment, but let me pass this test of humility, and please restore to me Your blessing. And restore Lady Magdalen to her rightful place as well.*

Lady Magdalen didn't deserve to be treated this way by her servants, by people she trusted. But because she was so kind and good, he also needed to guard his heart. He didn't want to end his life as his father had. Besides, he owed it to his people to marry well, and he couldn't marry a poor baron's daughter, no matter how kind and fair of face she was.

Agnes did not send for Magdalen all afternoon as she waited in the servants' room in the highest level of this part of the castle. Apparently she'd be sharing the chamber with four other women, as five beds were in the room and four of the beds had bedclothes, while the fifth was a bare mattress, probably filled with pokey straw, like the mattress she'd been sleeping on in the outdoor servants' quarters.

She did not have any of her things, as she'd left them in Agnes's rooms, so all she had to do was look out the window. But she would not complain about that. The ocean was visible over the tops of trees, and a small part of the white cliffs as they curved around. She could also see the far meadow and the small forest that separated it from the cliffs and the water. At the farthest point was the sea, sparkling as if it were made of stars.

"This place is so beautiful. I can see why a greedy person would try to take it." She soon began to feel greedy herself, wishing she could climb up the highest tower of Wolfberg Castle and see more of both the countryside and the ocean. One of the other servants told her there was a harbor just out of sight where ships brought goods from other lands and fishermen brought their catches to sell. She'd never seen a ship before.

The sea was so full of power and hope and possibilities. Here in Wolfberg, her mother could not make her feel small or use words to crush her.

When it was time for the evening meal, Magdalen hurried down to the servants' dining hall. Katrin was arriving at the same time and pulled Magdalen aside. "Your Steffan, the shepherd, is working in the kitchen as our new fetch-and-carry boy. What happened to him? Why was he in the castle looking for you? And why does he want me to call him Stoffel and pretend he is daft?"

"Did he tell you all that?"

"He said he had to pretend to be daft in order to get the job."

"That's right. It is too difficult to explain. Is he coming to supper?"

Just then Steffan walked into the room. He looked tired, his shoulders slumped. She could not tell in the dim room if he was pale, but his eyelids drooped.

She hurried toward him. "Are you well?"

"I'll survive."

"Perhaps this was a bad idea." Magdalen stood in line with Steffan to get their food. She spoke just loud enough for him to hear her over the noise of the other servants.

"No, it is good. I am in the castle. It's only a matter of time before I can get the things that will prove my identity."

"But you are injured and unwell. They will work you too hard."

"I just need a good night's sleep. I shall be well in the morning."

He was so resolute she did not question him further. At least no blood seeped through her rudimentary bandage on his forehead.

She should not care so much about him, since he didn't intend to marry her. At least, that's what her mother would say. But from a practical side, he was her only ally, the only person in Wolfberg who knew she was Lady Magdalen. A decidedly impractical part of her, however, worried that his head injury would fester and, combined with his exhaustion, would make him sick.

But even Agnes had said it: Magdalen had always been a compassionate person. It didn't mean she had romantic feelings for Steffan.

Katrin sat beside Magdalen and kept up a nearly constant chatter, which was for the best since it prevented Magdalen from talking to Steffan about what his plan was and what she could do to help him. They should not risk someone overhearing them.

When the meal was nearly over, Magdalen turned to Steffan. "Where will you sleep?"

"On the top floor with the other menservants."

"I will help you find your thing you've been looking for. But I think we should wait until another day."

"You might be right."

"You will not try to find it without my help, will you?"

He turned his half-closed eyes on her. He opened his mouth just as a man rose behind him.

"Hey, you, shepherd boy." The man nudged his shoulder.

Steffan looked down, probably trying to look submissive.

"The work's not finished. I need you to fetch some more water and wood."

Steffan stood and went with the man. She wanted to intervene, to tell the man that Steffan was injured, that he needed rest, but she did not think her interference would be welcomed by either the overbearing man or Steffan.

Was this how Avelina had felt before she came to Thornbeck, that because she was a servant, no one would listen to her or care about her opinion? Avelina had been a servant most of her life, and she had not been inclined to stand up for herself. Magdalen had actually scolded her for not demanding respect from other people, especially Lord Thornbeck.

Her cheeks heated at the thought. How silly and unworldly she had been then. She had not realized how difficult it was to be a servant. Even when Magdalen was not a servant, knowing she had the right to demand respect—especially from her mother—and actually doing so were two different things.

Katrin touched her arm. "Do you think Steffan—Stoffel—is well enough to work?"

"I don't know."

Katrin sighed. "Now I'll have to find a new boy to look at. There are precious few handsome ones. The blacksmith's apprentice is pleasant to look at, but he's bedded half the maidservants." Katrin wrinkled her nose. "A man who is fair of face is usually empty of conscience. That's what my mother says. But that is not a lovely thought, is it?"

Magdalen frowned and shook her head. "Why did you say you'd have to find a new boy to look at? Stef—Stoffel will be around more than before."

"I assumed you and he were sweethearts now."

"*Nein*, not at all."

"Oh, good." Katrin did not seem fully convinced as she ate her food.

Magdalen impulsively squeezed Katrin's arm. "Thank you for being my friend, and Stoffel's friend too. Please watch out for him as much as you can when he's in the kitchen."

Katrin hugged her back. "I can tell you are worrying, but all will be well." She lowered her voice. "Your shepherd will be well."

Magdalen shook her head. "Katrin . . ."

"Never mind. I shall see you in the morning."

Katrin went back to the kitchen to finish her work for the day and Magdalen went back upstairs to see if Agnes needed her.

Magdalen reached the corridor that led to Agnes's door. Should she knock? Would Agnes be in the Great Hall having her evening meal? If she wasn't, she might be vexed with Magdalen for disturbing her. Agnes was not accustomed to having servants invading her room constantly as Magdalen had been.

"There you are." Agnes approached her. "Come to my chamber for a moment. I need you."

"Yes, Lady Magdalen." She plastered a smile on her face and followed Agnes to her room.

"I need your help unbuttoning my gown." Agnes presented her back to Magdalen.

Magdalen began the task, pushing Agnes's hair aside to reach the buttons that started at the base of her neck and went all the way down her back. She could not help wondering who had buttoned them for her but refrained from asking.

Agnes stepped out of her gown. Dressed in her underdress, she said, "Take the gown and hang it over there. In the morning I will want you to bring me my breakfast. Then I will instruct you as to your duties for the rest of the day. Now I wish you to fetch me a fresh pitcher of water, then leave immediately. I will not need you for the rest of the night."

"Yes, my lady."

After Magdalen hung up the dress, she took the large water pitcher from Agnes's chamber and left.

Downstairs in the kitchen she found Steffan carrying in an armload of wood for the kitchen fire. He dumped it by the oven.

"Is that Lady Magdalen's water pitcher?" Frau Clara strode into the kitchen. "Kitchen boy." She looked at Steffan. "Go fetch a fresh bucket of water for the lady's pitcher."

Steffan looked at her.

Magdalen set down the pitcher. "I'll go with him." She hurried out the door before Frau Clara could protest.

It was nearly dark outside as they made their way to the well. Steffan looked all around. Everyone must have gone to their beds for the night.

"You need a good night's rest," Magdalen told him.

"I would agree with that. But tomorrow, sleep or no sleep, I will break away and search for my portrait."

"May I help?"

"Perhaps. Where will you be tomorrow?"

"I have to bring *the lady* her breakfast. After that, I'm not sure. I had at least two hours this afternoon with nothing to do. If I'd known where to look I could—"

"You will be free until the cook gets her breakfast prepared, *ja?*"

"Ja."

"But I do not want to endanger you." He glanced away and shook his head. "If Lord Hazen caught you snooping around the castle, you would be in just as much danger as I am."

"I do not think he would kill me, since he doesn't know who I am. Whereas with you . . ."

Steffan hauled the water bucket back up, pulling the rope hand over hand, his upper arms and back flexing against his shirt in the waning twilight. When the bucket reached the top, he unhooked it from the windlass. The Duke of Wolfberg had grown some muscles since she danced with him at Thornbeck.

"Come. We should go inside."

"So you think the portrait is in Lord Hazen's room?"

"I think it could be, since that room belonged to my parents. I used to play there when I was a boy, and my steward said he hid it in the place where I used to play as a small child. But you should not go there. I want you to promise me you won't."

She wanted to tell him that she was not a child and she was not betrothed to him and therefore could do what she wanted. But they were already entering the kitchen.

Steffan lifted the bucket and tilted it to pour into the pitcher.

"Thank you, Stoffel," Magdalen said. "I shall see you tomorrow."

Behind her Frau Clara told him, "You may go to your room. Climb to the top of the stairs and go to the room on the left."

Magdalen walked slower, waiting for Steffan to reach her. When she was halfway up the first flight of stairs, he caught up.

"Are you well? Perhaps you should see a healer."

"Lord Hazen sent away the only good one." His voice was deep and gruff.

"Is there a physician or barber who could look at your head?"

"I just need to sleep."

She didn't say anything the rest of the way up. When they arrived at the third level, he nodded at her and continued up. Her heart squeezed painfully as he passed out of sight, his shoulders slumping.

"There you are." Agnes stood in front of her open bedchamber door.

Magdalen hurried toward her with the pitcher of water.

"What took you so long? Are you consorting with that simple-minded boy?"

"I was concerned about his injury, but he is going to bed now."

"He is not your concern. Your only concern is to please me." Agnes raised her chin.

"How may I please you, my lady?" Magdalen couldn't quite keep the irony out of her voice.

"You may bring me my water."

Magdalen entered the room and set the pitcher on the table.

"I have no more need of you this evening. You may go."

Magdalen left the room, refusing to curtsy to her. When

she reached the stairs, she hurried up, but at the top Steffan was nowhere in sight.

She sighed, went into her shared bedchamber, and thankfully one of the other maidservants had put a sheet on her bed. Magdalen closed her eyes, clasped her hands, and prayed silently for Steffan's well-being.

Chapter Sixteen

The next day Steffan's head felt much better, except for a tiny pain over his eye, but every muscle in his arms and legs was screaming for his full attention.

He got dressed slowly, with Lord Hazen's personal servant telling him to make haste and get down to the kitchen to stoke the morning fire.

Steffan walked down the corridor, but the first step he took down the stairs made him gasp in pain. He grimaced with every step, and when he reached the next level, Magdalen was waiting for him.

"Where is your bandage? Is your head still hurting?" She spoke softly.

"What are you doing up so early?" he groused. She looked quite lovely in the torchlight, with her reddish-blonde hair glowing around her head and her eyes wide and anxious.

"I came to see how you were faring. Is your head still bleeding?" She stood on tiptoe to inspect his forehead.

"No."

"It does not look so bad." She glanced behind her down the

corridor, then leaned close to his ear. "I can go to Lord Hazen's rooms and search for your portrait."

"No." He drew back to look into her eyes. "If he thinks you suspect his scheme, you will quietly disappear and no one will ever discover what happened to you. You must stay away from his rooms."

He gave her his most severe scowl, but she did not seem very intimidated.

"You cannot go searching if you are working all day in the kitchen. I do not think your getting a job working in the kitchen was a good idea, but if I can find what you need—"

"No. It is too dangerous. Do not do it." To emphasize his point, he took hold of her arm.

"But I will wait until Lord Hazen is away from his chamber, until I know he won't be back, and I can—"

"You cannot know when he will return."

"But I have so much more time and freedom than you do. It will be easy. Besides, I am a house servant. It will not seem so suspicious if I am in his chamber cleaning."

Forcefulness was not working. "Please, Magdalen. Do not do this." He took her small, soft hand between his and peered into her eyes.

Perhaps that had not been the best idea either, because now she was gazing up at him, her pink lips parted, as if she was startled. What would she do if he kissed her?

He could not be thinking about her like that.

"Please wait." He let go of her hand. "I shall come up with a plan. There is no need to rush into something. It will be better to be patient. Please, Magdalen. Trust me and wait."

She bit her lip. "Very well. I shall try not to endanger myself or you."

"Thank you." He turned away.

"Wait."

He stopped.

Her eyes were wide and her brows were drawn together. "Please be careful. I am praying for you."

How long had it been since he'd felt someone truly cared for his welfare, enough to pray for him? Not since his grandmother died and he left for Prague. His sister, Gertrudt, married a prince a year ago and went to live in Burgundy, which was many days' journey on the other side of the German regions. Most people only cared what Steffan could do for them. Since Jacob was gone now, too, Steffan was truly on his own.

He continued down the steps, biting back a groan. He did not wish her to know how much pain he was in. Not only were his ribs sore from getting punched by the guard but he was also in pain from carrying firewood and buckets of water.

Steffan had befriended Magdalen, had bought her food and paper and ink, but he had also deceived her by not intending to find a courier for her letters. And yet, she could still look at him with great concern in her eyes, had carefully bandaged his head, and rose early to check on him.

She deserved a husband who would cherish her. Was Steffan even capable of cherishing a woman? He'd seen the way his father loved his mother, so much that when she died he was a broken man. Anger welled up at his father for the kind of weakness that would cause him to leave Steffan and his sister with no one but his grandmother, servants, and a less-than-honorable uncle.

But perhaps what he was really feeling was fear, fear that he would follow in his father's footsteps. He never wanted to feel that kind of devastation.

That old familiar emotion—fear or anger, they felt about the same—rose inside him. It was as if he'd fallen into another abandoned well—trapped, in danger, and helpless.

No. He was not helpless. He would defeat his uncle and cousin and would once more feel powerful, calm, and content.

Steffan just had to stay away from Magdalen until he could get back his rightful power and send her home. Perhaps he would even find her a husband among his peers.

He finally reached the kitchen where Magdalen went to fetch the food for Agnes and Alexander. Meanwhile, he carried in two loads of wood and then several buckets of water, as the cooks were already preparing the day's food, beginning with several loaves of bread.

After picking up the second load of wood, he noticed an older man standing at the edge of the trees that bordered the bailey around the castle. The man's face was familiar. Could it be? He looked very much like the horse groomer Ansel.

Steffan pretended not to stare at the man, but he was certain he was Ansel. His clothing was ragged and patched, and he looked much thinner than the last time Steffan had seen him.

His heart clenched. Poor Ansel. But Steffan had no choice but to ignore his old servant and go inside with his load of wood.

Soon the smell of warm bread filled the air. The cooks removed the loaves from the large brick oven, and Steffan stoked the fire with more wood.

He started out the door to get another load of wood. The bread loaves were sitting just inside the large window casing, and Ansel was there, staring at the cooling bread. The gray-haired man snatched a loaf and stuffed it inside his shirt. But as soon as he turned around to flee, a guard grabbed the back of his neck.

"Thief!"

Steffan hurried outside.

"That is the Duke of Wolfberg's bread!" the guard yelled. "How dare you steal from the duke?" He raised the hilt of his sword to strike him.

"Wait!" Steffan leapt toward them, throwing his arm between Ansel and the guard.

"Get out of the way," the guard growled through clenched teeth.

"Will you injure this poor old man over a loaf of bread?" Steffan's blood was boiling up inside him, especially to think he would do this in the name of the duke—in Steffan's own name.

"No one steals from Wolfberg Castle." The guard, whose face was twisted in a menacing scowl, still held on to Ansel's neck.

"Let him go. It was only bread."

"Will you take his beating for him?" The guard tightened his grip on Ansel, the older man's eyes widening. He looked so frail, as if the guard could easily break him in two.

"If you let him go, then yes, I will take his punishment."

The guard looked hard at Steffan, but only for a moment. He let go of Ansel with a shove. Ansel stumbled and broke into a run.

Steffan barely had time to raise his arm to protect the wound on his forehead before the guard slammed the hilt of his sword into Steffan's shoulder, then punched him in the mouth. The next blow was to Steffan's chin. Stars exploded before his eyes.

He fell to the ground. Blood, salty and metallic, ran over his tongue. He braced himself for the next blow. A sharp pain exploded in his side as the guard kicked him once, then again.

Steffan lay still, waiting, finally opening his eye. The guard was gone.

Steffan lifted his head and spit a stream of red on the ground.

His shoulder burned, his face ached, and his ribs throbbed. At least he hadn't lost any teeth. He lay his head back down on the ground. Perhaps he could get a few moments' rest before anyone came looking for him.

⌒

Steffan opened his eyes to three people standing over him and the sun shining brighter than it had when he'd closed them.

"He's awake now. You can cease your fretting." The head cook glanced at the person beside her, then looked back down at him and thrust a cloth at him. "Cover your mouth with this. You're bleeding. Now go upstairs and get cleaned up. You can come back to your duties after the midday meal."

Magdalen and Katrin were hovering beside the cook. They stretched their hands to him. "Let us help you up."

They each took his elbow and pulled him into a sitting position while the cook went back inside the kitchen.

The world started spinning. His head and lip throbbed, and his shoulder still burned, but not quite as much as before. He closed his eyes, and when he opened them, the world had almost stopped spinning. He spit out the blood that had been collecting in his mouth, careful not to get it on the maidens' shoes. He heaved himself up with the young ladies helping him.

"What happened?" Magdalen asked.

"What are you doing here?" He cringed at her coming to his rescue yet again. He wasn't sure he could bear staring into her concerned face one more time.

"Katrin came and got me from the dining hall. She said you were badly injured."

"I am not badly injured." But his lip was so swollen that his words were slurred.

Katrin said, "I saw him defending an old man who was stealing a loaf of bread from the kitchen window. He offered to take the old man's punishment if the guard would let the man go. It was the bravest thing I've ever seen." Katrin's voice cracked on the last two words and she burst into tears.

Magdalen stared up at him. "Oh, Steffan," she breathed. She took the cloth the cook had given him from his hand and wiped his face. "Your wound from yesterday is bleeding again."

"It's nothing." Katrin's crying was making him so uncomfortable, he chuckled. "You two act as if I'm the first man to ever bleed or get a few blows from a man twice his size."

"Katrin!" the cook yelled out the window. "Get back in here. I need you. That other maiden can take care of him."

Katrin ran back into the kitchen.

"You heard her," Magdalen said. "I can take care of you. So come."

She steered him back toward the kitchen and walked him through, her arm around his back and his arm around her shoulders. Most of the servants were eating their breakfast, so no one was there to see his bloody face.

"Wait here." Magdalen propped him against the wall. She ran off into the dining hall.

He'd been beaten by two different guards. He only hoped that someday he would see both those guards' faces when they discovered the man they had wrongfully beaten was the Duke of Wolfberg.

Magdalen came hurrying back, her expression sober, as when she had walked back to the stables with her mute friend, Lenhart, intent on defending him from the men who were mistreating him.

Her fierceness made him stand up a bit straighter and pay closer attention.

"I got you some breakfast." She held a bundle in her hand. "You can eat it after we clean up your face."

Now that he was standing on his own, she seemed uncertain as to whether to put her arm around him and serve as his crutch. But she only hesitated a moment. She took him by the wrist, laid his arm across her shoulders, and started toward the stairs. He didn't protest.

They walked slowly, his sides burning as if on fire every time he took a breath. He tested his jaw again. It was still a bit sore but felt much better than earlier. His lip was still bleeding as he held the cloth against it. He would at least be able to rest until the midday meal, a few hours.

A pang of guilt stabbed him as he thought about how kind she was being, how determined she was to help him. What spoiled, privileged nobleman's daughter was so uncomplaining and willing to help someone who was dirty and bloody?

He thought of his own sister. He couldn't imagine her even touching him in the state he was in. He could just see her wrinkle her nose and recoil from him, having never done an hour of actual work in her life.

"You don't have to help me," he said, even as his foot caught on the next step and he stumbled.

"I want to. Besides, I don't have to assist *my lady* for a few more hours."

Finally, they made it to the fourth level of the castle.

"Let me make sure no one is in the men's bedchamber." He removed his arm from around her shoulders and opened the door. "Anyone here?"

Chapter Seventeen

Magdalen followed Steffan inside. She forced herself not to think about his pain, what he had done, or what had been done to him, but to concentrate on tending each injury.

He went straight to a bed and lay down, moaning as he did so.

Never had she been inside a man's bedchamber or near his bed. She halted midstride. But no one was around and this was Steffan. He would not harm her.

He took the cloth, which was nearly saturated with bright-red blood, away from his mouth. His bottom lip was terribly swollen, and the lower half of his face was bloody.

"It appears to have stopped bleeding." She tried to look at him as a task, to be cold in her assessment of him. She did not want to break down in tears as Katrin had done—which had brought tears to Magdalen's eyes as well.

"I am well," he said. Or at least she thought that was what he said. It was hard to understand him, and his lip might still be swelling.

"I wish I had some ice or snow to put on your lip."

He quirked an eyebrow at her. "Wrong time of year."

"And your other injury only bled a bit." She pointed to the cut over his eye. But dried blood stained the side of his face.

Footsteps shuffled down the hallway, coming closer.

Magdalen turned and watched as one of the other men-servants walked through the doorway with a bucket and a cloth.

"I thought you might need this." He headed over to the table against the wall and poured some of the water into a pitcher and some into a pottery bowl. Then he handed the cloth to Magdalen.

"Thank you, Dietrich," Steffan said.

Dietrich came over and looked down at Steffan. "I've seen raw meat that looked better than your face. But you won't die."

"Ah, that's very encouraging," he managed to say in spite of his fat lip.

"We all heard what you did," the man said. "That was . . ." He paused, nodded, and raised his brows before he said, "Very brave." He tilted his head to one side. "Stupid, but brave."

Steffan seemed to be trying not to smile, not to stretch his lips. "*Ja. Danke.*"

"I must go back to my duties and leave you to your lovely healer." He winked at Magdalen.

"Thank you for the water," she said, then realized what he'd called her. She felt herself blushing and went over to get the bowl of water so she'd be facing away from Steffan. She took a deep breath, then carried the bowl back to him and set it on the bed.

She squeezed the cloth out over the bowl. "I feel as if I've done this before." She had to make light of the situation because she felt her heart twisting in pity and admiration as she started to wash the blood from his cheeks and beard.

She stroked the side of his face where the cut over his eye had left traces of blood. She would not think about how he had defended an old man and willingly allowed himself to be beaten so the thief could go free. She would not think about how unfair life was at the moment to both Steffen and her, about how he was the only person who knew her pain.

She dabbed at the cut over his eye. He winced.

She might have told him something that Hegatha had once said, that the cut might not scar if it did not scab over. But she did not trust herself to speak.

She wiped the blood from the whiskers on his chin with the cloth. His eyes were half open, watching her face. She pretended not to notice and dipped the cloth into the bowl of water and squeezed it out, turning the water pink.

Her heart beat faster and her breath became shallow. She tried to think of something to say to break the tension in the air as she dabbed at the spot just below his bottom lip.

"You aren't doing very well at not drawing attention to yourself."

He did that thing again where he quirked one eyebrow up. Even beaten and bloody, he was handsome, with intelligent eyes emphasized by distinct black eyebrows.

"All the servant girls will be in love with you before the day is out, as Katrin will tell them all about your noble and chivalrous deed."

He pushed himself up on one elbow. "I need to spit."

She nearly laughed. His statement finally broke the taut feeling in the air. Magdalen turned away to get a cup and the slop bucket she had spied by the door.

She held the bucket for him while he spit. Then she filled the cup with fresh water from the pitcher and handed it to him.

He swished some water around in his mouth, then spit it in

the slop bucket. He repeated the action, then drank the rest of the water in the cup.

She took the cup and then remembered the breakfast she had snatched for him—a bread roll and a piece of cheese. She removed it from her pocket and handed it to him.

He unfolded the cloth and bit into the bread, still half sitting up. Magdalen retrieved pillows from two other beds and placed them behind his back.

"Thank you."

Her cheeks were beginning to burn again. "I think I should go now."

He swallowed his bite. "Finished doctoring my wounds already?"

"If I could do any more for you I would. God will do the rest of the healing, no doubt."

His brown hair was tousled and lying across his forehead in a wavy swath, a healthy color back in his cheeks as he ate his roll and cheese, and his intense brown eyes were staring back at her. If it weren't for his enormously swollen lip, she might be tempted to do something very improper, like bend down and kiss him.

She took a step back. How foolish her thoughts were! She was no immature girl fancying herself in love with every young man she met. Then she remembered that she was angry with him for not sending her letters.

What she should be thinking about was how to get their identities back.

"I can go and see if Lord Hazen is in his rooms, and if he isn't I can—"

"No."

He leaned forward and grabbed her wrist, holding it loosely.

"I don't want you getting in trouble with him. He is a dangerous man."

"But it makes more sense for me to look for the portrait. He thinks I am only a house servant. He would not be so alarmed if he saw me—"

"If he thought you were trying to steal from him, he would. He would suspect I was still alive and that I had sent you. He would torture you and use you to get to me. It is entirely too dangerous. I forbid it."

Magdalen pulled her arm free from his grasp. She was not used to anyone touching her without her permission or talking to her this way—at least, no one except her mother. If Steffan treated her like her mother, it was a good thing he didn't want to marry her. She'd rather die than be married to someone for the rest of her life who treated her as if she didn't matter, as if she didn't deserve respect.

"You have no right to forbid me from doing anything," she said, her voice low as she fought off the anger that had stolen her breath. "I have a stake in this too."

He sighed. "Forgive me. I am in no position . . . You are right."

His contrite tone made her breath return and her heart stop pounding.

"I am used to being in control," he went on, "and I wanted to feel as if I could get myself out of this situation. Perhaps you are in a better position to look for the portrait. But even if one of us finds it, we should probably leave it where it is for now, as we have nowhere to hide it. We will need someone powerful to help us fight Lord Hazen and get our places back, so the portrait is only the first task."

He was staring her in the eye now. "I want you to be cautious.

There is no need to feel any urgency about the portrait just yet. Take your time, and if you are absolutely certain Lord Hazen is not in his chamber and will not be returning soon, I suppose it will be acceptable if you take a quick look."

"I will be careful."

"And make sure his guard and personal servant are not nearby. They may be greater impediments than Lord Hazen himself."

"Of course. I shall be cautious of them as well."

He reached out and took her hand. "Please. Don't get caught."

Her heart was a lump in her throat. Did he care so much about her? No, he probably just did not want Lord Hazen's suspicions to be aroused.

She slipped her hand out of his loose grasp. "Do not worry. I understand the seriousness of our situation. If I cannot safely enter and leave Lord Hazen's chamber, I shall stay away."

"Good. Thank you."

Agnes would not expect her for more than an hour, so Magdalen found one of the other servants who shared the fourth-level bedchamber with her. She was carrying sheets down the stairs from the third level.

"Hilde, I would be pleased to help you change the linens on Lord Hazen's bed. Is he still in his chamber?"

Hilde halted on the steps and stared, mouth slightly ajar. "Lord Hazen? He is down in the Great Hall breaking his fast. I changed his linens already, but you can change them next week."

"Thank you, Hilde. But please don't tell anyone I asked to

do that. They might be jealous, or you might get scolded by Frau Clara. It can be our secret."

Instructing Hilde not to tell might have the opposite effect. But it was too late. Magdalen couldn't take the words back.

She ran up the steps to Lord Hazen's chamber and paused in the corridor. No guard stood in front of the door, which was half open. She hurried toward it and peeked inside. No one was in sight, so she went toward the water pitcher, as if she were taking the pitcher to refill it. But no one called out to her, and she faced the rest of the room.

The bed was enormous and draped all around with dark curtains. A couple of trunks stood near the bed, but would Jacob have hidden the portrait in one of Lord Hazen's trunks? That wouldn't make sense.

She let her gaze travel around the room looking for possible hiding places. The thing that caught her eye was what was set against the wall. Stacks of small wooden coffers were laid out in the shape of a large rectangle. Most of the boxes would require a key to open. The small coffers were of varying sizes—some as big as three handbreadths and others as small as a black walnut with its green hull still on.

They were too small to hide a large portrait, unless it was folded or rolled up, but Steffan had not said how large the portrait was. She had assumed it was several handbreadths tall, as befitted a wealthy duke, but some portrait painters preferred a smaller canvas.

She decided to search the larger places first. She opened a trunk and rummaged around inside. Nothing except clothing. She ran her shaking hands around the sides and inside the lid, but found no secret compartments. She did the same with the second trunk. Still nothing.

She stood and looked around, but the wooden coffers were drawing her to them. Magdalen walked across the room, intent on the little coffers. Even if the portrait was not here, she might find something important. She reached for one of the top boxes and the lid lifted easily. Inside was a foreign coin and three buttons. She closed it and opened the next one. It was larger and held a pair of shears one might use for clipping hair.

Her hands were shaking harder than before as she reached for a large one. She shifted two smaller ones so she could lift the lid. Inside was a large book, a book she recognized.

Her father's mining book. She lifted it to find a second one. They'd both been missing since just after her father's death. But how did they get here?

"Magdalen."

She jumped and spun around, her heart pounding out of her chest. Steffan came through the door toward her.

"Dear heavenly saints," Magdalen whispered. "I nearly died of fright."

Steffan's footfalls were silent as he walked toward her. He wasn't wearing any shoes.

"My father's books." Magdalen pointed down at the box.

Steffan leaned over to inspect them. "Quickly. Let's check all the boxes."

They lifted the lids of all the coffers on top, then moved them one at a time, but they began encountering locked coffers. In fact, many of the others were locked.

As quickly and carefully as they could, they restacked the boxes as they were before.

Magdalen whispered, "He could return at any moment, and you cannot let him see you." She wanted to take her father's books, but she had no good place to hide them. Besides, she didn't want Lord Hazen to know someone had discovered them.

"I'm not arguing," Steffan said as they both hurried to the door and looked out.

She did not see anyone, but the sound of footsteps resounded on the wooden stairs. Someone was coming.

Chapter Eighteen

She put a hand on Steffan's back as they both rushed out the door and ran until they reached the servants' stairs. Magdalen started to go up, but Steffan caught her arm and motioned her to follow him as he went down one flight of stairs. Then Steffan dashed into an open doorway and pulled her against the wall. He stood with his finger over his lips, still holding on to her arm.

She was breathing hard but trying to stay quiet. The room they were in was dark, as the shutters on the windows were closed. She listened, very aware of Steffan's nearness, his hand on her arm, his shoulder pressing against hers.

"Did they see us?" she whispered.

"Wait."

They stood silent and unmoving. In the dim light, his face was pale. Sweat beaded on his upper lip.

"You are in pain," she said.

He said nothing for a moment. Then, "I am well enough."

They stood for several more moments. Finally, Steffan said, "He must not have seen us, or else my uncle would have his guards looking for us. I think we can go now."

Her breathing had finally slowed to normal as she followed

Steffan out of the room and back up the stairs. He was moving slow and breathing hard. She followed him all the way up to the room he shared with the other menservants, then touched his arm.

"Let me see you." She got in front of him. At least he wasn't bleeding anywhere, but his puffy lip was purple.

"You should lie down." She went and poured him a cup of water and brought it to him where he sat on his bed. "Is there anything else I can do?"

He shook his head and drank the water.

"You should not have been out of bed and engaging in dangerous activities." She stood by his bedside.

Steffan pulled the cup away from his mouth. "And I told you to be patient and wait for a good opportunity."

"It was a good opportunity. Hilde told me he was not in his chamber."

"Who is Hilde?"

"The servant who changes his bed linens."

"And when does she change his bed linens?"

"Every Wednesday. She said I could change them next week."

He was either looking down or his eyes were closed. "I am sorry for my ill temper. You did well. And if Lord Hazen did not notice us running down the corridor or see anything amiss in his chamber, then he will have no reason to suspect that anyone is sneaking around and searching through his things. He will not be on his guard, and we shall have an advantage. I thought of another place where I used to play as a child, so I will need to look there if it's not in my parents' old bedchamber."

"I can look in Hazen's bedchamber next week when I change his linens, and we can also sneak in when we know he's in the Great Hall or doing something else."

He nodded but didn't say anything for several moments.

"I should go. Agnes will need me soon."

"Magdalen?"

"Yes?"

"Thank you."

She had a sudden urge to reach out and smooth the hair off his forehead, but of course, that would be foolish, not to mention awkward. How brave he had been to take a beating from that burly guard. What kind of duke would take the punishment for an old man who was stealing bread?

But she didn't want to let her heart soften toward him. He may have done a noble deed, but he was still a duke who had rejected her.

Magdalen sat in Agnes's bedchamber waiting for her return. She wanted to search for Steffan's portrait, but she was afraid Agnes would come back and find her gone, and she wasn't ready to anger her.

With nothing to occupy her, her mind wandered to the letters she had written to Lady Thornbeck and her mother. Where were they? She had given them back to Steffan, but she wished she had asked him where he'd left them. He didn't have a chance to collect his things before he ended up here in the castle.

If Agnes or Lord Hazen found those letters and read what she had written—the truth about what was happening here in Wolfberg—she and Steffan would both end up dead.

She needed those letters. She needed to *send* those letters! But how would she find a courier, and if she found one, how would she pay him?

Voices drifted in from the corridor.

"I don't want you to be ashamed of me," Agnes said.

Magdalen tiptoed toward the door and listened.

"How could I ever be ashamed of you?" a man answered.

"I only care about what you think," was Agnes's breathy comment.

No one said anything for several moments and Magdalen imagined that they were kissing. *Ick.*

A bit later, the man said, "I have to go to my father now."

"You mean your uncle?"

"Oh, of course. My uncle. He wants to speak with me."

So, Steffan's cousin was still lying to his "wife" about who he was.

"Will I see you later?"

"*Ja.*"

Magdalen started tidying up, moving to the other side of the room, picking up and putting away some articles of clothing that Agnes had left on the floor or draped over the furniture.

"What are you doing in here?" Agnes said.

Magdalen looked over her shoulder, pretending surprise. "I was just cleaning. You told me you would need me."

Agnes huffed a breath, as if undecided about whether she should scold Magdalen. But she said nothing as she wandered over to a cushioned chair and sat down. Magdalen peeked at her occasionally as she folded Agnes's clothes. Agnes stared at the wall with a pucker between her eyes, her lips pouty. Finally, she got up and came toward Magdalen.

"In two weeks Lord Hazen is giving my husband and me a wedding celebration and inviting the nobles from all over the northern regions. But your mother's invitation will have to get lost. I cannot risk her being here, of course. And your friends, the Margrave of Thornbeck and his lady—that invitation will also be misdirected. My father has promised to take care of that."

Magdalen forced her expression to remain unchanged.

"You are very quiet," Agnes observed. "I heard that your imbecile friend, the shepherd who is so attached to you, was beaten by a guard again. You should keep a better watch over him."

What a cruel, mean-spirited . . . "What would your husband say if I were to tell him that you are not Lady Magdalen after all, but are only a stable worker's daughter and a servant?"

"If you dared to tell him such a lie, my father would—"

"Your father the baron, who is now in heaven? Or your father the stable worker?"

"He isn't a stable worker anymore. Lord Hazen promoted him to be the assistant to the captain of the guard." Agnes actually smirked.

"So you don't mind if your new husband discovers your deception?"

Her smirk disappeared. "You won't tell him. You wouldn't want Lenhart or Stoffel to be harmed." But fear shone from her eyes.

"Do you care so much what your husband thinks? You know you aren't really married to him, since you were married under a false name." Should Magdalen tell Agnes that her husband wasn't the real Duke of Wolfberg?

"Please don't tell him. He would be hurt if he found out I lied to him. And you do not understand how ruthless Lord Hazen is."

Magdalen felt a tiny pang of pity for Agnes at the anxiety on her face. Could Agnes actually care that Alexander would feel hurt at her deception? Probably she was only afraid of what would happen to her and Erlich when Lord Hazen discovered the truth.

"You cannot tell him, Magdalen. Vow that you won't."

"Very well. I won't tell him—yet. But in exchange you must not allow any harm to come to either Stoffel or Lenhart, because as soon as you do, I will tell your husband everything."

"Well." Agnes tossed her head, turning half away from Magdalen. "You have no proof. He won't believe you."

"Perhaps I do have proof. Proof I can show to Lord Hazen."

Agnes's lips parted and her chest rose and fell.

"But you must tell your guards not to beat Stoffel again, and tell your father and the stable workers to be kind to Lenhart."

Agnes clamped her fists on her hips. "I cannot tell the guards not to beat some particular servant. What would they think? They might tell Lord Hazen. And I certainly can't tell the stable workers what to do."

"And why not? You are the Duchess of Wolfberg. I should think it would be well within your authority."

"What would Alexander say? If I were to single out two obscure servants and tell the guards and other workers to give them special treatment, he would think I had lost my senses."

Magdalen shrugged. "If you do not wish to risk it, that is all well and good. I shall tell the duke and the baron the truth."

"Very well. I shall speak to the guards and the stable workers."

Magdalen had never done this sort of bargaining before. It felt foreign, but her situation, as well as that of Steffan and Lenhart, was desperate.

She smiled. Avelina would be proud of her.

"You were ruthless enough to steal my place in life, but Agnes, surely you are too shrewd to fall in love with the duke."

Agnes crossed her arms in front of her chest. "You probably think I'm evil for what I did to you. But it was all my father's idea.

He was tired of being told what to do. He said, 'Why couldn't we be the ones telling others what to do?' He made it sound easy and as if we were entitled to do it. Why did you have all the privileges? What had you ever done to be the daughter of a baron? Nothing. But when I met my husband . . . I would do anything to keep him from discovering the truth."

Perhaps Agnes did love Alexander, in her own warped way. Was Alexander evil? Or was he only a pawn of his father's? Steffan called Alexander a whey-faced imbecile, and yet Agnes seemed to care what he thought of her.

"You need me as well, to protect you." Agnes made her voice sound gruff, but the fear lingered.

As if Magdalen would ever accept help from Agnes. But if she and Steffan were not able to find his portrait so he could prove his identity, Magdalen would need help to prove that she was Lady Magdalen. She couldn't expect to get that help from Agnes, however.

Regardless, in two weeks guests would arrive in Wolfberg to celebrate the fake marriage of Agnes and Alexander.

Chapter Nineteen

Magdalen glanced around the dining hall while waiting in line for her food. Where was Steffan?

He walked in, and she moved to the end of the line with him.

"In two weeks," she said softly, "there will be a wedding celebration. Lord Hazen will invite all the nobles, but Agnes's father will make sure my mother and Lord Thornbeck will never receive their invitations."

He said near her ear, "It was very clever of you to discover that."

"I want to send my letters." She glanced around to make sure they weren't attracting attention to themselves by whispering together. "Where are they?"

"I put them somewhere safe before I came into the castle."

"I can retrieve them and find a courier to deliver them."

"You might get caught leaving the castle. I'll fetch them."

"Forgive me if I do not trust you."

Steffan stared down at her, a pained look in his eyes.

They had reached the front of the line and took the proffered bowl of food. The people sitting in front of them were quiet and kept looking across at them, so neither Magdalen nor Steffan spoke as they ate. Then Katrin came and sat on the bench beside Steffan.

"Are you well?" she asked. "I found out the man you saved was once a servant here at the castle. He was sick during planting season and was unable to plant his vegetable garden early enough. He and his wife were nearly starving. You probably saved his life."

Steffan did not look Katrin in the eye.

"I hope your head will be all right. I knew a man who was dizzy and had trouble walking for the rest of his life after a few blows."

Steffan swallowed the bite he was chewing. "I assure you I'm not dizzy."

"I am very glad to hear that. Maggie." She leaned behind him to talk to Magdalen. "All the house servants seem to think your name is Agnes. That is very strange."

"My mistress, Lady Magdalen, insists on calling me Agnes. It is very odd, but one cannot argue with one's mistress."

Katrin gave her a strange look, as if she was thinking something she could not say aloud, and turned around to eat her food.

Lenhart suddenly loomed in front of them on the other side of the table.

"Lenhart! I'm so pleased to see you. Are you well?"

Lenhart came around the table and embraced Magdalen. How good it was to see a familiar face, someone she trusted completely. She hugged him tight.

Steffan could not imagine his own sister, Gertrudt, hugging a male servant.

Both Magdalen and Lenhart were smiling with their whole

faces—their whole bodies, actually. Could the pain inside Steffan's chest be . . . jealousy? Magdalen trusted this boy, but she did not trust him, and rightfully so.

"Where are you working? Are you still in the stables?"

Lenhart shook his head. He held up one hand, then brought his fingers out straight and his thumb up to meet them. He moved his hand as though the tips of his fingers were a beak pecking the ground.

"You're tending the geese? Oh, that is good! Be careful, though. One goose likes to bite. His name is Gus, and he has a black spot on the top of his beak."

She went on to explain which other geese were prone to bite and which ones liked to be petted.

"Come and get your food," the grumpy kitchen servant called out.

Lenhart went to fetch his bowl of food, then sat between Steffan and Magdalen.

No respect. Even when Steffan was in Prague, his wealth made people respect him. Now . . . he had no control over anything or anyone in his life, and no one gave him any special treatment, not even Magdalen, the one person who knew who he was.

Magdalen was always kind to him, but she didn't treat him as she should a duke. Magdalen, the girl with pretty green eyes. Magdalen, who was smiling so warmly right now at Lenhart, who was attentive to Katrin even when she talked too much. She had been so gentle and concerned about his wounds, washing his face and bringing him fresh water to drink.

What could Steffan do to make her smile at him the way she was smiling at Lenhart?

This was a foolish way of thinking. He'd always said he would honor his grandmother's wishes, which was never to marry beneath his station, to think of his people's needs above his own, and here his people were, some of them starving and being mistreated by Hazen's guards.

Steffan had been a fool to listen to his uncle and go to Prague, leaving his people in the hands of his evil uncle. He would not be so unwise again, and he would not lose his head over a woman.

He clenched his spoon so tightly, the handle broke.

"Are you well? You look a bit pale." Katrin leaned toward him, staring hard.

"I am well." Steffan sat up straighter.

Magdalen and Lenhart stood up as if to leave. She looked down at Steffan. "I hope they will not work you too hard today. I do not think you are yet recovered."

Her wavy hair framed her face as she stared down at him. She was one of the fairest maidens he'd ever beheld. He'd hardly be alive if he didn't notice. But that only increased his resolve not to fall in love with her.

Hazen trudged up the stairs. His head had been aching since he'd arisen from bed that morning, and now it was as if needles were stabbing him behind his eyes. He'd have to send someone to the village to buy some healing herbs.

His mind kept revisiting the fact that his guards whom he'd sent to kill Steffan had not yet returned. He had not given them the bulk of their payment, and it could only be collected when they'd shown proof of his nephew's death. Many things could have delayed them, but such a long delay did not bode well.

Someone was walking on the level above him. Then his son's wife appeared on the staircase. She saw him and stopped.

"Lady Magdalen. Come. I would like to speak with you. Let us continue down to the library."

She hesitated, then complied.

Tideke, his guard captain, stood at the bottom. Hazen motioned for him to follow him into the library, then closed the door.

"One of the servants will be expecting me." She glanced at the closed door and took a step away from him. "And my husband, the duke, will be looking for me."

"I only want to ask a few questions." He committed the fearful look in her eyes to memory so he could enjoy it later.

"Of course." She crossed her arms and then immediately uncrossed them.

"I was wondering if you thought your husband had lost some weight since seeing him in Thornbeck two years ago. Has he changed at all?"

The color drained from the girl's lips. "I . . . no, he looks very much the same. I always thought he was very handsome, and so he is. Very handsome."

He simply stared at her, hoping she might become so nervous she would reveal something. But she only squirmed and glanced about the room.

"How often do you anticipate that your mother will send you letters?"

"My mother? In a few months she will probably write. I do not like writing letters, so she will probably not write me very often."

He had heard Lady Magdalen's eyes were green and her hair was tinted red. This girl had blonde hair and hazel eyes.

"Who was the servant girl who came to Wolfberg with you?"

"Servant girl? Oh, her name is Agnes. She is a terrible servant. I sent her away to work outdoors."

"I see. But you have a new servant helping you in your rooms. What is her name? Maggie?"

"Y-yes."

"Is she not the same girl who came here with you?"

"No, she is not. Who is telling these lies?" Her bravado suddenly rose and her cheeks reddened.

"Lies?"

"As I said before, I must go. People will be looking for me." She eyed the door.

How dare she think she could fool him? He motioned to Tideke.

His guard stepped forward and grabbed her around the neck, pulling her up on tiptoe. Tideke smiled as though relishing the frailty of her bones, his thumb pressing the middle of her throat.

She gasped and grabbed at his hands, her eyes nearly popping out of her head.

Hazen took notice of the way her face turned red, and he imagined he was the one squeezing the breath, the life out of her as the look in her eyes became more and more panicked.

Tideke must have lessened the pressure because she drew in a noisy breath.

"I rule Wolfberg, and those who are disloyal to me will not be allowed to live, whether one is the wife of the duke . . . or merely a servant girl. Do you understand?"

"Yes."

"I do hope you will not disappoint me."

She gasped, still clutching at Tideke's hand.

"If you promise to be loyal, only to me, you may go."

She seemed to try to nod.

Hazen jerked his head at Tideke, who let go of her neck.

She gasped and coughed, then scurried to the door, snatched it open, and ran down the corridor.

This girl was not Lady Magdalen. His son was a fool.

Magdalen's step was lighter as she mounted the stairs to Agnes's room carrying a pitcher of fresh water. Already Agnes had moved Lenhart from the stables to watch the geese, probably suspecting Erlich would not cease mistreating Lenhart if he remained nearby. And if Lenhart and Steffan could stay safe, she could concentrate on finding Steffan's portrait.

She also needed to get those letters sent to her mother and Avelina and the margrave so they could come and help her, preferably before the wedding celebration, which barely gave her enough time.

Magdalen entered Agnes's room and set the pitcher on the table next to the basin. There was no reason to think Steffan's portrait was hidden in this room, but Agnes was nowhere in sight, and Magdalen had thought of her necklace every day since Agnes had taken it. She was determined to have it back.

She looked in the bottom of the large cabinet where Agnes hung her clothing. There was nothing there except shoes and a small box. She snatched up the box and opened it. Inside were ribbons of various colors. Magdalen pushed them aside, but there was nothing else except some metal hairpins scattered on the bottom.

She closed the cabinet and went to the trunk on the other side of the room. She raised the lid and found her box where she kept her favorite rocks that she had collected. She looked inside it, but her necklace was not there. She definitely wanted that back when she was Lady Magdalen again, but she had nowhere to hide it at the moment.

She set the box to the side and kept looking, finding more shoes and different odds and ends. Then her eye caught something—a little leather side pocket attached to the inside of the lid. Magdalen stuck her hand inside it even as she heard footsteps in the hall coming her way.

Her hand felt velvet. She pulled it out. The footsteps were so close Magdalen didn't even look to see what was in her hand. She closed the lid to the trunk, stood up, and slipped it in her apron pocket and quickly moved away from the trunk.

Agnes entered the room. She was breathing sharp and fast, her hand over her heart. Her face was pale, and tears leaked from the corners of her eyes.

"What is the matter, Agnes?"

She drew in a loud, labored breath. "He knows."

"Knows what? Who?" Magdalen approached her.

"Lord Hazen," she said gruffly. "He knows I am not Lady Magdalen."

"How could he know?"

"Did you tell him?"

"No. It was not I." Magdalen searched her mind. Who knew that Agnes had taken her place besides Erlich and Steffan? There was Lenhart, but he couldn't speak and most people avoided him as if he had the pestilence.

"He's going to tell Alexander, I just know it." Agnes's voice rose in pitch with each word until she was almost screeching.

"It's all right. Keep your voice down, and tell me what Lord Hazen said."

"He asked me a lot of questions. He asked me if you were the servant girl who came with me from Mallin. He knows! You must have told him!"

"I did not tell him."

"I thought it was a good idea to bring you into the castle, to keep you close so you wouldn't run away and tell your mother what happened, especially when my husband said he didn't remember what you looked like. But somehow Lord Hazen figured it out. I thought he was going to have me killed!" Tears ran down her face as Agnes clasped her hands together.

"What do you mean?"

"He had his guard choke me!" She pointed to her neck. Small red marks showed on her pale skin.

"And what else did he say?"

"He said I must be loyal to him. He frightened me so much." She let out a sob.

"And what did you say?"

"I said I was the daughter of the Baron of Mallin. I said whatever he had heard was a lie. I demanded he tell me who had said such a thing, but he wouldn't tell me. I just pretended I didn't know what he was talking about. Should I tell my father? He will try to kill Lord Hazen. And then Alexander will never forgive me." Her tears suddenly dried up. Her eyes grew huge, and her face changed to a shade of ashen gray.

"Calm down. Take some deep breaths. It might help to wash your face. I brought some fresh—"

"Listen to me." Agnes grabbed Magdalen's forearms. "If he

asks you, vow to me that you will tell Lord Hazen that I am Lady Magdalen."

Magdalen did not wish to tell Lord Hazen anything. She knew the man was evil after what he did to Steffan. He might kill Agnes—if it was discovered that she had forced the real Lady Magdalen to switch places with her, Agnes's life was in danger anyway.

Magdalen said, "I think it is best that Lord Hazen not know the truth and that your father not know that Lord Hazen suspects your true identity. Do you agree?"

Agnes's mouth hung open for a moment, then she said, "Yes."

"Then let us agree that neither of us will tell Lord Hazen our secret, and neither of us will tell your father about what Lord Hazen said today."

"I agree. But why are you doing this? Why would you not want Lord Hazen to know the truth about who you are? You surely don't care what happens to me after what my father and I did to you."

She did not owe Agnes any explanation at all. "I have my reasons, one of which is . . . Even after what you did to me, I don't want to see you killed, since you might repent someday."

Agnes stared at her a moment, then burst into tears again.

"Come. Wash your face." Magdalen led her over to the pitcher and basin where Agnes washed her face and then went to lie down on her bed. Agnes soon began breathing loudly and evenly.

Magdalen went into the small changing room adjoining her bedchamber and took out the velvet object she had found in Agnes's trunk.

It was a small red velvet pouch that was closed at one end by a drawstring. Magdalen pulled it open and dumped the contents in her palm. Her necklace lay in her hand.

Chapter Twenty

Steffan climbed the stairs after his work was done. His feet were heavy, and he could barely keep his eyes open. How would he ever have time to look for his portrait when he was so exhausted he could barely put one foot in front of the other?

"Steffan!" a whisper came from his right.

He lost his balance and started falling backward. A hand caught his arm and pulled him back solidly onto the step.

"Sorry to startle you." Magdalen emerged from the dark staircase.

"Are you well? Do you need my help?"

"No, I am well." She came closer and accompanied him up. "I wanted to tell you that Lord Hazen suspects that Agnes is not Lady Magdalen."

For some reason, her raspy whisper made his heart beat faster. "What else does he suspect?"

"I don't know, but apparently someone told him something to make him suspicious. Do you know who it could have been?"

He was so tired and she was so near him her arm kept brushing against his. "No. Do you have any ideas?"

"The only people who know are Agnes's father, us, and Lenhart."

Warmth and compassion imbued her voice. What made her so caring? He already knew she did not have a kind and compassionate mother. His grandmother had never let him doubt that she loved him, but she'd also been rather stern. And he did not remember much about his own mother except that she kissed his cheek every night at bedtime.

"I can't help wondering if someone—even Lord Hazen—might have overheard you and me or Agnes and me talking."

"Hmm, yes."

"You are very tired. I should let you go to bed. But I am anxious to get those letters sent by courier."

"Do you know a courier?"

"Well, no, but—"

"The letters are safer where they are. What if Lord Hazen were to search your possessions?"

"I suppose you are right." She sighed. "And we probably should not be talking on this dark stairwell. Someone might be listening. I will try to talk to you tomorrow."

"Very well."

They were on the fourth level now, walking down the hallway to their rooms. Before they parted, he reached out and grasped her hand. She turned and faced him, looking up into his eyes. Her green eyes sparkled in the light of the one torch.

"Be careful. If you feel you are in danger, come to me. I will protect you."

Her lips parted and her mouth hung open. She just stood there.

"*Gute Nacht,*" he whispered.

"Schlafen Sie gut," she whispered back, then hurried to her room, leaving him at his door.

Magdalen sat on a stool making alterations to some of her own gowns. Agnes had her sewing a higher waistline on one of the dresses.

"I can't let Lord Hazen think these dresses were made for someone else," Agnes said.

Agnes should be making her own alterations to the dresses, but she claimed she was too afraid of getting caught doing menial work by Lord Hazen. Fortunately or unfortunately, Magdalen's mother had ordered her to learn to sew from the other house servants just in case she needed to know it someday, as sewing was one of the only tasks a lady of means was allowed to perform.

As Magdalen ripped out the seam, she tried not to hate Agnes's teeth, which jutted out slightly, or her smirk, which she'd enjoy wiping from her face, or her laugh, which sounded like a dying animal. It was difficult not to hate her for stealing Magdalen's identity. And yet, she could be thankful that Agnes *had* taken her place, since Lord Hazen no doubt would have forced her to marry his son—or murdered her when she protested that he was not the real Duke of Wolfberg.

"God," she whispered, "forgive me for hating Agnes. I want to curse her, but I know that I must not hate anyone. Give me the power over my hatred to forgive her. I can pity Agnes for her evil father and be thankful that my father was kind and good. Besides, I know Agnes will be punished for her deception and wrongdoing when she is caught and I am restored to my rightful station."

The prayer made her feel calmer, but then she stuck her finger with the needle. She put her finger in her mouth as someone approached, their soft footfalls on the flagstones of the corridor announcing the person to be a small woman wearing soft-soled slippers.

Katrin appeared in the doorway.

"Katrin! I wasn't expecting to see you."

"Maggie, how do you fare? I was sent to assist you in your work."

"You were?"

"Yes, Lady Magdalen sent me." She looked pointedly at the dress in Magdalen's lap and then at the stack of dresses beside her. "She said you had some mending I could help you with."

"How generous of Lady Magdalen." Ironic to be praising Agnes for allowing someone to help her resew her own dresses to fit the person who had usurped her.

Katrin picked up a dress, and Magdalen showed her how to rip out the seams in the middle of the dress in order to sew a higher waist, since Agnes was shorter and thicker in the middle than Magdalen.

"Where was Lady Magdalen off to?" Katrin asked.

"Oh, she went for a walk in the gardens with her husband."

"It is a pleasant day for a walk. Tell me about your home in Mallin. That is where you are from, isn't it? How did you come to Wolfberg?"

"You know I came here—" She had to swallow before saying the words. "With Lady Magdalen." Perhaps she should just tell Katrin the truth. It would be easier for Magdalen, but the truth was a secret that would be a heavy burden for poor Katrin to have to carry around.

Katrin kept sewing.

"I left my mother and sisters in Mallin. They saw it as my opportunity for a better life." That much was true.

"But why were you sent to take care of the geese when you first arrived?"

"My mistress was displeased with me. But she decided she wanted me back as her personal servant."

"Oh."

"Mallin is a beautiful place, with rocky hills and trees. My friends—I mean, Lady Magdalen's friends, the Margrave of Thornbeck and his lady—sent us some sheep and goats so the people of Mallin would have a new way of earning money and feeding themselves, but many of the sheep contracted some kind of sickness and died. Our people used to work in the mines, but the copper ran out and the mines are standing empty now."

"I see."

"What about you, Katrin? Have you always lived in Wolfberg?"

"No, I came here from Arnsbaden. Lord Hazen cannot do without my family."

"Lord Hazen?"

"Oh, look at this. I'm not sure I'm sewing this right."

Magdalen examined the dress. "Oh yes, that is right. Your stitches are very even."

"Thank you. I am good at mending. My mother used to make me do all my little brothers' mending, and they were always putting rips in their clothes. I mended them until their clothes were nothing but rags sewed together. I didn't have a father, as he died before my last brother was born."

They sewed for quite some time, both talking about their childhoods and sharing memories. It was nearly time for the evening meal when Agnes rushed in the door and went straight to the wash basin to splash water on her face and wash her hands and neck.

When she dried her face and hands, Agnes stared at Katrin as if she had never seen her before, which was strange since Katrin said she had sent her.

"I am going down to the Great Hall for the evening meal with the duke and Lord Hazen." Agnes pointed her nose in the air. "You may finish those dresses in the morning."

Agnes left and Magdalen and Katrin put away the dresses, with Katrin telling her a tale from when she had played a trick on her brothers. Then they went down to the servants' dining hall. She wanted to say something to Katrin about how strange it was that the cooks and Frau Clara had allowed her to spend all afternoon with Magdalen, helping her mend Agnes's dresses, but she didn't want to interrupt Katrin's story.

The next morning Steffan sneaked up to Lord Hazen's chamber. His uncle was at breakfast, so he needed to search fast.

A thought had come to him last night when he was half asleep in his bed. His uncle once hid something on the back of a framed portrait on the wall. Steffan had seen him retrieve it when he didn't know Steffan was looking. And now he remembered a few paintings and wall hangings in Hazen's bedchamber.

He once again made his way down the corridor on bare feet and slipped into the room—and found himself face-to-face with Magdalen.

Their eyes met, but they did not speak. She turned away from him and opened a trunk on the floor and started looking through it. Steffan strode to the first painting—a portrait of Lord Hazen—and lifted it from the bottom. He felt along the back of it and all around the frame, looking for anything that might be attached or hidden inside. He found nothing unusual. Next he went to a large tapestry hanging on the wall next to his uncle's bed. He lifted it, getting under it, feeling all around, but there did not seem to be anything there either.

There was one last portrait on the wall, a portrait of Steffan's grandfather. He lifted it, but it came off its hook into his hands. Steffan turned it over, feeling all around the inside of the frame. Still he found nothing.

He bent to set the painting on the floor when he heard footsteps.

Steffan froze. The steps were firm and steady, getting louder.

His blood raced through his limbs. He lifted the painting, his hands shaking. He aimed to place the painting back onto the little hook as he plastered his cheek against the wall. The portrait slipped off. He tried again, willing his hands not to shake. On this second try it slipped back on and held.

Magdalen stood on the other side of Lord Hazen's large curtained bed frantically motioning at him. Then she sank down and disappeared.

He dashed toward the bed, falling to his hands and knees, then onto his belly as his momentum sent him sliding underneath it.

He suddenly felt as if he'd fallen into a tight hole. It was dark and cold, and he could barely breathe. Something closed in above him, with the hard stone beneath him. He was trapped. His heart beat painfully in his throat, cutting off his air.

Calm down, calm down, calm down. He was not in a hole. He

was under his uncle's bed. He focused his eyes on the light to his right, where he had just slid under the bed. He could slide out just as easily, whenever his uncle left. *Just breathe.*

Sweat beaded at his temple and between his shoulder blades.

Magdalen. He had to think about Magdalen. She was in danger too. His uncle already suspected that the servant girl pretending to be Lady Magdalen was an imposter. If he found them in his room, hiding under his bed, he would kill them both.

Her shoulder was pressed against his. She must have been there the whole time, but he'd been too panicked to notice. He reached out and took her hand. She held on tight.

His uncle went to one side of the room, then the other. Was he looking for something? Was he looking for *them*? Under the bed was a rather obvious place for a person to hide. He'd surely find them if he was searching for them.

His footsteps moved toward the bed and stopped.

Steffan kept his eyes wide open, straining to see as he concentrated on remaining motionless. Suddenly his uncle's feet moved again, this time toward the door and then down the hall, growing fainter.

"Let's get out of here," Magdalen whispered.

Steffan crawled toward the light and to freedom. But as he freed himself from the bed, his back scraped against the bottom of the wooden bed frame. He stood and a metallic *ping* sounded behind him, something hitting the stone floor.

Steffan squatted and picked up a small key. He felt above it, along the underside of the bed, and felt something sticky. The key was also sticky. Lord Hazen had been hiding the key under the bed.

He hurried to the stacks of locked coffers on his uncle's trunk.

Magdalen had already found her father's mining books in these coffers. What else might Hazen be hiding?

He moved the unlocked boxes out of the way, Magdalen helping him. He grabbed a locked coffer and inserted the key. It didn't fit. He tried another box and another. He tried almost all of them.

"Make haste!" she whispered. "He could come back at any moment."

Steffan wanted to tell her he was hurrying, but he didn't take the time. He just kept trying the key in all the little wooden boxes. He had only two left. He tried the key in the first lock. It slipped in, but it wouldn't turn. Then he tried it in the very last box. It slipped in. And turned. And opened.

He lifted the lid, and there was a piece of rolled-up parchment lying on the bottom. If it was locked with the key hidden, it must be important, so Steffan grabbed the parchment and stuffed it in his pocket. Then he closed the box and locked it.

Magdalen was already busy stacking the boxes back up exactly the way they had found them. Only it was impossible to know exactly how they had been arranged. There were so many of them. He hoped Lord Hazen had not memorized how they looked either.

When all the boxes were neatly stacked up again, he took Magdalen's hand and ran for the door.

Voices could be heard somewhere ahead, probably on the staircase. He ran the other way, pulling Magdalen with him, toward the corridor that led to the east wing.

His heart was still beating hard, but it was also soaring high. He had not been able to locate his portrait, but he had found something that might be valuable. At least some of the pounding of his heart was from the hand holding on to his and the pretty, daring girl to whom it belonged.

They went up three short stone steps to the east wing. He kept an eye out for guards. Not seeing anyone or hearing a sound, he opened the first door he came to and pulled Magdalen inside with him, then closed the door behind them.

Chapter Twenty-One

"Where are we?" she whispered.

"In my sister Gertrudt's room. We're safe for now." Her hand was soft and warm inside his. They stood very close. Her bright eyes stared up at him. The two of them were like comrades on a crusade. He wanted to tell her he thought she was clever and brave, that he felt fortunate to know her.

Instead, he said, "Come, you can see a beautiful view from here." He let her hand go and walked to the other side of the room, to the window that faced the sea. He unfastened the shutters and let in the late-day sunshine.

Magdalen drew closer, her mouth forming a circle. They stared out at the dark-blue sea meeting the pale-blue sky. "It is very beautiful." She drew even closer, her nose touching the glass that had been installed only a few years earlier, and looked straight down. "Even the trees are beautiful. Green, then blue, then more blue."

His heart tightened as he stared at her lovely profile, but he was not a silly boy mesmerized by a girl's comely face. He should be thinking how to help his people, how to help the servants whom his uncle had cast out.

"What are you thinking about?" She did not take her eyes off the view out the window.

He sighed. "I was thinking how, because of my uncle, I killed two men."

Compassion suffused her expression as she turned her gaze on him.

"That was not your fault," she said softly. "You had no choice."

"Perhaps. But as long as my uncle is free to send men to murder me . . ."

She turned her whole body toward him and placed a gentle hand on his arm. "We shall pray he is captured before anyone else is hurt."

Just as he was allowing himself to enjoy her touch, she took her hand away.

"When I was the Duke of Wolfberg, I had so much power, but I did not appreciate the power I had to do good. And then I let my uncle come in and take over while I went to Prague. But when I have my place back, I'll not waste my power again."

"I believe you."

She had such a sweet smile, and it reminded him of the time they'd spent together in Thornbeck talking and dancing. He'd thought her a pleasant dance partner and enjoyed talking to her, but he'd been very aware that she was only a baron's daughter.

Her eyes widening, she reached out and tapped him on the arm. "We should be looking at what you found in the box."

How had he forgotten? *No more foolishness, Steffan.*

He took the parchment out of his pocket.

He unrolled the paper, then held it up facing the window so they could both see by the light streaming in.

"It's some kind of map," Magdalen said.

"I'm not sure of what or where, though." They both leaned closer. "These are hills." He pointed.

"And forests here, and a stream," Magdalen indicated. "But how can we tell where this is if there are no names anywhere?"

"Something is here." Steffan traced a line of dots with an X at either end.

"This looks strangely familiar." Magdalen suddenly gasped. "This looks like the map my father had in his library. And look at these small circles here, here, and here." She placed her finger on the map. "This is a map of Mallin's copper mines. These circles are the openings to the other mines, and the one with the Xs is another mine that has two entrances."

"Are you certain?"

"I used to wander all over those hills as a child, and I often went with my father to visit the mines." She looked up at him with a wide-eyed smile. "I am certain."

He couldn't help smiling back at her.

Her smile faded, and she returned her attention to the map, holding one corner. "But why go to the trouble of stealing this map and my father's books? All of the copper was mined out a few years ago. What is Lord Hazen looking for here?"

They both studied the map.

"I just remembered." She pulled something out of her pocket and held it out. "It's my necklace. I found it in Agnes's room. My father gave it to me before he died. But I think it's only jasper. He didn't tell me it was valuable. He only said it was a pretty rock he found in one of the mines."

Steffan reached out and held the pendant against his palm. "It looks like a fairly ordinary stone, but I suppose it could have some kind of significance."

"I've been thinking about something else," she said, a crease between her brows. "There must have been some reason for your uncle to send my mother a letter proposing marriage, planning for me to wed his son in your place. Why did he do it? What is he after?"

"Since you have no brother to inherit your father's title and land, he must want his son to inherit whatever he thinks is valuable in that mine."

She nodded, then pulled the necklace over her head and absently dropped the stone inside the neckline of her dress. "What do you think we should do now?"

"I would love to examine these mines for what my uncle thinks is so valuable. But first we need to be able to prove our identities, and we need someone powerful to prove them to, which would be easy enough if your mother and the Margrave of Thornbeck came to the wedding celebration my uncle is planning."

"But Agnes told me her father will make sure the invitations are lost. And without an invitation, my mother and the margrave might never visit me."

The truth of it made his heart sink, for the obvious reason, but also because her mother did not seem to care about her.

"Then we must make sure they come here. We must get word to them."

"That is exactly why I wrote those letters and asked you to send them." Her eyes were narrowed as she stared at his face.

"I did not want to send for help until I was sure I could prove who I was." And he still could not, which was why he should be searching for his portrait.

She looked as if she might say something, then took a step away from him. "We should go. Someone might find us in here."

The room probably had not been touched since his sister left to marry nearly a year before, so it was unlikely anyone would find them. But she was angry with him for not sending the letters.

"Yes, we should go. And I shall hide the map in a safe place."

"In the same safe place you've hidden the letters?"

He didn't answer.

"You should tell me where you're hiding them."

"So that when Lord Hazen kills me you can still send the letters?" He hoped she would at least smile at his bad jest.

She huffed out a breath, then pressed a finger to her chin, glancing up at the ceiling. "*Ja.*"

He sighed. "I will go now to place this in the same box as the letters, which I buried under the large rock under the tree we sat beneath. Do you remember that day?"

"That was the day you told me about getting trapped in the old well when you were five. You were thinking about that when we were hiding under the bed, weren't you?"

"What makes you think that?" *How did she know?*

"It was the look on your face. And if I had fallen in a well I would have been terrified to be in a tight, dark space."

Her voice was always so soft and compassionate, and something about her green eyes made him want to draw closer. But he could not let himself get close to her, either physically or in any other way. He could not marry her, and he would not do anything to hurt such a kind, noble maiden. "I hope I did not embarrass myself too much."

"Not at all. You were very brave, and we escaped safely, so all is well."

He cleared his throat. "Perhaps it is time. I will go out tonight and find a courier for the letters. Come."

He led her to the door, opened it, and cautiously looked out.

The corridor was clear, so they went back to the west wing of the castle. As they parted to go to their separate duties, he impulsively touched a finger to her cheek, just grazing her skin. It was as soft as he thought it would be.

"Be careful," he said.

She stared back at him, probably thinking he should keep his hands to himself. He turned away and hurried down to the kitchen and his work.

Magdalen's insides trembled as she brought her hand up to her cheek. Why had he done that? It was just a little brush of his finger on her face. So why did it make her heart flutter? She'd felt the same way when they were in his sister's room, when he held her hand longer than necessary, his long slender fingers wrapped around hers. And when they'd stood looking out at the sea together, she had felt so close to him, as if their thoughts were melding and he was as drawn to her as she was to him.

Foolish. As foolish as her belief that he had wanted to marry her based on their meeting at Thornbeck.

Magdalen went to her stool and sat down to work on resewing her dresses to fit Agnes. Katrin had not joined her today. No doubt she was needed in the kitchen. The cooks would already be preparing for the great company of guests coming to Wolfberg Castle in the next two weeks.

The work was monotonous, but at least she had been able to dispel the bitter thoughts about Agnes by imagining her letters reaching her mother and Avelina in Thornbeck, imagining their outrage at the thought of Magdalen being so wrongly treated.

"God," she whispered, "please help Steffan find couriers to deliver my letters. Give him success, and give the couriers and their horses speed and safety on the journey." She squeezed her eyes shut. Everything depended on those letters, for even if she and Steffan could prove who they were, it did them no good if they had no one to prove it to, no one who could defend them against Lord Hazen.

Surely God would not let her down.

The thought of her father's death, as well as her brother's, sprang so sharply into focus that tears stung her eyes. She had tried to deny it, even to herself, but she felt so hurt that God would allow her father and brother to die. And she did not understand why she and Steffan were being mistreated now.

When she'd confessed her pain and disappointment to the priest in Mallin, he said, "God cares for His creation, and He cares for you, Lady Magdalen. It is written in the Holy Scriptures, so it is surely so. You must not doubt, but believe."

"But if He cares for me—"

"That is why we call it faith—His loving-kindness is not seen or fully known at times, but we have faith that it exists."

Faith. She had to have faith that God's loving-kindness existed even in the situation Magdalen was in now. But it was so much easier to have faith when her father and brother were alive, when she was not serving her usurper.

Footsteps approached the room, but they did not sound like Agnes's soft shoes. They were louder and sharper and quicker.

Lord Hazen appeared in the doorway, a strange, lax look on his face. He strode toward her.

Chapter Twenty-Two

"What are you doing there, servant girl?"

A chill went down Magdalen's arms. "I am mending some clothing for my mistress."

"Mending Lady Magdalen's dresses?" He came over and picked up the dress she had just finished, then lifted one from the pile that had not yet been mended, and he seemed to be comparing the two.

"Tell me if I'm wrong, but it looks as if you are cutting these dresses and shortening them. Why would Lady Magdalen need her dresses altered? Has she grown . . . shorter?"

Magdalen's stomach twisted. "I only do as I'm told, my lord."

"*Ja.*"

She resisted the urge to look up at him as he stood near, but she imagined his small, dark eyes squinting down at her, his enormous forehead wrinkling, the tufts of steel-gray hair puffing out on either side of his head.

"You were with Lady Magdalen when she arrived at Wolfberg, were you not? I believe the lady said she was displeased with you. She had you sent out to tend the geese."

Magdalen's hands began to sweat as a trembling started in

her legs. If only she could trust this man who had discerned the truth about who she was. But of course she couldn't. He was evil, and at the very least, he would have Agnes put to death.

"And Lady Magdalen said your name was Agnes, but the other servants say your name is Maggie. Do you not think that is . . . strange?"

He didn't seem to expect an answer as he moved away from her. She peeked up through her lashes. He stopped at the water pitcher and poured himself a cup of water and drank it.

She was only pretending to sew now, as her hands were shaking so badly she could not make a stitch.

"I asked Lady Magdalen all these questions, and she strenuously protested my insinuations. I was hoping you might tell me the truth." He lifted the cup to his lips again, all the while keeping his eyes trained on her.

"I do not know what you want me to tell you, my lord." She managed to hold her voice surprisingly steady. "I am content to sit here and sew for my mistress."

"Hmm. But one must wonder why you are so content, when you are the real Lady Magdalen."

Magdalen allowed herself the nervous laugh that bubbled up. "Forgive me for laughing, my lord, but that is an amusing thing for you to say."

"And why is it so amusing to you?"

"Well, the Duke of Wolfberg should know if she is Lady Magdalen or not, because he met her and danced with her at Thornbeck Castle less than two years ago."

She refused to look up at him, keeping her gaze on the bundle in her lap. But he stayed silent so long, she finally took a peek. He was glaring at her.

"What do you know of that party at Thornbeck Castle?"

"Very little, my lord. Lady Magdalen took her childhood dry nurse Hegatha with her. I only know what she told us servants."

"No one makes a fool of me. I shall uncover the truth." His voice was raspy. "I shall not be bested, by you or that empty-headed imposter who calls herself Lady Magdalen." Lord Hazen strode from the room.

At least he didn't seem suspicious of Steffan. But it was just a matter of time before he figured out everything. The shrewd man must have a spy among the servants.

A few minutes later, Agnes entered the room with a smile on her face. She barely glanced at Magdalen before she sank onto a chair with a low squeal.

"You seem very pleased today." Should she tell Agnes what Lord Hazen had said? It seemed cruel to ruin her good mood.

"I hope you fall in love someday," Agnes said on a blissful sigh. "Then perhaps you will know how wonderful it feels."

Magdalen looked down to keep from rolling her eyes to the ceiling. Instead, she concentrated on one of the letters she had written. She imagined Lord Thornbeck reading it, his face turning red from anger, and the scowl he often wore. She imagined Steffan being raised to his rightful position of Duke of Wolfberg, and his cowardly cousin and Agnes being thrown in the dungeon.

Yes, Agnes. Perhaps someday I will feel as delighted as you do right now.

But what would happen to Magdalen? She would have her identity back, but she'd also have to go back home to Mallin with her mother, who never said a kind word. At least she and Lenhart would be safe, and she would be with her sisters and her people. She had always wanted to help them prosper, to make sure they had enough to eat and warm clothes to wear. Perhaps . . . perhaps a way to provide for them would present itself. Perhaps she would marry a kindly, rich old man who would help her people prosper. But for her to find true love? Highly unlikely.

She imagined Steffan smiling, sitting in the place of honor on the dais in the Great Hall of Wolfberg Castle, welcoming his young, noble wife, whoever she might be. Yes, Steffan would fall in love.

Her heart twisted inside her. *God, am I so unworthy? Am I destined to see everyone else content, everyone except me?*

Someone was coming down the corridor, shoes slapping on the flagstone floor, almost running.

Alexander appeared in the doorway. His face was scrunched in a strange expression, as if he was not sure if he was angry or anguished.

"Darling, is something wrong?" Agnes stood and took a step toward her husband.

"Yes, I should say there is something wrong." He seemed to be barely containing his emotions as he looked at Agnes and then at Magdalen.

Agnes glanced her way. "Go in the other room, girl."

Magdalen hastened into the adjoining room, but she left the door slightly ajar so she could listen.

Alexander stared down at his hands as if he'd never seen them before.

"What is it? Please tell me." Agnes sounded as if she was crying. She walked toward him, closer, until she was right in front of him. "Did I do something wrong?"

He didn't lift his head but reached out and grabbed her around the waist, then bent to bury his face in her shoulder.

"Darling." Agnes caressed his shoulders.

They stood like that so long, Magdalen rolled her eyes and huffed.

Finally, they pulled apart and Alexander said, "Lord Hazen told me you're not Lady Magdalen. Is it true?"

"What? I . . ."

"It is true." He put a hand over his face. "He says I have to marry the real Lady Magdalen, as soon as he's sure he's found her."

"But what about me? I love you. Doesn't that mean anything?" Agnes's voice rose to a high pitch as she clutched at his arms. She started to sob. "You don't love me."

He put his arms around her again. "I do love you, but Lord Hazen . . . You don't know how he is. He will have his way."

The two of them actually seemed to have fallen in love. Would he tell Agnes that he was not who she thought he was either?

She put her ear up to the opening.

Alexander said, "I vow that I will do whatever I need to do to protect you."

Magdalen's heart twisted painfully. Would anyone ever love her like that? She hated that Steffan's face loomed in front of her whenever she closed her eyes, the way he looked after he took the punishment for the hungry man who stole the loaf of bread. He was selfish and irritable, but he brought her food when their breakfast had been inedible. And her knees went weak just thinking of the way his brown hair hung over his forehead and the warm expression he sometimes had when he looked at her.

But she would be foolish to fancy herself in love with him. Steffan was like most other lords and noblemen. He scorned marrying for love.

She wiped her face with her hands and her nose with her

apron. She pushed the door open and walked out into the bed-chamber.

"If you are going to be in here any longer, I need to take my mending with me into the other room."

Agnes and Alexander broke apart while Magdalen stalked to where her dresses lay. She took her time gathering them. Alexander whispered something in Agnes's ear, then departed.

Agnes burst into tears. She went to the bed, lay down, and closed the curtains.

Magdalen put the dresses aside. Why alter her own dresses when Agnes might not be in a position to order her around much longer? But the thought of Lord Hazen forcing her to marry Alexander, or to at least pretend to be his wife . . . She closed her eyes and prayed.

Magdalen did not see Steffan at the evening meal. Katrin helped her sneak some food, hiding a bread roll and a wedge of cheese in her apron pocket. When Agnes allowed her to retire to her own bed for the night, Magdalen waited in the corridor until she saw Steffan walking toward her on his way to the menservants' bedchamber.

"I saved you some food."

He walked past his door until he was only a step away from her. She gave him the cloth bundle.

"Thank you." He opened it and immediately bit into the bread.

"Did you find a courier?"

He shook his head. "It's as if Lord Hazen has sent away every man and horse besides his own guards and the horses in his own stable. I may have to steal a horse and deliver them myself."

"Go yourself?"

"Of course. I know how to ride a horse."

"I hadn't thought of that." She tapped her chin, then remembered that was something Avelina used to do when she was thinking.

"Has Agnes said anything else about Lord Hazen being suspicious?"

Magdalen took a deep breath and let it out. "He came to speak with me today. He knows Agnes is not me. And he knows—or thinks he knows—that I am Magdalen. He's threatening to get rid of Agnes and force Alexander to marry me."

They both glanced up and down the corridor to make certain no one was nearby.

"That changes things, then."

"What do you mean?"

"I don't think I should leave when you're in so much danger."

"I'm not in danger. That is, I don't think I have anything to fear from your cousin. He's in love with Agnes, as strange as that seems."

"Yes, but my uncle . . . Who knows what he might do to you?" He leaned closer. "You could come with me."

It was not her life but her heart she was worried about. "I think I'd better stay here."

"But are you sure Lord Hazen won't do you harm?"

"He wants his son married to Lady Magdalen. Agnes is in more danger than I."

"I can protect you." He took a tiny step closer to her.

She leaned away from him. "I believe you. I think." She smiled to try to dispel some of the awkwardness of the moment. Why was he getting so close? They weren't Agnes and Alexander, and Steffen did not care for her.

He seemed to catch her hint and took a step back. "I don't want anything to happen to you. I will try to find a courier and come back so I can watch over you. But I am not sure if I'll be able to."

She wanted to tell him he needed watching over more than she did. His lip still looked swollen and the cut over his eye was still healing.

He looked down at the floor.

"You are very kind to want to protect me. I already know what a courageous man you are."

He lifted his head, and the corners of his mouth quirked up. "You think I am courageous?"

Yes. "Sometimes."

"You are very good-hearted. Some women in your position would have stabbed Agnes in the heart while she slept, but you actually seem to feel compassion for her."

Magdalen covered her mouth to stop the smile that spread over her face at the thought of stabbing Agnes in her sleep.

"And you have been most kind to me, even though I'm not sure I deserved it." He continued to stare into her eyes. "You certainly did not owe me anything."

"Well, your brown eyes and smile are hard to resist." It was true, but she probably should not have told him that. A spark seemed to light up those brown eyes.

"I suppose I should prepare for my journey tomorrow, if you're certain you are safe."

He had a vulnerable look on his face, as if he was hoping for something . . . a word from her? A gesture? She just watched him. Such a strange man.

"I shall pray for you."

"Thank you, Magdalen."

The way he said her name . . . She backed away from him, said, "Farewell," and went into her room.

The other maidservants were already in bed. Magdalen undressed quickly and quietly, pulling her loose kirtle over her head. Dressed in her plain gray underdress, she blew out the remaining lit candle and crawled into bed.

"Maggie, Maggie, wake up!"

A loud whisper next to her head forced Magdalen's eyes open.

Katrin stood there holding a candle and candleholder, illuminating the whites around her eyes. "You're in trouble, and so is Steffan."

Magdalen sat up. "What do you mean?"

"Lord Hazen knows Steffan is the duke and you are Lady Magdalen, and he plans to kill Steffan today."

"How do you know this?"

"I heard him talking. It's true. You must believe me."

"Steffan will be safe. He is leaving this morning to seek help."

Katrin's eyes widened. "You must warn him now, before it's too late, and you should go with him unless you want to marry Alexander."

Magdalen stood, snatched up her overdress, drew it over her head, and grabbed her bag. "How did Lord Hazen discover this? Who told him?"

"I don't know. But please make haste." Katrin helped her throw her few possessions into the bag.

Magdalen ran to the door and into the corridor. She pushed open the door to the male servants' sleeping chamber. All was quiet except for the faint sounds of men breathing heavily in sleep and Katrin crying and sniffing behind her.

Magdalen stepped inside, her heart pounding. Thankfully she knew which bed was the duke's.

"Steffan. Wake up." She touched his shoulder.

He drew in a quick breath and jolted upright. "What?" He grabbed her arm, still half asleep, blinking at her in the dark room.

"Lord Hazen knows everything. He's planning to kill you."

"How do you know?" But he was already standing up, then bent and reached for something at the foot of his bed.

"Katrin told me. She overheard him."

Most people slept without clothing, especially when it was warm, but thanks be to God, Steffan was wearing hose.

He pulled on a shirt, grabbed a bundle out from under the bed, then hurried toward the door.

Katrin stood in the corridor looking small, her shoulders hunched and her head down.

"Come with us." Magdalen tugged on Katrin's arm. "If he finds out you warned us, you will be in great danger."

"Are you sure?" Katrin whispered back.

"Yes," Steffan said. "Make haste."

She nodded and followed them down the stairs. At the very bottom Steffan led them to the door that was never guarded but always locked. He started unlocking it with a key. As soon as he got it open, he ushered them out in front of him, then locked the door behind him. He turned to Magdalen. "Go to the stables. Find Lenhart. He will be sleeping with the horses. Get him to saddle three horses for us and a fourth for himself."

"Where are you going?"

"To my hiding place to dig up your letters and my sword."

"But we didn't get my father's mining books!"

"We can't go back now." He took off toward the pasture where they used to graze their geese and sheep, and she and Katrin hurried toward the stables.

Chapter Twenty-Three

The sky was still dark, with only the barest bit of light to usher the night away. Magdalen's gaze darted all around the castle bailey, but no one was in sight.

She ran into the stables and said softly, "Lenhart? Are you here?"

A rustling sound came from the back, then a dark figure strode toward them. As he got closer . . .

"Lenhart! Thank goodness! We need you to saddle four horses."

He suddenly turned and disappeared into the dark barn and soon came back holding a saddle and smiling broadly.

Magdalen and Katrin helped him saddle the horses, tightening girths and making sure they were ready. Magdalen's father had shown her how to saddle a horse when she was very young, but now she was actually strong enough to perform the task.

When they were nearly finished, Steffan came running in, breathing hard with a large bundle under one arm and a sword at his hip.

They strapped their belongings onto the saddles, and all four of them took the reins of a horse and walked quietly through the stable yard. Would anyone stop them? Would someone warn Lord Hazen that they were leaving, the same person who had given him enough information about Steffan and Magdalen that he was able to figure out who they were?

God, please let the darkness hide us, Magdalen prayed as they skirted around the edge of the castle bailey toward the gate and bridge that led away from the castle. As they passed the gatehouse, the guard was slumped against the wall on a stool. Magdalen moved as quietly as possible, watching each step she took, even though it was still too dark to see very much.

They had proceeded several steps past the guard, with Lenhart taking up the rear, when a voice called, "You there! Where are you going?"

Katrin, who was beside Magdalen, gasped and whimpered. Steffan was in the lead, and he turned and whispered, "Keep going. Don't stop." He quickened his step, and they all followed suit.

The guard grumbled something undiscernible behind them. Magdalen listened hard, afraid to look behind her as they made their way down the castle mount in the semidarkness of early dawn.

"Let's mount." Steffan sprang onto his horse with such haste it took her breath.

She grabbed the reins of her own horse and quickly mounted. Lenhart had to help Katrin, but when everyone was safely mounted, Steffan took the lead and galloped his horse the rest of the way down the castle mount and through the still-sleeping town of Wolfberg.

They passed the cathedral where Agnes and Alexander had been married, passed the shops and houses along the main street, then took the southwest fork in the road that would lead them to Mallin.

Katrin did not seem as if she had much experience with riding a horse, but her face was scrunched in a look of determination as she stayed close behind them. Lenhart stayed close to her as well, often glancing over at her.

Thank You, God, for Lenhart. Please help us escape from Lord Hazen. Her heart was pounding, and she could think of nothing else to say. If the man would kill his own nephew for no other reason besides greed, he'd have no scruples killing all four of them if he caught up to them.

They had been riding for about two hours, Magdalen would guess from the position of the sun, when they drew near a village. Steffan slowed and guided his horse off the side of the rutted dirt road into the trees, eventually halting when they were out of sight of the road.

"You three wait here and I'll go into this village alone to buy us some food. We don't want anyone to see us together and tell Lord Hazen." He twisted and reached to the back of his saddle and took his money pouch from his bag. "I'll also try to find someone to take your letter to Thornbeck while we head for Mallin."

Their eyes met for a moment before he nodded and moved off toward the village.

They had not exactly discussed what they would do once they reached Mallin. Magdalen was eager to discover the mystery behind why Lord Hazen had taken her father's mining books and why he had a map of Mallin's copper mines. But she was not eager to see her mother and let her know what she had been doing for the past few weeks.

Lord Hazen was surely following them, or at least his men were. He might only be a few minutes behind them, and probably no more than an hour or two. But she prayed that somehow God would show them favor and put obstacles in their enemy's path.

Steffan soon returned with a large bundle of food.

"Did you find any possible couriers?" she asked softly as he passed the food bundle to her.

"Yes." He gave her the tiniest half smile. "I don't know how reliable this person is, but I paid him to deliver your letter. It is also possible that he might be intercepted by my uncle's men, but . . . we can pray he makes it to Thornbeck."

They ate quickly and then packed the rest and remounted their horses.

"How long will it take to get to Mallin?" Steffan's expression was tight, as if he was focused solely on the task at hand.

"On horseback we should be able to make it in two days, especially if we are able to change horses along the way."

He nodded once, then urged his horse to speed up to a fast walk.

They could not afford to exhaust their horses with too much galloping, as they rode all day, stopping only a few times to eat and get water for themselves and their horses. Steffan was able to buy a few water flasks at the last village and filled them up at the town so that, hopefully, they would not be caught without water if they could not find a stream.

As it grew dark, Katrin was drooping in her saddle, leaning over the horse's neck. Lenhart and Steffan were still sitting tall, but the hollowness around their eyes and the heaviness of their eyelids betrayed their exhaustion. Magdalen's back was aching—not to mention the pain in her backside—after riding all day.

They approached a village. Steffan said, "I know of an inn here where we can sleep for the night."

An actual bed seemed too good to be true, although she knew these inns were often crawling with lice and other vermin.

"I'll go in and rent the rooms," Steffan said. "Lenhart, you watch over the maidens."

Lenhart stood a little taller and his chest expanded. Katrin glanced up at the tall boy—truly, she should cease calling him a boy. He was nearly sixteen years old.

They let their horses graze the small amount of grass thirty yards or so from the inn while they waited for Steffan to return. Would he get them two rooms, one for Steffan and Lenhart and a second for Katrin and Magdalen? Or would there only be one room available?

Her face heated at the thought of sleeping in the same room with Steffan. Would it be uncomfortable? If he was only able to get one room, they would all behave themselves in a mature manner.

He came out of the front doorway looking rugged and handsome after riding hard all day, his hair tousled and a certain manly confidence in the tilt of his shoulders.

"Magdalen, if you and Katrin will go inside, Lenhart and I will settle the horses in the stable and feed them. Your door is at the top of the stairs, first one on the right. Lenhart and I will be in the next room down from yours."

She and Katrin entered the low-ceilinged inn. An older woman with a round face greeted them. "I shall take you to your room." The woman turned and started toward some stairs.

Magdalen felt the eyes of several men in the room watching them. She linked her arm with Katrin's and marched purposefully to the stairs and straight up the rickety wooden steps.

"Here you are." The innkeeper paused in front of a door. She turned the handle and pushed the door open.

Two thin mattresses lay on the floor of the bare room. Magdalen and Katrin stepped inside.

"Alma will be up soon with some water." The woman hurried away.

Magdalen examined the door and its handle. Before she could turn around, a woman came up the steps.

"I have some water for you." She carried a pitcher into the room and set it on the small table in the corner. "Two towels." She handed them the cloths draped over her arm. "Sleep well."

"Please, miss," Magdalen said, blocking the young woman's way. "Is there any way to lock the door?"

"I am sorry, but no. The owner has a guard who keeps watch over the place." With reluctance Magdalen allowed the woman to leave, and she closed the door.

Magdalen had a sick feeling in her stomach. Should she tell Steffan that she was afraid to sleep in a public inn with no lock on her door? Or pretend to be brave and unconcerned?

Katrin started washing her face and Magdalen joined her, using the water and one of the cloths. Truly, she was dirty and probably smelled like a horse, but she was so tired she hardly cared.

After they cleaned themselves the best they could, they sat on the straw mattresses.

"I still cannot figure out who could have told Lord Hazen about me," Magdalen mused aloud, "and especially about Steffan. Hardly anyone knew his real name."

Katrin only stared down at her dress and started scratching at a stain.

A knock came at the door. "It's me," Steffan said.

Magdalen opened the door. "There are no locks on these doors."

"I just discovered that myself." He frowned. "Come, we'll go downstairs and eat some supper and talk this over."

They sat at a corner table and ate the stew and bread set before them. The meat in the stew was mostly chunks of fat, but Magdalen ate it anyway. She did not want to faint tomorrow because she was too fine to eat rustic food.

They were all quiet during the meal, and when they were nearly finished, Steffan said in a low voice, "If you do not object, I think Lenhart and I should stay in your room tonight, for the purpose of making sure no one comes in."

"I think we would feel safer if you did." Magdalen hadn't realized how much she'd wanted him to say that.

Upstairs Steffan and Lenhart dragged their mattresses into the maidens' room, put them in front of the door, and lay down with their bodies between their charges and the world outside.

"They're heading south." Hazen's tracker pointed in the direction of Mallin.

Hazen clenched his teeth. He could not allow them to reach the baroness. If they were able to discern what was happening . . . He'd simply have to murder Lady Magdalen and marry her oldest sister. No matter what he had to do, he would not be thwarted.

"How far ahead are they?" Hazen asked as the tracker mounted his horse again.

"Two, maybe three hours."

Where were all his spies? Why did no one warn him for two

hours that they had stolen horses and escaped? They even took the mute boy with them.

Hazen and his men headed out. If they rode after dark they might be able to catch up with them the next day. And when he did, Hazen would not spare any of them. He would silence Steffan and the real Lady Magdalen forever. And the other noblemen and King Karl—the only people powerful enough to object to his plan—would never know.

⁓

Steffan awoke and scrambled up. Had he slept all night? He hurried to the window and opened the shutters. Dawn was beginning to lighten the sky. "Get up," he said softly. "We need to go."

He never should have slept so late. He'd intended to get going two hours before dawn, in case Lord Hazen was near.

Everyone groggily grabbed their things. They'd slept in their clothes, so it was only moments before they were leaving the little inn and saddling their horses.

He glanced over at Magdalen, who was saddling her own horse and tightening the girth, her hair coming loose from her braid. What baron's daughter was as full of grit and gumption as Magdalen? And she was so fair. Any man would be fortunate to have her for his wife.

They rode a long time. He didn't want to push the horses too hard, but when they did stop, he found a horse breeder who agreed to give them fresh mounts, and they left their horses with him.

With fresh horses, they were able to ride a bit faster and longer. The sun was just about to set on the second day of their journey when Magdalen called out, "Mallin is just ahead."

The area was mountainous, and the road wound around hills and valleys, slowing them down. They halted and Steffan took out the map, walked over to Magdalen, and held it out so she could see it. He pointed to the mine that was marked with an X. "Are we anywhere near here?"

"It's just over this hill, but we'll have to leave the road and traverse through the woods." She pointed toward the east. "Do we want to look in the mine first? To see what Lord Hazen thinks is so valuable? My mother's home is a bit farther over those hills." She pointed south.

"Since we are so close, I'd like to look at the mine."

Clouds had moved in, making it almost dark, even though the sun had not yet set. They moved off the road, and when the trees became too dense, they dismounted and led their horses.

The unusually long summer might just be relenting, as the wind that swept over them was cool. A cold rain right now would be quite unpleasant.

A sound like the beating of horses' hooves drifted to him from the road behind them. Could his uncle have caught up to them?

Steffan glanced over his shoulder. Lenhart and Katrin were still plodding along behind them. All their lives were at stake. His uncle would show no mercy if he found them. At this point, Lord Hazen needed them dead.

They came to a clearing in the trees at the top of a hill where they could see several rocky hills around them.

"He is here now," Katrin said suddenly, her eyes wide and wild. "We should turn ourselves over to him. Perhaps he will show us mercy."

The realization came over him like a bucket of cold water in his face. "You were the one who betrayed us to Lord Hazen. It was you, wasn't it?"

Magdalen's mouth fell open.

Katrin took a step away from them. "I never wanted you to get hurt. If I had not warned you, Lord Hazen would have killed you."

"Katrin?" Magdalen's eyes showed confusion and hurt. "Were you Lord Hazen's spy? Were you telling him about us?"

"I had no choice. Lord Hazen does not accept disloyalty from anyone. He would have killed me if he thought I was withholding information from him. But yes, he sent me to ask you questions, and he asked me if there was anyone around the castle with the name Steffan. But when I realized he meant to kill you, I came and warned you both."

"Get away from us." Steffan shooed her with his hand.

"The horses!" Magdalen said. "They're getting closer."

Katrin started walking backward. "Forgive me, but if I had not told him, he would only have found someone else to spy on you."

"Go on back to Lord Hazen." Steffan could not even look at her anymore.

Katrin took her horse and ran back the way they had come.

"Come!" Steffan took Magdalen's hand, his other hand holding his horse's reins, and ran toward the mines. Lenhart followed.

Chapter Twenty-Four

Steffan wasn't sure which way to go, so Magdalen took the lead through the heavily forested hills. The wind grew quite wild, shaking and twisting the limbs of the trees and whipping Magdalen's hair across her face. They pushed on, trudging up and down and around three more hills, no longer able to hear horses' hooves behind him.

Ten yards ahead of them was a hole in the side of a sheer face of rock. A well-worn but slightly overgrown path led up to it.

"Will the horses fit inside?" he asked.

"Yes. This is our widest mine."

They went inside, leading the horses. It was completely dark, but Magdalen found a torch on the ground and Steffan set about making a spark with a flint and steel and tinder to light the torch. When he finally accomplished that task, he held up the torch with one hand and the horses' reins with the other while Magdalen came in behind him.

"Wait." Steffan stopped. "If Lord Hazen knows we stole his map, won't this be the first place he'll look for us?"

"It is true. He may."

"I suppose we have little choice. We must either hide here or try to make it to your mother's house to get help."

Lenhart started making grunting noises.

"What is it?" Magdalen asked him.

Steffan could not see him in the dark mine, but Magdalen was closer to Lenhart and did not have the glare of the torch in her eyes.

"You want to go to Mother and try to get help?"

"That might be a good idea, but it is dangerous." Steffan held his breath.

"He wants to do it, and he knows this area very well. He should be able to get there before Hazen and his men, if they are headed for Mallin Park House." Magdalen turned to Lenhart. "Please be careful."

Steffan imagined the compassionate, concerned look on Magdalen's face, the look that was so often there. His heart squeezed.

Soon Lenhart was gone, and he and Magdalen continued into the mine.

The dirt floor angled down, but it grew sharply more angled, tilting so much that they had to walk leaning backward and slow their pace, taking small steps.

The air must be getting thinner because he could barely breathe. He tugged at the neckline of his shirt. And suddenly he was five years old again and trapped in a hole in the ground. The low ceiling and walls seemed to close in on him.

Magdalen touched his arm. "Are you all right?"

"Of course."

"Most people are nervous their first time in a mine. If you want to stay at the entrance, I can look around."

"No. I can do this."

How could he appear so weak and foolish in front of Magdalen? She who was so brave herself. They were supposed to be searching for what was so valuable that his uncle would force his son to marry Lady Magdalen for it.

He focused on his breathing—deep breaths in and out—and searching the uneven dirt and rock of the walls and ceiling. But he kept imagining the ceiling falling in on them, and his breathing went shallow again. His face started to tingle.

"Talk," Steffan said.

"What?"

"T-tell me what happened to this mine."

She placed her hand on his arm. "The copper ran out about five years ago. This mine is very solid, and there are two entrances. One of them is hidden and not everyone knows about it, but my father showed it to me once when I was a little girl. I used to take my sisters out here exploring. I know it well.

"I must say, I have no idea what Lord Hazen might think is valuable here," she continued. "I have never known of any other kind of mines in this area except copper. Perhaps there is some sort of treasure hidden here that Lord Hazen knows about, but I cannot think why he would not have simply sneaked up here and taken it. Why go to all the trouble of marrying his son to me to acquire it?"

Her voice was calming. His breathing was almost back to normal. He swallowed, ignoring the cold sweat down the middle of his back.

"Tell me about those long bands of gray and red in the wall there." He pointed to their left.

"I don't know what that is. Copper ore is sometimes a gold

color, sometimes green, but that doesn't look like copper. But it could certainly be something else, some other kind of valuable metal, perhaps."

Steffan stepped closer to the wall, holding the torch high. He had seen something like this before at the university when they'd studied mining and metals.

"I think you are right. This could be iron ore—the silver bands here—and the red bands in between could be jasper. They are often found together."

"Oh! Red jasper like my necklace. Are they valuable?" She stepped closer.

"Iron ore is, and if there is iron ore in this mine, that could be what my uncle was searching for. There is a way to melt iron now. With taller furnaces and men operating large bellows, it is possible to heat iron ore hot enough to melt it and get rid of all the impurities. The pure iron will be in high demand."

Concentrating on the rock was helping to slow down his breathing.

"Is iron ore difficult to find?"

"Yes, that's what makes it even more valuable."

They continued on in their descent into the earth. But Steffan concentrated on the walls now as he walked, becoming more and more convinced that Magdalen's father had not recognized the iron ore in these rocks after their copper ore ran out, and that was exactly what his uncle had found and wanted. Possibly all these abandoned mines contained the sought-after iron ore.

Finally, the floor evened out and they were walking on level ground.

"I know you are uncomfortable." Magdalen's voice reverberated off the walls. "Do you want to leave?"

"Not unless you want to."

"I like it down here. But we have to go out eventually. Shall we turn around?"

They started moving Magdalen's horse backward so they could turn her around in the narrow cave-like mine. Now that he was thinking about leaving instead of about the minerals in the mine, he started to sweat again and his breaths came in short gasps. He forced himself to focus on getting Magdalen's horse headed in the opposite direction.

Shouts echoed through the mine. They were coming from the direction of the mouth of the mine.

Magdalen grabbed his arm. "They found us."

Chapter Twenty-Five

Steffan listened to the men's voices carrying through the long, dark tunnel toward them. Magdalen pressed herself to his side.

"You said there was another entrance. Where is it?"

"Uh." Magdalen seemed to freeze. Then she pulled on her horse's reins and turned her back in the direction they had been going. "I'll show you. Hurry."

They set off at a brisk pace. They came to a Y in the mine and Magdalen turned to the right. The floor started angling up now. They were climbing a hill of rock.

Behind them a voice called, "You cannot escape."

"It's Lord Hazen."

"He's here?" Her voice was breathless. She clutched his arm tighter.

He needed to stay calm. Sweat dribbled into his eyebrows and he wiped it with his thumb.

They came to another Y and Magdalen stopped.

"Which way?"

"I don't know. Oh, Steffan, I'm so sorry. I can't remember." She put her hand to her head.

"Don't worry. Just think back to when you were a child playing in here. Think." He tried to sound calm and use a gentle tone. His blood was starting to pulse faster in his veins even as the torch was flickering and burning less bright, threatening to go out. He took deep breaths as images flashed before him of being alone in the deep, dark, slimy well.

She pressed her thumb into her temple, staring down at the floor. Finally, she said, "I think we need to go left."

They turned themselves and the horses to the left fork and hurried several dozen feet into that tunnel, until Magdalen suddenly groaned.

"This doesn't look right. We're starting to go down, aren't we? This is wrong." She halted. "We have to go back."

"Are you sure?"

"No, I'm not sure, but . . . I think so. Oh, I'm so sorry."

"Don't worry. We will make it. Just breathe." *Just breathe, Steffan.*

They backed the horses all the way up. Any minute Lord Hazen and his men could be upon them. They were trapped.

Sweat beaded on his forehead and ran down his temples. But he forced himself to focus. He had to get Magdalen safely out of here. Thankfully the horses were calm as long as he kept the torch away from their eyes. And the torch was growing dimmer and dimmer.

Finally, they were back at the fork. This time they took the right one, which climbed gradually higher. After they took a dozen or so steps, the torch flickered, sputtered, and then went out, plunging them into darkness. It pressed in on him on all sides.

"I can't see." Magdalen's voice broke through his panic.

She seemed to be groping as her hand skimmed his arm, then she grabbed him with both hands.

"We have to keep going. I'm putting my hand on the wall." He kept talking to keep them both calm. "It might be for the best. If Lord Hazen's men have no torches, it will take them awhile to reach us. They'll have to make one, and they won't be able to see us now that our torch is out."

"*Ja*, that's true."

He scraped his hand along the wall to make sure they didn't get lost or collide with the wall while Magdalen clung to his arm that held the horses' reins.

"How will we know when we are close to the opening?" he asked.

"It's not easy to find, unfortunately, but this tunnel ends just past the opening above us. We just have to go to the end and then take a few steps backward and we should find it."

They kept walking for what seemed like an eternity. Occasionally he heard a muffled shout somewhere far behind them. It was only a matter of time before Lord Hazen's men reached them.

"We should pray," he said.

"Oh God, oh Jesus, help us," Magdalen whispered softly. "Help us find the opening. Help us escape and reach safety. We lift our eyes. Where does our help come from? Our help comes from the Lord."

His heart skipped a beat at hearing her quote the Holy Scriptures.

Breathlessly, she kept talking, softly but quickly, as if she was saying whatever came to her mind. "Jesus, name above every name, keep us safe and give us victory over our enemies. Thank

You for Steffan's courage and for these horses who will take us to safety. Show us the way out of here and confuse our enemies so they cannot find us."

Steffan's head scraped on something and his chest constricted, so tight he could barely breathe. He was forced to lean down as he walked. Would he finally be suffocated in a dark hole under the earth, as he had so many times in his nightmares? Or would he humiliate himself by screaming like a baby afraid of the dark?

No, Magdalen was thanking God for his courage. He could not let her down.

"Thank You, God, that Your power is greater than any other," her voice rattled on. "Thank You for rescuing us from our dire situation. Our lives are in Your hands."

Now he was alternately running his hand along the wall and the ceiling overhead. Finally, he couldn't resist asking, "Is the ceiling supposed to be getting lower?"

"Oh yes." There was a joyful lift to her voice. "That means we're close to the opening."

Good. Because he was sweating like he was three feet from the sun, reliving every nightmare he'd ever had.

"Thank You, God, that we're getting close. Please help us find it. Guide us in the dark."

"I think I felt something." A crack or fissure in the ceiling. As they moved farther he felt another crack. He stopped and grabbed her hand. "Here, take the reins." He put them in her palm. Then he used his fingers to feel around the crack.

"Close your eyes." Dirt rained down as he pushed with all his might. Something gave way and let in a stream of light as well as dirt. He coughed, then pushed again and the opening widened.

He threw off the covering. He stood up straight and stuck his head out.

A misty rain was falling in a small clearing that surrounded the spot, with two long wooden planks propped against a tree not far away.

"Boost me up," Magdalen said, already lifting her arms over her head. "Once I get out I can get my father's boards and get the horses out."

He stooped and grabbed her around her knees and lifted her. After all the wood and water he'd been carrying, she felt quite light. He held her up until she'd had time to grasp the top of the opening, then he boosted her again. She scrambled up and out of the opening.

"Watch your eyes," she said, and suddenly a huge section of the ceiling overhead started peeling away.

For several moments he heard nothing except the wind blowing outside, and leaves swept into the opening, making the horses stamp their feet and snort restlessly. Had she been captured by Lord Hazen's men?

"Watch your head," she said as a wooden plank appeared above him. He moved the horses a little farther out of the way as she slid the hewn plank in until it touched the floor of the mine. Then another plank appeared, and he helped guide it down beside the first one.

He tugged on the first horse's reins and led him up, walking on the planks until they were both safely out of the hole. He handed the reins to Magdalen and went back down for the second horse.

Magdalen smiled in triumph. "We made it."

Steffan was a bit pale, but he heaved a sigh. "Let us go. Lord Hazen's men could spot us at any moment."

"Should we close the opening?"

He was already bending down to grasp the first plank and haul it up. He got both of them up before she could even offer to help, then they placed the wooden covers back over the hole, kicking leaves and dirt over them. They each took the reins of their own horse.

"We need a place to hide." Steffan looked intently in her eyes, standing so close they were almost touching.

"The only place I can think of is in one of the mines."

"Choose one that was not on the map."

She closed her eyes and pictured the map in her head. Yes, there was one in the valley on the other side of the village. "Come. I know which one."

She tugged on her horse's reins, leading her toward the top of the hill. Once there, she let the horse take her time going down the other side, as it was steep and the rain made the ground slick.

They crept along, making their way down the heavily forested, leaf-covered hillside. When they reached the base of the small ravine, Magdalen turned right, in the direction of one of the older mines.

"Mount up!" Steffan grabbed her by the waist from behind and practically threw her into her saddle. She looked over her shoulder. Four or five men on horseback were galloping toward them in a straight line along the ravine.

Magdalen urged her horse into a run. Steffan leapt on his own horse and was right behind her.

How would they ever lose them? Would they be able to get away? If they went to the mine she had planned on hiding in, the men would see them and trap them inside, as that mine did not have a second entrance.

Magdalen let her horse run the length of the ravine, and when it abruptly turned back to the left, she turned with it. But instead of following it all the way, knowing they were blocked from the view of Lord Hazen's men, she steered her horse straight up the side of a short hill, then plunged down the other side.

The rain poured down now. Her horse slipped but then regained her footing.

Trusting that Steffan was right behind her, she drove her horse hard along the side of a less steep hill, avoiding the rocks along the way. Thankfully the trees were sparser here as well, though she still had to duck to avoid limbs.

She found a dirt trail that led them to a small wooden house in a clearing. She kept going and passed the house, rubbing the rain out of her eyes.

Now that she was at a level place, she looked behind her. Steffan was there, very close, and Lord Hazen's men were nowhere in sight.

She steered her horse back toward the left. They looped around the side of the hill where the old mine was located. Would it be better to go to Mallin Park House? To the large stone home where her mother and sisters lived? Her mother did not have any guards and very few male servants who could help defend them. Thinking about her little siblings made her keep to her path around the hill and toward the mine.

She came to the old crooked tree at the entrance. She drew her horse to a halt and dismounted as a chill shook her body. Her horse let her lead her into the opening of the mine as Steffan dismounted.

She waited for Steffan to follow her. When he didn't, she stepped to the opening and looked out. He was pushing on a dead, rotten tree. The base of the trunk gave way, sending the broken tree crashing down in front of the entrance. He led his horse over the tree and inside the mine.

Chapter Twenty-Six

Magdalen shivered in her wet clothes. Steffan ran his hands over his arms to brush off the excess water, then shook his hair.

"The rain is good," he said. "They will have a harder time finding our trail." He was staring out at the world outside the dark mine tunnel behind them.

"It might be good in that way, but I am cold." Her skirts were weighed down with water, and drops ran from her hairline, one forming on the tip of her nose. She hastily wiped it off.

"What do we have that's dry?" He opened up his saddlebag. It was leather and looked like it had been oiled to make it shed water. "I have some dry clothes. Check yours."

She knew before she opened the soaked bag tied to her saddle that all her clothes would be drenched. And they were.

"I have an idea." He turned to his horse. "Let's take the saddles off the horses and you can wrap up in their blankets. They won't smell very good, but at least you'll be warm and dry."

They worked together to unsaddle the horses and brush them off the best they could. They were still warm from the hard ride.

"You'll have to take off those wet clothes. You can put on some of mine."

If he had said the words in any other way than the innocent tone he used, she might have either blushed or been defensive. But he was right, of course.

"You go first." She motioned him farther into the mine.

He took a bundle of clothing and stepped into the dark mine. When he came back out moments later, she was surprised he already had his dry clothes on and he carried his wet ones.

"Here." He reached into his leather saddlebag and handed her some clothes. "I know they won't fit you very well, but they'll be better than those wet things."

She shivered as the chill seemed to seep into her bones. She took the clothes and went to change.

She fumbled with the men's clothes in the dark, almost falling down trying to put on the hose. Thankfully it was the footless kind, but it was so loose she was afraid it might fall off. At least the linen shirt he gave her was soft, and it was so long it hung past her knees.

"Are you all right in there?"

Her teeth chattered when she said, "I'll be there in a moment." With stiff fingers she tied the laces at the neck of the coarse tunic, picked up her wet clothes, and joined him.

Steffan glanced at her but didn't say anything. Her cheeks grew hot as she imagined her appearance in his clothes. And her hair must look like a bird's nest after it had come loose from its braids on their wild ride.

"I'll take that now." She reached for the horse blanket he was holding. He gave it to her and she wrapped it around her shoulders.

"Do you want the other one as well?"

"*Nein*, this will do. I'll be warm soon and the horse can have it back. She'll likely be cold after a few more minutes."

"Don't worry. They are well for now." He was rubbing her horse's head and neck with a cloth. Steffan's hair was soaking wet and dripping from the ends.

"You're drying off the horse instead of yourself."

"We can't afford for the horses to get sick." He looked at her over his shoulder and smiled.

If she had to be stuck in an abandoned mine being chased by evil men, she was glad it was with a man who would not make advances on her. Yet he was kind enough to make light of the situation, to constantly tell her, "Don't worry," and to care more about her and the horses than himself.

But why did he have to be so handsome? With his dark, wet hair curling against his temples and forehead, his brown eyes shining in the dim light of a rainy twilight as he brushed the horses, her mind went back through the last two years when she'd dreamed he would ask her to marry him. She'd been so overjoyed when his letter arrived. Until the day he'd told her that he did not send that letter and that he did not wish to marry her at all.

Tears stung her eyes as she remembered his rejection. Foolish tears. She had no time to dwell on such a thing when their lives were in danger.

Magdalen went back to spread her wet clothes on a rock just inside the opening of the mine while her thoughts kept spinning, like a spider weaving its web. She couldn't seem to stop them.

Steffan would naturally want someone wealthier than she was. A simple baron's daughter from impoverished Mallin was not someone who would tempt a powerful duke. But he was not a powerful duke now. He was a man running for his life.

"Lord Hazen must be truly evil," she said as she tried to wring the water from her hair. "Did you not know how evil he was when you were a boy?"

"I was not well acquainted with him until I was older. He and my grandmother did not like each other, so I rarely saw him when she was alive."

The rain was coming down more heavily now. She stood beside him while he continued to brush off the horses.

"Alexander was a sickly child and very pampered by his nurses. On the rare occasions we were together as children, he was forever getting some slight injury and blaming me for it. I did not have a good opinion of my cousin."

"When was the last time you saw him, before you went away to Prague?"

"About three years ago, before my grandmother died, Alexander and Uncle Hazen came for a visit. When they left, my grandmother told me never to trust my uncle. 'He is greedy,' she said. 'Greedy men are dangerous men.' But she could be rather cynical sometimes, and it never entered my mind that my uncle would try to kill me." After a moment he went on. "During that visit I remember I actually felt sorry for my cousin."

"Why?"

"He seemed afraid of my uncle, defeated by him, as if he could not stand up to him and was not allowed to have his own opinions or do what he wanted."

"That is sad."

"But I should not have felt sorry for him. I should have told him what an immature child he was for not standing up for his own desires and goals. Now he's his father's puppet in stealing my inheritance."

"It is very unjust." But what bothered Magdalen the most, when she allowed herself to think about it, was how her usurper, Agnes, had found love with Alexander. How unfair that they were enjoying married love when Magdalen, even when she did get her identity back, would be unlikely to ever be loved in marriage.

But she certainly did not plan to talk to Steffan about that.

"No more unjust than what was done to you. What did you say Agnes's father's name was?"

"Erlich. He's one of Lord Hazen's assistants, so he got what he wanted as well."

"Sometimes it seems the wicked prosper more than the righteous, but I have to believe that they will get what they deserve eventually. And in our cases it will be in less than two weeks."

"Do you think so?"

"Yes, but not unless we stay out of sight of Lord Hazen and his men. I think these horses are well enough, since I have no hay or oats or grass to give them. Let us lead them farther in so they will be less noticeable, and we shall sit where no one passing by can see us."

They did as Steffan suggested, and she found herself sitting with her back against the rock wall of the mine beside Steffan.

"Did you go away to Prague at your uncle's urging? I suppose that was when he got rid of everyone who would know that Alexander was not you."

"He did not urge me to go at first. I wanted to go . . ." His forehead creased as he stared through the opening, into the rainy night. "I had a notion that I could help my people prosper if I went to the university. We were already prosperous, but I thought

I could bring new sources of income to our town and region if I increased my knowledge."

"That was very noble of you."

"And I selfishly wanted to travel and learn things my tutors couldn't teach me. My uncle was supportive. I thought he sincerely wanted me to help my people. Now I know he just wanted me out of the way. How imprudent I was."

"You could not have known. Wicked people are good at being deceptive, I imagine."

"That's true enough." He seemed to rouse himself and turned his body toward her. "What about you? How did you end up with a mercenary servant who would steal your position? She must know she won't get away with it."

"Agnes said it was her father's idea, but I never would have thought he could do something so evil. He's been with our family since before I was born."

He was looking down at her so intently that it made her heart flutter.

Foolish girl. He does not fancy you.

"Did they harm you?"

"No, they just threatened Lenhart and me if I did not do as they said. I wanted to fight back, but I had no weapon. I felt help-less and angry because I did not know how to stop them."

"It wasn't your fault. You had no idea they would do such a terrible thing, and understandably so. You could not have been prepared."

"I suppose not." He couldn't know how much it meant to her to hear him say, "It wasn't your fault."

"And were you relieved that you did not have to marry?"

"I . . ." She glanced up at him. He was watching her closely with those dark-brown eyes. Why would he bring that up? "I was willing to marry you because I thought it would help my people. I hoped you would increase their prosperity."

"So you were sacrificing yourself for your people."

"Most men think women are eager to marry anyone who asks them."

"I would never assume such a thing."

"Oh, I think you did assume that about me."

"Well, you were crying when you saw that your servant was marrying the supposed Duke of Wolfberg."

He had her there. Or perhaps not. "I was crying because I did not know what to do. I was a goose girl, another person had taken my position, my authority, my freedom, and even my clothes. I suppose you think I was desperate to marry any man claiming to be a duke."

He lifted his hands in surrender. "Forgive me. You had many better reasons to cry than not marrying me. Or my look-alike cousin. In fact, I'll be the first to say that I was a selfish, spoiled young man who was easily led by my cunning uncle."

He ended with a sad look on his face, but she could not help jabbing him a little. "Was?"

"You are very amusing." He lifted just one brow, and one corner of his mouth followed. "I believe I have learned a lot about sacrifice and empathy since having everything I've ever known stripped away from me."

"You still had a heavy purse to buy whatever you needed." She wasn't sure why she was goading him. Was she bitter about his rejection?

A slight smile graced his lips and he nodded. "Perhaps I would have learned even more had I been poor as well."

Why was he being so humble? It was making her want to scoot away from him, even as it drew her to him. Was he trying to impress her? Well, she would not fall for his charm.

"I believe"—he leaned toward her, an intense expression in his eyes—"that I have learned to value the truly valuable, and what is truly lasting and valuable is not money."

"Oh!" she cried out as the realization struck her as if she had just run into a stone wall. "Do you know what this means?"

"What?" His gaze fastened on hers.

"Now that we have found the iron ore in the mine, I don't have to marry in order to provide for my people! They will be able to start mining again! Oh, and they can build one of those new furnaces you were talking about. Mallin will be a prosperous place again, more prosperous than before."

As she talked, the smile on his face faded.

"I won't have to marry some wealthy duke or baron, some old man I barely know." She laughed and clapped her hands. "Are you not glad for me?"

But Steffan did not look glad at all. He leaned away from her and no longer met her eyes. "Oh yes, of course."

But his lack of enthusiasm could not dampen her joy. Mallin would be prosperous again!

Chapter Twenty-Seven

Steffan leaned back against the wall of the mine and watched the joy play across Magdalen's face.

He had not thought for a moment that once he was a duke again and in his rightful place, she might not want to marry him. Now, to see her so joyful about not having to marry at all . . .

She didn't need him, and she obviously did not want him either.

He closed his eyes. He was tired. He was slightly cold and his hair was still wet. He was stuck in a mine running from his evil uncle. And now Magdalen, the girl he had thought was so sweet and beautiful, the girl he imagined would love to marry him if he would have her, was thrilled she would not have to.

Of course she was glad. He had rejected her. He'd told her, when she finally realized he was the duke and that his cousin was an imposter, that he had never intended to marry her.

But she had not been in love with him. She'd barely known him and had not seen him in two years. He could see that she felt hurt by what he'd said, but she shouldn't have. And now that he knew her better, had been through so much with her and had seen her compassionate nature . . .

After bragging about all he had learned since his selfish days as a spoiled duke, he did not want to look like a selfish, spoiled duke now. Of course she was glad that this discovery would help her people.

"Tell me more about what you learned."

"What?" His eyes popped open.

"At the university. You said you learned about mining and iron ore and a new way of melting it."

"Oh. Of course."

While the old Steffan wanted to be angry with her for not wishing to marry him, and the old Steffan might have even been gruff with her, how would the new, less selfish, less spoiled Steffan respond? It was sad that he had to think this hard about it. But the way she was staring at him, with that sweet smile of hers lifting her perfect lips . . . he wanted to be better than the old Steffan.

He started telling her about mining iron ore, about the process of melting it and turning it into iron tools and weapons. While he talked about things other young women might find dull and tiresome, she nodded or asked a question every so often. Her green eyes sparkled with such interest. Perhaps she was interested in more than just mining. Perhaps she was also interested in him.

But that was only the arrogant Steffan rearing his head.

"It's quite dark now," Magdalen said. "The rain has lessened too."

"We'd better try to sleep. But before we do that we should move deeper into the mine so Lord Hazen and his men can't see us if they pass by with a torch." His stomach sank even as he said the words. The last thing he wanted to do was move farther into a dark mine. But he also didn't want to die at his uncle's hands and cause the death of this innocent lady.

"I am very tired." She yawned and covered her mouth. "But first I have to . . . go out and take care of something."

"Of course. Don't go far, and keep an eye out for Lord Hazen and his men."

She nodded, left her blanket on the floor, and hurried out the opening. She stepped over the fallen tree and disappeared into the darkness. Overhead the clouds were dissipating, but there was very little light.

He set about gathering blankets for their makeshift beds, trying to think how he might make Magdalen's sleeping spot as comfortable as possible.

Where was she? She was taking a long time. It was still raining a bit so he would have thought she'd be quick.

He dropped the blankets and raced to the entrance. He stepped over the fallen tree trunk and looked all around. All kinds of man-eating animals resided in the forests of these regions of the Holy Roman Empire. Bears, wolves, wild cats—all were known to attack people. In addition, Lord Hazen and his men were probably nearby.

"Magdalen?" he whispered as loudly as he dared. No answer.

He went back into the mine and retrieved the sword he had brought with him. Then he came out with his sword drawn, his jaw clenched, ready to defend her.

Magdalen moved to find some bushes to squat between, far enough away from the entrance of the mine. Leaves and limbs pulled at the tunic and hose she was wearing, though she tried to avoid them as best she could to keep from getting her dry clothes wet.

Just as she finished taking care of her needs, she realized she was near the *Hünengräber*, or giant's tomb, which was in a small clearing in the forest that she had often visited when she was growing up. In the waning light, she could just make out the large boulders set up like a tomb in the middle of the forest.

The *Hünengräber* had been there since before anyone could remember. Hegatha had always warned her never to disturb it or even go near it. Magdalen asked her, "Why not?"

"It's where the giants left their treasure, and now it's guarded by fairies and trolls. I was told when I was a child, and now I'm telling you—nothing good comes of disturbing a giant's tomb."

Magdalen obeyed, for she never liked to incite her nurse's displeasure.

"But what a superstitious notion that is," she whispered now as she looked at it, a superstition left over from the ancient country's heathen ways.

She drew nearer to where the huge stones were stacked and placed so as to create a little aboveground tunnel leading under the largest stone, which lay across the tops of the long, upright boulders that stood on either side.

As she left the path and went around to the back side of the giant's tomb, an opening led underground, with smaller flat stones holding back the earth, as it were, leaving a space large enough for someone to walk into if they stooped. The ground at the mouth of it was covered in leaves and weeds, but the interior was too dark to tell what lay inside.

Magdalen had no time to go exploring a giant's tomb, with

Steffan waiting for her and a misting rain falling. She turned to head back to the mine when something growled.

A long, white-striped head poked out of the giant's tomb. Magdalen jumped back. "Don't worry, Mr. Badger," she said as soothingly as she could as she backed away from him. "I am going. Moving away . . . See?"

The badger made another sound, slightly less threatening than his growl, then waddled away.

Magdalen moved back up the little mound to the trail. The badger had probably been foraging for earthworms in the cool, damp earth.

Magdalen picked her way through the darkness, trying to avoid brushing against the wet limb of a beech tree. She heard a rustling in the bushes beside her. Was it another badger? Badgers could be aggressive. She certainly did not want to make one angry.

Suddenly, a man loomed beside her. Two hands came toward her face. Before she could scream, hard fingers clamped over her mouth, gouging into her face.

Her heart pounded painfully hard. She clawed at the man's hands.

He growled in her ear, "Cease that or I'll slap you." He shook her so hard she couldn't see for a moment.

If only she could scream, Steffan would come and save her. But the man's hand over her mouth made it impossible.

Terror like liquid heat seeped into her veins. What would this man do to her? Was he one of Lord Hazen's men? He would surely take her to Lord Hazen and torture her to force her to tell them where Steffan was hiding.

The man chuckled in her ear. "Lord Hazen never said I couldn't have a little fun with you before I take you to him."

She started fighting him again, raking her fingernails over his hands and arms.

The man let out a yelp. Just as his grip on her face relaxed, something solid slammed against her temple. Her whole body, bereft of strength, melted as everything went black.

Steffan hurried through the wet brush. Was he going in the right direction? He started to call out her name when he heard a man's voice speaking low. It sounded threatening. He headed toward it. Two figures standing very close emerged up ahead. One was a large man and the other was a woman.

His heart crashed against the wall of his chest. Magdalen was struggling against the man's grip on her face. The man slammed his fist against her head, and she went still.

Steffan charged forward, his sword raised over his head.

The man dropped Magdalen's limp body on the ground and drew his sword. Steffan struck, but the man blocked his blade. Steffan struck again and again, beating him back.

Ice flowed through Steffan's veins as he was reminded of the last time he'd wielded his sword. He fought for his life then, and now he fought for Magdalen's. He could not let this man go back to Lord Hazen and his men. He could not allow him to escape. And after what he saw him do to Magdalen, he had no desire to.

Steffan used both hands and struck his most powerful blow. The man lost his footing and his balance. As he fell he tried to stab Steffan in the stomach. When he did, he left his upper body unprotected, and Steffan plunged his sword through his enemy's heart.

The man stared up from the ground. His hand shook, then loosened. His sword dropped and he lay unmoving.

Steffan pulled his sword free of the man's chest. Then he hurried over to Magdalen and fell to his knees beside her.

Chapter Twenty-Eight

The water on the cold ground was seeping through her borrowed clothes. Magdalen groaned at the pain in her head. Someone was putting an arm under her shoulders. Then she remembered the guard who struck her in the head. She opened her eyes, clenching her hands into fists and tensing her whole body.

"Magdalen."

"Steffan!" A sob caught in her throat and sounded like a squeak.

"It's all right now. That man is dead." He leaned over her, a dark but welcome shadow. One arm was underneath her shoulders, and his other arm slid under her knees. He lifted her as if she were no heavier than an armload of firewood.

Her hands slipped around his shoulders. They just naturally seemed to fit there. In the barest bit of moon- and starlight, she could see the intense look on his face as he carried her through the brush and trees. How thankful she was that he had come. To be safe and warm in his arms, when she might have been brutalized by that terrible man.

He stepped over the fallen tree and into the mine. Then he set her gently on the floor and knelt beside her. "Are you all right?"

He moved her hair away from her face. "You have a big bump on your head."

She couldn't take her eyes off his face, even though she could barely make out anything more than his outline. She should say something. Instead, she shuddered, still feeling that man's hands on her mouth, his hot breath in her ear. Was she truly safe? Steffan said he killed him.

"Magdalen? Are you all right? Did he hurt you?"

By his tone she knew he meant a different kind of hurt than the bruise on her head.

"Nein." Her voice was so raspy as to be barely audible. She swallowed and tried again. "He didn't hurt me." She bit her lip to keep it from trembling, trying hard not to start sobbing. If Steffan had not come, that man would have done unspeakable things.

Her head ached, but that was nothing compared to the way her heart squeezed.

A tear, followed by another and another, spilled down her face.

Steffan put his arms around her and pulled her close, still kneeling beside her.

She buried her face in his chest and sobbed softly.

Steffan's heart clenched at her sobs, at the way her shoulders shook, at the hot tears that soaked through his linen shirt. He sat back on the floor of the mine, settling her comfortably against his chest. "You're safe now," he whispered against her hair. "I won't let anyone harm you."

"I'm so sorry." Her voice was watery and punctuated by another soft sob.

"For what?"

"I've ruined your clothes."

"Don't worry. I have other clothes." He stroked her hair—a dangerous move, as it was so silky.

"I'm sorry you had to kill that man."

"It was necessary, and certainly not your fault. It's Lord Hazen's fault."

Oh, God, what if I had not gotten to her in time? What if the man had dragged her away and my uncle had tortured or even killed her?

Sweet, lovely Magdalen. How would he have been able to bear that? He suddenly realized he did not feel any remorse for killing that man. Of course God forgave him. God helped him save her.

She finally ceased crying and sat up, pulling away slightly, and wiped her eyes with her hands. He picked up the blanket she had left when she went outside and wrapped it around her shoulders.

"Thank you." Her voice was small, and she took a shuddering breath and sighed. "Thank you for saving me."

In her bowed head, her slumped shoulders, and her downcast eyes, he read her determination not to ask him to comfort her. She would not expect anything from him. And somehow that thought stabbed him like a knife.

He liked being with her. He liked talking to her. And he very much liked holding her in his arms. He had told himself over and over that he couldn't marry her, that he owed it to his people to follow his grandmother's advice and marry for political gain. But it was all a lie. The reason he told her and himself, repeatedly, that he wouldn't marry her was because of fear. He was afraid—no, terrified—of falling too deeply in love, of loving someone the way his father had loved his mother. Her death had destroyed him.

Did Steffan dare to risk marrying for love? It was not hard to imagine loving Magdalen . . . very much.

His breath quickened.

He wasn't certain he could overcome this fear, or even if he should.

"I've made you a bed a little farther into the mine," Steffan said, "and I will sleep at your feet, so if anyone comes exploring, they'll face me first."

"You are being very kind." She couldn't meet his eye. He *was* being very kind. Should she be embarrassed? Gratified? Humbled? Or annoyed that she had let him see her cry? She did not want to feel indebted to him, this man who was handsome and brave and strong and intelligent, mostly because she knew when this adventure was over, when they both had their lives back, she'd never see him again. And he probably wouldn't care.

She should say, "How very chivalrous of you" and smile saucily at him. His brows would raise in that amused way of his. But she did not feel very saucy.

"Can you walk?" He spoke so gently, it made a tear fall from her eye. At least he couldn't see it.

He touched her shoulder, so she took his hand and he pulled her up. Unable to see anything at all, she clung to Steffan. Soon, he stopped her.

"Here is your bed." He guided her hand down until she felt something soft on the ground.

"You seem to have found the right spot."

"I counted my steps so I would know exactly where I was."

"That was wise." She could hear his retreating footsteps in the silence, which seemed to meld with the darkness and press in on her. And she hadn't fallen in a dark well as a child like Steffan.

When his footsteps returned, she asked, "Are you well? It's very dark."

"I think I'm beginning to forget my fear of dark holes."

"That's fortunate. I think I am beginning to *have* a fear of dark holes." She tried to chuckle, to let him know her fear was nothing serious, but it came out as a nervous sound.

"Don't worry. I shall be near."

"Thank you." Magdalen lay on the blanket he had spread out for her. He had even made her a small pillow.

"I hope my clothes will be dry by morning," she said.

"You are not enjoying wearing men's clothes?"

"I am grateful for them, but I am not used to them. I shall be glad to give them back to you." How much more awkward this moment would be if she believed Steffan might want to marry her. It was good that he did not.

"How is your head feeling? Are you in much pain?"

"Only a small headache."

After a short pause he said, "Are you certain you are well?"

"Yes." But she didn't feel sleepy. In fact, she was afraid to fall asleep, afraid she would dream about the man who had grabbed her.

"Can you believe that about Katrin? She betrayed us. And I had no idea." A pang went through her middle at the remembrance of what Katrin had done to them.

"I did not realize she was our betrayer either, although I did have some suspicions."

"Did you?" Magdalen must be a poor judge of character.

"She was the obvious person, though she seemed so kind and innocent."

"And yet I never suspected her. I do not easily trust people, but I was completely fooled. Is it not strange that she warned us to flee?"

"*Ja.* Perhaps my uncle wanted us to flee."

"But why? What purpose did that serve? *Nein,* I think she warned us because she was a little in love with you."

He made a sound of air blowing between his lips. "That seems unlikely."

"Not at all. You were the only handsome young man among the servants. That is what she once said."

"You think I am handsome?"

Magdalen laughed a short, quick laugh. "I suspect you know you are handsome. Leastways, Katrin thought you were."

After a pause, Steffan said, "I suppose she had little choice but to inform on us. My uncle probably brought her to Wolfberg from Arnsbaden, and she felt her loyalty was owed to him. He probably threatened to murder her family if she did not ferret out information for him."

Tears rose to Magdalen's eyes again. "I feel as if all anyone ever does is betray me."

"I have not betrayed you."

"I felt a bit betrayed when you took my letters but did not send them as you promised."

After a slight pause, he said, "That was wrong of me. I deceived you. Please forgive me. The letter to Thornbeck has been sent now."

"You did save my life tonight. That can make up for a lot of sins, I suppose. I forgive you."

"Indeed, we are fortunate all the clanging of swords did not bring Hazen's men upon us."

"The forest is rather good at muffling sound. I suppose it is all the trees and ferns and moss and endless bushes. But you did save me." She let the tone of her voice take on the seriousness she was feeling. "And I am very grateful."

"And I am grateful God let me be here when you needed me."

Did he long to reach out and hold her hand the way she was longing to, so much so that her hand ached? How good it had felt earlier when he'd held her in his arms, so tender and warm. If only he would hold her like that again.

But she must not long for that. She should be trying to think of what to do next. That was what her friend Avelina would do. "What is our plan, now that we've likely found what Lord Hazen wanted in our mines?"

"We can hope that Lenhart made it safely to your mother's house, and that my courier is able to deliver your letter to Thornbeck—or that at least one or the other will reach their destination. Therefore, we should try to get back to Wolfberg to be there when they arrive."

Magdalen thought for a moment. "That sounds reasonable."

"And now I suppose we should go to sleep. We will need our wits about us tomorrow."

She thought back on how she had wiped the blood from his face when he'd been beaten. Twice. How she had sympathized with him when he was afraid of small dark places. And now to hear the gentleness in his voice, the kindness and sympathy, it caused a strange tugging at her heart.

She should stop thinking these thoughts and go to sleep.

After what seemed like a long time, she heard Steffan's breathing grow loud and even. Soon she drifted off to sleep as well.

Chapter Twenty-Nine

Steffan awoke with a start. What was that sound? And why could he not see? Had his fire gone out in the hearth?

Then it came to him—sleeping in the servants' quarters, trying to get his place back from his cousin and uncle, and being on the run with Magdalen.

"Magdalen? Are you there?"

The only answer was a small cry, then, "Steffan!"

"I'm here. What is wrong?" He scrambled to his knees and crawled to where he thought she should be. He reached out his hand and touched her.

Her hand grabbed his, and then he heard a tiny sob. He put his arms around her. Would she be shocked and pull away? She didn't, but instead leaned her head on his shoulder. He could feel her breath on his neck.

"What is wrong? Did you have a bad dream?" He'd had enough of them to know how they could make your heart race and keep you awake for a long time afterward.

"Something was chasing me, a wild animal." She pressed her face closer to his shoulder and took deep breaths. "I couldn't get away. I tried to move. I think I kicked my foot against the wall and woke myself up."

Holding her in his arms made his chest expand, and a strange sensation overtook him. She was holding him back, with her arms around him. The darkness seemed to whisper to him that he could kiss her and no one would know, that she would not push him away.

It was a dangerous thought.

"I know it sounds foolish, but that dream frightened me so much."

"It's not foolish at all. Dreams can be very frightening." When he was very young, after he had fallen in the well, his sister had often comforted him.

"I knew it was a dream. After all, there are no animals that walk upright like a man and have red eyes and fangs that drip blood and saliva. I even kept telling myself to wake up."

"I think those are the worst, when you're telling yourself to wake up but you can't. I'm sure you dreamed that because of what happened tonight."

Gertrudt had told him once, after a servant girl burst into tears after he chastised her, "Women don't want brutal honesty. They prefer a gentle, encouraging word. You had better learn that before you get married, or I pity your wife." Did he sound gentle and encouraging?

"I'm sure you're right. What do you do when you're afraid?"

"Lately a Scripture passage keeps springing into my mind. 'I lift up my eyes to the mountains—where does my help come from? My help comes from the Lord, the Maker of heaven and earth.'"

"Oh, I know that one. It's in my Psalter. I especially remember this part: 'The Lord will keep you from all harm—he will watch over your life; the Lord will watch over your coming and going both now and forevermore.'"

"That's excellent." Hearing her quote Scripture made his heart leap, just as it had earlier when they were trying to get out of the mine. He'd never felt this way about any woman before. But then . . . his heart beat faster as an image of his distraught father invaded his thoughts, a memory of him sobbing over Steffan's mother's grave, and of the vacant look in his eyes in the weeks and months following her death.

If something happened to Magdalen, would he grieve as his father had?

"Do you know another passage of Scripture?"

He blinked to dispel the memory. "My tutor used to make me memorize scriptures. I liked this one: 'Not by might nor by power, but by my Spirit,' says the Lord Almighty. 'What are you, mighty mountain? Before Zerubbabel you will become level ground.'"

"Oh, I like that. I wanted to ask you before, how do you know so much Scripture? I only know a few passages that the priest taught my sisters and me, besides what's in my Psalter."

"I only had a Psalter and a Book of Hours before I went to the university, but we studied all the Scriptures there. I even had the entire Bible translated for me in German."

"Oh."

She didn't say anything else. Did she disapprove? Did it surprise her?

"I wish I could read it in German."

He considered telling her that she could, and often, if she married him. But Magdalen might still be excited about *not* having to marry.

His heart sank a little.

"When all is well again in Wolfberg, you can stay as long as you like and read it." There. His sister would be proud of him for his gentle invitation.

Magdalen swallowed the lump that came into her throat. He was talking of her staying in Wolfberg to read his Bible, as if she were no temptation to him at all, just a common guest like any other.

Why did she care? She'd promised herself she'd never care for him in that way. But the tears that pooled behind her eyes were proof that she had broken that promise.

At least he couldn't see her.

"I think, when I am back in Mallin, I shall commission someone to translate a copy of the Holy Writ for me. I shall be rich enough after our mines are operating again." She'd have her own Bible. She wouldn't need to read his.

"Oh. Yes, you could do that."

Why did he sound sad? Men were beyond comprehending.

They lay quietly in the dark. Why wasn't he talking? Had she hurt his feelings by not accepting his offer to come and read his Bible?

"Is there anything you need?" he asked. "Can I get you your water flask?"

"Thank you, but I am well."

"I'll let you go to sleep then." Neither of them spoke.

With the assurance that Steffan was nearby keeping watch over her, she drifted back to sleep, trying not to think about the man who had attacked her or the bad dream that had awakened her.

Magdalen and Steffan stood just outside the entrance with the sun shining down through the trees. The horses were grazing on what grass they could find, and Magdalen prayed Lord Hazen's men would not find them at this mine, which was not on his map.

"That looks very bad." Steffan's tone and expression were both somber as he stared at the side of her forehead.

Magdalen carefully touched the bump on her head, then tried to cover it with her hair. "It doesn't hurt."

He gave her that quizzical, doubtful raise of one eyebrow.

"It feels sore if I touch it, but it doesn't throb like it did last night. I am well now." She smiled as cheerfully as she could.

"Are you sure you do not want to try to get to your home in Mallin?"

"I want to go to Wolfberg. If Lenhart was able to make it home without getting captured, then I don't need to go. And if my letter reaches Thornbeck, Avelina and Lord Thornbeck will come to Wolfberg, and I want to be there when they arrive."

"It will be dangerous."

"I would rather face danger than explain things to my mother. So what is our strategy?"

"I think our goal is covertness rather than speed. But we do need to go into the village to replenish our supply of food and water. You can go with me, but someone might recognize you and draw attention to you, and Lord Hazen could be nearby. Will you be all right to stay here while I go?"

"I think so."

"I will come back for you as soon as I can." He stared at her, running a hand over his short beard. "I was about to promise you that I will come back, but the truth is, I could get captured by my uncle and his men. Many other things could happen, and I don't want to leave you."

Did he care about her so much?

He touched her shoulder, looking into her eyes.

She couldn't stop staring at his lips. His bottom lip wasn't swollen anymore. When had it healed? His mouth was very close, and coming closer.

She closed her eyes and held her breath. Was he going to kiss her? She should not let him, but . . . she wanted him to, and she would let him.

His lips touched her cheek. They were warm and gentle. He then pressed his cheek against hers before pulling her into an embrace, his arms around her and her face pressed against his shoulder.

It felt so good to feel his warmth, his tenderness . . . But did he not notice that she had closed her eyes and practically invited him to kiss her? And not on her cheek either.

What kind of silly, wanton girl was she? No. He could not know that she'd hoped he would kiss her, that she'd expected him to kiss her lips.

She took several breaths.

Oh, but he must have seen the way she closed her eyes, that she was still thinking about kissing him. Her face burned. What was wrong with her?

She pushed away from him.

Chapter Thirty

Steffan's heart was still pounding after he decided at the last moment to kiss her cheek instead of her lips. Magdalen had pushed him away after he embraced her. Wise girl.

He hurried to pack their belongings on the horses. Magdalen helped by strapping the first bag to the back of her horse's saddle.

He'd always been told, by his priest, his tutor, his grandmother, and even by Jacob, that he should never kiss a maiden. The only woman he should ever kiss was his betrothed on their wedding day. Kissing, they said, was for senseless, indiscreet men, for wayward sinners, and for the poor, who had few pleasures in life.

He had been sorely tempted several times in the last several hours, especially seeing how Magdalen had clung to him after he saved her the night before and after her nightmare. Not that it was her fault. He had wanted to comfort her. But to feel her breath on his neck . . . and then this morning, to see her stare at his lips and then close her eyes. He wouldn't be breathing if he had not been tempted.

What would Magdalen think if he tried to kiss her? He was fortunate she had not slapped him for kissing her on the cheek. Did she think of it as a brother kissing a sister? He shuddered. That would be worse than getting slapped.

He ran a hand over his face. If there were a stream nearby, he'd go dunk his head in it. Maybe the cold water would clear his thoughts.

Together they finished readying the horses.

"I don't think anyone will recognize me if I pull the hood of your tunic up over my head," she said, stuffing her hair into it.

He nodded. "It is a good disguise."

As they rode into the village, they did not speak to each other, and Magdalen kept her face mostly covered while he procured supplies for their journey.

He let his gaze scour the men milling around the marketplace for Lord Hazen and his soldiers, and he was certain Magdalen was doing the same. Just as they were about to leave, he spotted two of his uncle's guards asking questions of a group of villagers in the middle of the street.

He kept his head down while he stowed the last of the provisions in his leather saddlebag. Magdalen pulled the hood as low as possible.

Soon they were on their way back to Wolfberg.

By midafternoon the next day, they came to the path leading to Rosings Abbey.

"We will stop here for a meal, and you need to rest." Steffan didn't like the look of exhaustion in Magdalen's eyes and the way her shoulders drooped.

"I don't want to slow you down to take care of me. I'm afraid Lord Hazen will catch up to us." Her pretty green eyes glistened with impending tears.

"Listen." He leaned forward, drawing his horse alongside hers, and took her by the wrist. "It doesn't matter that we are traveling a bit slower. We have at least a week before the guests arrive in Wolfberg." He caressed her wrist with his thumb. "And secondly, I like taking care of you."

She shook her head and made a sound that was a cross between a laugh and a snort.

"You took care of me, remember? And I let you. And now you have to let me take care of you."

"Your swollen lip is better." She smiled. "The cut over your eye is almost healed."

"Now, don't worry. We will eat our food and sleep, and in the morning you'll feel better. If God so wills, Lord Hazen would not find us even if we stayed at Rosings Abbey for a week."

When they reached the abbey, the nuns sent Steffan to another part of the convent. They gave Magdalen a hot bowl of rabbit stew and showed her to the same room where she had slept on her way to Wolfberg, before Agnes and her father forced her to change places with her.

With her stomach full from the stew and some wheat bread and butter, Magdalen lay back in her narrow but comfortable bed and read from the Psalter that one of the nuns' young servants had brought her. She had not seen her own Psalter since Agnes took her things.

As she read the familiar psalms of David, she was suddenly jealous that Steffan had read the entire Bible. What secrets and knowledge and wisdom did he have that she did not? He did seem rather more patient and gentle than other young men—not that she'd met many young men.

A knock came at her door. "Come in."

A middle-aged nun entered looking quite sober, her brows drawn together. She sat on a stool next to Magdalen's bed.

"My dear, the other nuns tell me that you are traveling with a young man who is not your husband, just the two of you."

"It is true."

"There are many things that can happen to a young woman traveling alone with a man who is not her husband. I would like to set you on your guard."

"I thank you for that. If I were with almost any other young man, I might have cause to be alarmed or even afraid. But you see, this young man, whom I shall call Stoffel, is very . . . noble-minded, and not the kind of young man to take advantage of anyone, and he knows I have no intention of allowing anyone to take advantage of me. I shall not marry except for true love, and neither he nor I are in love." She smiled to show that she was in no way being oppressed or coerced. But as she said the words, a twinge of pain stabbed her heart.

"Are you sure he is not in love with you?" The woman squinted and tilted her head as she stared into her eyes. "I was there when he was told he would have to separate from you. The look on his face—"

"Oh, I can assure you that you are mistaken. We are only friends, like brother and sister." So why did tears threaten and sting her eyes? Steffan was not in love with her, but she . . . she could certainly see the wisdom of this woman's words. It was unwise for a young woman to travel alone with a young man— especially a young man like Steffan—because she was in danger of falling in love with him.

But she did not feel the need to share that information.

"I sense that you are troubled. Is there anything I can help you with?" Only the nun's face was visible, and from the slight wrinkles around her eyes, Magdalen guessed she was probably a little younger than Magdalen's mother's forty years.

"I don't think so. I am trying to get something back that was taken from me. But I don't think there is anything you could do to help, although I thank you for your willingness to offer."

"Sometimes we must wait on God for help, and I believe God wants you to wait on Him now, for true love as well as getting back what was taken."

Magdalen smiled. "Thank you. I'm sure you are right."

Chapter Thirty-One

Magdalen's heart thumped harder as they drew near to Wolfberg Castle. They could not let any of the guards see them entering, so they left their horses at a stable in the village at the base of the castle mount. Steffan led them on foot around the front gate through the woods.

Neither of them spoke. Magdalen followed as he dodged around trees and bushes. She was completely lost, but he grew up here, so he knew where he was—she hoped.

"We have had quite an exciting quest, have we not?" He raised one brow.

She couldn't help smiling at him. "Yes, if you think running for our lives and nearly getting killed or captured is exciting."

"You should admit that you enjoyed our adventure."

She drew in a quick breath. "Highly presumptuous. I suppose that is the way with dukes."

"Other dukes. I am merely being honest and prompting the same honesty from you."

"Oh, is that what you call it? Very well, I do enjoy being with you. It is the most excitement, as you call it, I've had my entire life. But you seem to think it is nearly over. We still have to defeat your evil uncle and cousin. We have no assurance that we shall have any allies in our fight, and Lord Hazen and his men could return at any time."

"I like to think we have survived the most difficult parts."

They moved through the trees down a shallow hillside until they came to a rushing stream. It was narrow enough that he was able to leap over it. He turned and extended his hand to her. She grasped it and jumped across. Then they moved up the hill.

"We'll spend the night inside the castle, but we'll have to hide out here in the woods until it gets dark."

"Inside the castle?"

"I know every inch of Wolfberg Castle, including one place I don't think even my uncle knows about."

"At least he wouldn't think to look for us in the castle."

She couldn't help watching his face, noting every nuance of his profile, memorizing each line and curve of his jawline and nose and brow and lips. Ever since he kissed her cheek, she'd been half afraid, half hopeful he might kiss her again. But she could not encourage such a thing.

Twilight was falling as they neared the meadow where they used to graze their sheep and geese. They hid in the shadows and watched the new goose girl herd her gaggle of geese along the path and out of sight on their way to the goose pen. The sheep were nowhere in sight.

They sat and ate some of the food they had been given at the abbey. Then they went to the place under the rock where Steffan had hidden his important things. He dug up his metal box, dumped everything into his traveling bag, and waited for nightfall.

When it grew quite dark, they crept toward the castle. As they watched from the cover of the trees, a guard strode by, keeping close to the castle. Several minutes later, he came by again.

When the guard was out of sight, they hurried to the small door at the rear of the castle that was always locked. Steffan took out his key, opened the door, then locked it behind them.

They were inside.

Steffan and Magdalen both wore their servants' clothing, so they would not stand out too much, but all servants should be in their beds at this hour. They had to move with stealth and hope no one saw them.

Steffan headed down a corridor Magdalen was probably unfamiliar with as he made his way to the east wing of the castle. He found the door he was looking for. It was locked. He took out his key and opened it.

How fortunate that he had taken this key with him when he went to Prague.

The door led to a small room and a winding staircase that went up and around in a circular fashion. They walked to the staircase and started up.

"I've never seen a staircase such as this," Magdalen said. "It almost makes me dizzy."

They came to a small window. They were in the highest tower of the castle. Magdalen stepped onto the stair beside him and they both looked out.

The view of dark-blue waters seemed to go on forever, and from here they could see a glimpse of white cliff faces jutting into the edge of the water.

"You are so fortunate to grow up in a home as magnificent as Wolfberg Castle, and one from which you can see the ocean . . . I can't think of anything better."

His heart grew so big it filled his chest. But he replied, "I am glad you approve of the view."

"I like the hills where I live, with the thick forests, but you have both forests and sea. Did you miss it when you were in Prague?"

"I did. For a long time it was hard to go to sleep at night without that distant roar."

"What was it like to be with men who were focused on learning?"

"Some were not always focused on our studies. Some were more focused on pursuing . . . women and drink."

"But not you?"

She just assumed he did not pursue the sins of the flesh. His heart expanded again at the thought of her faith in him.

"I had seen them, the way they looked when they came back from a night of drinking and carousing—sick and dirty and barely able to hold up their heads—and I was not tempted to join with them."

"That was wise and mature of you."

"I had two friends who felt the same way. We sometimes played tricks on the other fellows, and we went to dances and festivals. We enjoyed our time together."

"Were they also dukes?"

"My two closest friends were earls' sons, but we kept our titles a secret." He suddenly wished she could meet them.

"What were their names?"

"Mertein and Claus."

"The best friend I ever had was Avelina—Lady Thornbeck—but

I only was able to be with her for two weeks. She promised she would send a group of guards to escort me to visit her after her baby was born. But then I sent her a letter telling her I was going to marry you." Without pausing, she stood. "Shall we go on the rest of the way? It cannot be much farther, can it?"

"No, not much."

They were quiet the rest of the way up. He could hardly wait to show her the view from the top.

He did not even have to use his key, as the door was slightly ajar. He pushed it open, and once they were inside, he locked the door behind them.

"No one ever comes up to this room, but there is also a secret hiding place, which I will show you later."

The room was relatively clean, in spite of being unused for so long. Some broken furniture and other clutter—old clothing and a couple of trunks, some tools and some paintings—were stacked against the wall.

She started toward the window. She had already noticed the view. "Oh, it is beautiful from up here."

All the windows had been inset with glass several years before, but the thick panes caused a somewhat distorted view.

"Better to see it unobstructed." He used considerable force on the metal clasp. It finally gave way, and the window swung outward on its hinge, opening a one-foot-wide by three-feet-high space, letting in the cold evening air.

"I can hear the sea. That sound is so different from anything I've heard before." Magdalen leaned on the windowsill and let her head hang out. She brought her head back in quickly. "I don't suppose it's wise of me to let anyone see us up here." She grimaced. "But I can hardly wait to see what it looks like in the morning light."

Air filled his lungs at her delighted smile. How could he bear to let her leave after this was over? Could she ever love him? He kept remembering her joy at not ever having to marry. How much time did he have to talk to her before Lord and Lady Thornbeck would arrive, ready to save her from her nightmare? How soon would her mother come with her own men to take her back to Mallin?

He turned away from her. "I'll go find some food for us."

"Are you sure that's safe?"

"I will do my best to avoid anyone seeing me. The only people who should be roaming around the castle this time of night are the guards, and there shouldn't be many of those."

"Be careful."

"I can only lock and unlock the door from the outside. I'll try to come back as soon as possible."

She suddenly put her arms around him and hugged him tightly. "I will pray for you."

"Thank you." He hugged her in return until she pulled away. But then he kissed her cheek, just as he had done a few mornings ago.

His heart pounding, he turned away before he could see her reaction.

He had two choices before she left Wolfberg. He could simply bid her farewell, or he could ask her to stay forever. But he was sweating just thinking about it.

Magdalen searched through the things in the room until she found an old tarp and a sheepskin and a few old, worn blankets.

She used them to make two beds for them, along with the blankets in their bags they had brought with them. Oh, how long it had been since she'd had a proper bath and clean bedding! For this alone Lord Hazen deserved to be punished.

As she lay on the floor looking up through the window at the sky, Magdalen's mind was fixed on Steffan. It had seemed so wise for her to keep her feelings about him a secret. After all, what could she say? *I think if you loved me, I could love you too?* That she would like to marry him because she thought he was a good, kind man and she felt this strange longing for him?

She could not say any such things. Nor would she. She would not humiliate herself over a man who had once told her people should marry for a better reason than love.

Then why did he kiss her on the cheek, twice? Some families, certainly, were more affectionate than her own. Her mother never kissed her, but she and Avelina had kissed each other on the cheek. Magdalen kissed her sisters on the cheek sometimes. Perhaps Steffan thought of her as a sister and that was why he kissed her. But she had met Steffan's sister, and Gertrudt had not seemed particularly affectionate.

Her mind and heart were full of him. "Oh God," she whispered, "take this longing out of my heart, or let him care for me as much as I care for him."

Three soft raps came at the door, then she heard the key clicking inside the lock, and the heavy wooden door opened.

"I brought some food." Steffan entered and opened his bag. "Oh, you made us beds." He smiled.

He sat beside her, and they ate and drank and then lay down.

She made sure the beds were not too close together but still close enough that she and he could talk.

"Just knowing Lord Hazen could come back any moment makes me nervous," Magdalen whispered from her makeshift bed. "I don't know if I'll be able to sleep."

"Shall I sing for you?"

"That would be lovely."

"But you might not like my singing, and I'm not sure if I can sing quietly enough."

"Oh no, you cannot *not* sing now. You must."

"Will you laugh at me if I sing poorly?"

"Probably. No, please, do sing something. I'm sure you have a lovely voice."

"Well, there is a ballad that Engel, one of the nursery servants, used to sing to me at bedtime." He began to sing. When he reached the end of the first verse, he stopped.

"You sing beautifully. Won't you sing all of that song?"

"That's all I remember. Are you not sleepy now? Have I not put you to sleep?"

"If you sing it again, I think it will."

"Very well." He sang it again, and her eyes locked on his as she watched his face in the scant light that came in through the window glass. His eyelids were beginning to droop, and he lay down.

"Thank you. You have a good voice." Truly, he had sung very well, so well that she was afraid to say just how impressed she had been.

Steffan mumbled something she didn't understand, and then she heard the regular, even breathing that signaled he was already asleep.

⌘

They spent the next morning talking quietly, and Magdalen's heart nearly burst every time she looked into his eyes. It felt as if he wanted to tell her something. Several times he opened his mouth and she thought he was about to confide something important, but then he would give a slight shake of his head and look away.

Steffan said, "I need to show you something, in case our secret place is found out and Lord Hazen tries to come up here." He led her over to the cluttered side of the room where a broken table lay top down on the floor. He moved the table with care so as not to make too much noise—and showed her a tiny handle in the wooden floor. When he lifted the handle, a three-foot square came up with it, revealing a hole in the floor.

"It's called a trapdoor. A ladder leads down to a small room. My father showed it to me before he died, but I was too afraid of dark holes to go down in it and explore, and I don't think anyone else even knows about it. So if you hear anyone coming, I want you to hide here."

"And you."

He shrugged, then nodded.

The hole was very dark. Poor Steffan. How would he manage hiding in such a dark, tiny hole? She would just have to pray that they would never need to.

"I'm going down to the west wing to try to spy on Alexander and Agnes. I want to see what they know."

"Don't be gone long. Please?"

He looked back at her. Then they both seemed to step toward each other. She hugged him and he kissed her cheek. Then he departed while her stomach flipped around inside her.

When Steffan returned half an hour later, they took out the food that Steffan had scavenged the night before.

"Tell me everything you heard Alexander and Agnes say."

He sighed and his brows drew together.

"What is wrong?"

"Nothing, but . . . it was very confusing."

"Confusing?"

He stared down at the bread in his hands. "I always hated Alexander, even though I haven't spoken to him much in years. So to hear the way he speaks to Agnes . . . it doesn't make sense."

"What do you mean?"

"He said he knew it was wrong to pretend to be me, but he didn't know what else to do. He was afraid of his father."

"He must have told Agnes the truth."

"Which was shocking enough—"

"*Ja*, since he didn't have to tell her the truth. She wouldn't have known, since I didn't tell her."

"But he also said he was glad he had done it because it had led him to . . . fall in love with her."

Magdalen absorbed this information in silence. She could not imagine anyone falling in love with mean-spirited little Agnes.

"But I still want to plant my fist in his face."

"Agnes doesn't deserve . . ." She almost said, "Doesn't deserve to be loved," but that sounded cruel.

"What she did to you was wicked and unjust."

"Perhaps they are both sorry."

Steffan gave a slow nod. "But it's best not to trust them."

Ugly thoughts and feelings churned inside her. Her longings felt so unfulfilled. Was it right that Agnes had gotten exactly what Magdalen had wanted? Agnes had gotten true love and wealth by stealing them. Would her wrongdoing be rewarded?

Would Magdalen be punished for not taking what she wanted?

For not fighting back and for being too kind and gentle to kill Agnes in her sleep? Magdalen had refrained from telling Lord Hazen the truth partially because she did not want him to execute Agnes. Still, she wasn't sorry she hadn't killed Agnes.

"Wait for the Lord," she whispered.

"What?"

"In the Psalter it is written, 'I remain confident of this: I will see the goodness of the Lord in the land of the living. Wait for the Lord; be strong and take heart and wait for the Lord.'"

He sat quietly for a moment, then took her hand in his and squeezed it. "That is what we will do. We will be confident in the Lord's goodness, and we will wait for the Lord."

Her heart soared at the way he was looking at her, at his warm eyes and sweet smile.

"Besides," he went on, "the way of the wicked will not prosper for much longer. We shall regain our proper places soon, and they shall get what their actions deserve."

Would he take revenge on his uncle and cousin? Or did he only mean that they would be justly punished?

He let go of her hand, and they both went back to eating.

"What else did Alexander and Agnes say? Did you learn anything?"

Steffan opened his mouth, but then raised his hand, as if to keep her from talking. Then she heard it too—the noise of many bridles clinking, horses' hooves, and men's voices.

He helped her to her feet and they both looked out the open window.

"Don't get too close," he said, his hand on her shoulder. "We don't want them to see us."

Many men on horseback made their way through the castle

gate. She caught a glimpse of Lord Hazen near the front, his head high.

As she strained her eyes to recognize the faces of the people entering the gate, she said, "I see Katrin. She's to the right of Lord Hazen."

"I see her." Steffan's voice was grim.

"Do you think your uncle knows we're in Wolfberg?" Magdalen put her arms around herself, resisting a shudder.

"He at least suspects it. We should be extra quiet and careful. And if he comes looking up here, we will hide under the floor."

She recalled Lord Hazen's arrogant face. The man would do anything to keep Wolfberg, she was quite certain. He would not hesitate to murder the true heir.

Chapter Thirty-Two

Steffan watched Magdalen as she sat on the floor of the round tower room stitching up a tattered blanket and alternately looking out the window at the beautiful view.

How long would they be alone together in this room? It was getting more and more difficult not to tell her his feelings. And yet, part of him never wanted this time to end. But when help arrived, it would end. It could happen any day. Lord Thornbeck could come riding up to the castle with all his guards and soldiers. The guests would arrive soon as well, and Steffan would expose his uncle for the evil schemer that he was—if his uncle didn't kill him first.

"Tonight I'll go look in one of the tower rooms for my portrait."

"Is that one of the places you played as a child?"

"Yes, but I don't know if it's the place Jacob meant. It could be a place I no longer remember. It could be anywhere."

"I want to help you search." Magdalen's green eyes were placid but intent, her lips full and perfect.

"You are very beautiful. Honestly, I was surprised when Lord Thornbeck did not ask you to marry him."

She laughed, her eyes sparkling as she covered her mouth with her hand. The sound of her laughter made his chest expand.

"I cannot say any handsome young men have ever asked me to marry them, except for one earl who later broke our betrothal when he realized our copper mines had run out. And your uncle."

"I am sorry that happened to you. Please forgive me."

"There is nothing to forgive. You did not create the misunderstanding. Lord Hazen did."

"Yes, but—"

"Do not give it a moment's thought. Besides, even though I will no longer need to get married, I shall be in high demand by impoverished noblemen everywhere, as soon as they hear that our mines in Mallin have iron ore." She smiled triumphantly.

She was right. The thought of those impoverished noblemen caused heat to rise up the back of his neck. How dare they look at Lady Magdalen as a means to wealth? She was so much more than that. She was brave and kind and compassionate. They wouldn't be able to appreciate her . . . the way he did.

Still staring down at her mending, she said, "I suppose you will be glad to finally have your house all to yourself again when your uncle is defeated and your cousin is sent away."

He thought for a moment. "Now that you say it, it will be rather sad."

She looked up at him. "Why?"

"My grandmother is dead, as well as Jacob, and my uncle has dismissed all the servants that I knew and depended on. And I will also miss you very much . . . when you're gone." His chest constricted just saying the words.

She looked down again. "I should think you'd be glad to get rid of me. I must be a reminder of a terrible time in your life."

He stepped toward her. "I have enjoyed every minute I've been with you."

She stared at him, her mouth open. She said quietly, "I have enjoyed every minute with you too. I thought you were a bit unkind at times, but you're not."

"You thought me unkind?"

"But you are not."

"Why did you think that?"

"I suppose it was because you were very angry when I first saw you. And because you said you never intended to marry for love."

He sat back. "Is that why you were shouting at me before Agnes came to force you to work inside the castle?"

She pursed her lips. "It was because you were trying to keep me from going back home, and for completely selfish reasons. You only wanted me as a witness, to help you get your place back."

How did this happen? He hadn't wanted to start an argument.

"You are right. I was being very selfish. I was not thinking of you at all, and I am truly sorry. You had every reason to dislike and distrust me then."

"You *were* deceitful." She looked down, her voice quiet again. "But you had every right to say you didn't want to marry me. I was only shocked that I had come to Wolfberg because of your uncle's wicked plot."

This was getting worse and worse. Her face was drawn and sad, and she wouldn't even look at him.

"Magdalen, I was distraught and distracted that day. I did not know then what I know now. I feel very differently . . . about everything. Especially you."

She gave him a sidelong glance from beneath lowered lashes, then looked away.

"Besides that, I did run to your rescue that day when Agnes forced you to go inside the castle."

"I remember." Her grimace turned into a tiny smile. "Chivalrous to the core."

How did she make him feel warm, pleased, and unsettled all at the same time?

"It's getting colder." She shivered and rubbed her arms.

He leaned over and closed the window facing the sea and then walked to the window facing the castle gate and closed it too. It was nearly dark and would be a cold night.

Magdalen rubbed her arms. How much longer would they be in this tower room? Every time her hand brushed against Steffan's, every time he drew close and looked into her eyes, she wondered if she'd reveal her feelings to him without even intending to, if he could see it on her face, or if she would blurt it out. But that would make things uncomfortable for both of them.

"Shall we go look for your portrait now?"

He hesitated, looking out the window. "I suppose it is late enough. My uncle will be in the Great Hall now."

Magdalen followed Steffan out of the door and down the twisting spiral stairs. They did not even whisper, and soon Steffan stopped at a door. He tried the handle and it opened. They walked inside and he closed the door behind them. The room was quite dark.

"I will open the window," Steffan whispered.

She realized she'd been holding on to Steffan's arm, so she let go. He moved quietly across the room. She heard him unlatching some shutters, and then light spilled in as he swung open the shutter.

While Steffan took a small wax candle out of his pocket and

worked to light it, Magdalen strode to a pile of old tapestries illumined by the twilight coming in through the window and started looking through them. Dust rose from them, burning her nose, and she sneezed.

Steffan got his candle lit and set it on a small table beside a ragged old trunk in the corner. He opened the trunk and started looking through it.

Soon, Magdalen had looked through the entire stack of tapestries, and when she was certain no portrait was hidden among them, she moved to a wooden box. Perhaps the portrait was inside. She opened it easily, as there was a hole where the locking mechanism should have been.

She tipped the box over, but nothing was inside. The box did not even have any hiding places along the back.

"Are you finding anything?" She hurried over to where Steffan was taking things out of the old trunk and putting them on the floor beside it.

"Only a lot of junk."

Magdalen glanced around the room. There was nothing else for her to search, so she went over to the large fireplace and looked inside. Perhaps there was a hiding nook inside it, as it did not appear as though anyone had built a fire in it in a long time. She found nothing, but her bare feet were black with soot.

Steffan stood behind her.

"Oh! I didn't know you were there."

"Wipe your feet with this." He handed her a cloth.

"Good idea." They didn't need her black footprints leaving Hazen's men a perfect trail.

"The portrait isn't here." He planted his hands on his hips. "But we should keep looking."

And so they searched another room, as no one slept in that wing of the castle and it was mostly deserted even in the daytime. After half an hour, they were satisfied it was not in that room either. One by one they searched all the rooms in the east wing that were unoccupied and not near Lord Hazen or Alexander's bedchambers. They found old clothes, blankets, and toys that had belonged to Steffan and Gertrudt, but no portrait.

Magdalen reached up to push the hair out of her face, which had come loose from her braid, and found Steffan watching her.

"We should stop for the night."

"Is it still night?" She glanced at the window. The gray half-light of dawn was beginning to show through.

"Not for much longer." Steffan sighed. "At least we know where the portrait is not."

She would have laughed if she'd had the strength. They trudged back up the stairs. They were almost at the top when Magdalen stumbled. Steffan caught her arm and kept her from falling.

"Thank you."

"Are you well?"

"Just tired."

They both fell onto their makeshift beds and were soon asleep.

Steffan's back ached from all the searching he and Magdalen had done the night before, and he sat whittling a piece of wood. Magdalen was still asleep, but the sun was high and his thoughts would not seem to leave him alone.

A sound came from the door like a key turning in the lock. Steffan jumped to his feet, clutching his knife.

The door opened, and Alexander and Agnes stood looking at them.

Steffan leapt at Alexander with his knife aimed at his coward's heart.

"Please! Wait!" Agnes threw her arm across Alexander's chest.

Alexander held out a loaf of bread. "We mean you no harm. We brought you food."

"What sort of trickery is this?" Steffan glanced behind him to make sure Magdalen was all right. She stood by the window with wide eyes and her hand over her heart.

"It's no trickery. If we wanted to harm you, we would have brought my father up here. We simply wanted to tell you that we intend to help you regain your rightful stations."

"And why would you do that?"

Alexander's normally pale cheeks reddened. "I never wanted to pretend to be you. My father . . . he would not listen to reason. He has gone mad with greed and a sense that he deserves whatever he wants. And Agnes feels the same way I do."

"Is that true, Agnes?" Magdalen asked. He could tell she wanted to believe them, but after all Agnes had done to her, she was not certain if she should.

"I am sorry." Agnes took a step forward, then glanced at Alexander. "It was my father's idea all along. But I am sorry for doing it. I . . . I was wrong."

The boldness in Agnes's eyes put him on his guard. "No one turns from evil to good so quickly and easily." Steffan gripped the knife and stepped closer to protect Magdalen if necessary. "Who else knows we are here? Whom did you tell?"

"No one. Last evening we were taking a walk and we heard you laughing. We saw that this window was open, and it's normally closed. We also heard that some food had been stolen from the kitchen during the night."

Steffan glared at him, trying to think of how they might escape.

"I can understand your anger and mistrust," Alexander said, "but I tried to talk Father out of it. He had discovered there was valuable iron ore in Mallin's mines through a mining expert who had once been employed by the baron. This expert explained that whoever ended up mining the iron ore would become quite wealthy. So Father had me pretend to be you and marry the heiress of Mallin. If I had not gone along with his plan, he would have killed me."

"We have known each other since we were children, Alexander, and I have never seen you so humble, meek, and mild. Why the change of heart? Why do you care?"

Alexander did not answer for a moment, staring off to the right. He took a deep breath and let it out. "I know you don't believe me, but I didn't want you to be harmed. I didn't want that on my conscience. I am not the unfeeling person my father is. I am not like him."

Perhaps that much was true. Alexander never struck him as being the same sort of heartless, greedy person as Lord Hazen. Whiny and fearful, yes. But he had been a child. Perhaps he had grown up and decided to turn away from his father's wicked ways. Still, Steffan and Magdalen had been betrayed too many times not to be cautious now.

"My plan," Alexander went on, "was to protect Lady Magdalen from my father. I thought I could at least do that much to redeem myself in God's eyes. And then . . . I discovered the woman I married was not Lady Magdalen, but a pawn in her own father's scheme."

Magdalen crossed her arms and eyed Agnes across the room. She obviously was doubtful of his assessment of his wife's situation.

"Nevertheless, I fell in love with her. I told her the truth about who I was, and she told me the truth as well. I can't bear to think of my father trying to separate us." He put his arm around the girl's shoulders and drew her to his side.

"Changed by love." Steffan's voice conveyed ridicule, and he cringed at his own bitterness.

"Anyway, we brought you some food." Alexander held out a cloth bundle. "I understand why you would not trust us, but if there is anything else we can do for you . . . We want to prove that we are sincere."

Steffan felt the scowl fading from his face. But when he pictured himself walking toward Alexander and accepting the food from his hands, he also pictured his cousin shoving a knife between his ribs.

"You can put the food down there." Steffan pointed to the floor.

Alexander bent and placed the cloth bundle on the floor and the loaf of bread on top.

"Will you forgive me, Magdalen?" Agnes asked from across the room.

Magdalen was quiet, then said, "I do forgive you, Agnes, and I forgive your father, even though he's not sorry."

"Do you forgive me, Steffan?" Alexander held his gaze.

He didn't want Magdalen to think less of him. She was so generous herself. "*Ja*, I forgive you, Alexander." And then he felt a warmth inside and realized he really did forgive him. What else could he do? Christians were forgiven and therefore must forgive.

But the feeling flowing through him could not be from himself. He'd been angry with his cousin for too long.

But Steffan did not intend to let his uncle get away with what he had done, killing Jacob, and many others, no doubt. Hazen had not repented, and neither had Agnes's father. They deserved punishment, and Jacob deserved justice.

"Thank you." Alexander looked genuinely relieved and even smiled. "We will leave you now."

"Alexander."

His cousin turned to glance back at him.

"Does your father know we are here?"

He shook his head. "He knows you left Mallin and came this way, but he thinks you are hiding in the woods nearby. But you should be careful."

Steffan nodded.

The two of them backed out the door and were gone.

Magdalen shut the window, then latched it closed. "Oh, Steffan, I'm so sorry." She burst into tears, bowing her head and covering her face with her hands.

He crossed the room, wrapped his arms around her, and pulled her to his chest. "Why are you sorry? What heinous crime have you committed?" He said it playfully, hoping to stop her tears.

"It is my fault they found us. I was the one laughing. How could I be so careless?" She sniffed, her cheek pressed against his chest.

"Don't worry. If Alexander and Agnes are telling the truth, they will not tell Lord Hazen."

"Do you think they could be lying?" She lifted her head, her eyes shiny with tears and wide with fear. He wanted to protect her so much it made his chest ache.

"It is possible." Then he said, more softly, "It is hard for me to trust my cousin. I'm not even sure I should, but if they wanted to betray us, why would they bring us food and ask for forgiveness? It doesn't make sense."

She pressed her cheek against his linen shirt and patted his shoulder. "I know."

She was trying to comfort *him*. Again, his chest squeezed painfully. She was so tenderhearted. He did not deserve her. But he very much wanted to.

"All we can do now is wait on God to save us.

"And search for my portrait."

Chapter Thirty-Three

Magdalen held Steffan tight. He was just the sort of man she would want to marry—kindhearted enough to embrace her and comfort her when she cried, and honest enough to admit that he was struggling to trust his cousin's word.

Wanting to comfort *him* made her cease crying as she patted his back and rested against his warm, solid chest. His soft, linen shirt smelled so good—she drew in a deep breath of it—like outdoors and a particular warm smell that was distinct to Steffan.

She cared so much for him. Should she kiss him on the lips to let him know how she felt?

She lost her breath at the thought. She wasn't sure she could be that bold, nor did it seem very wise. Perhaps she should say nothing and enjoy their friendship. But if they were friends, should she not be able to tell him anything?

"Steffan." Her breath deserted her again and made it difficult to speak.

"Yes?" He caressed her shoulder.

"Everything is about to change, when Lord Thornbeck arrives and all the guests come. What will happen then?"

"What do you want to happen?" The intense note in Steffan's voice made her lift her head to look up at him.

"I . . . I don't know." But it was not the truth. She did know, but how could she tell him?

She stared into his brown eyes. He wasn't looking at her with that soft, sweet look he sometimes had. It was more of a bracing-for-the-worst expression. Her heart stuttered. "What is the matter?"

"Nothing. Go on."

"I . . ." This was foolish. He had already rejected her once. She would not humiliate herself by forcing him to reject her again. She blurted, "What shall we do with Alexander and Agnes when we are in our rightful roles again?"

She had an uncomfortable feeling inside, almost as if she had lied. But she'd only avoided saying what was truly on her mind. And it was a good question for both of them to consider.

Steffan lifted his head, his eyes suddenly alert. He grasped her arm.

A sound drifted in from outside. Steffan hurried toward the window and she followed.

They looked out, staying far enough back so no one could see them. A group of people were entering through the gate. Was that her mother riding on a horse? Mother said a lady should never take a long trip on horseback.

"It is my mother! My mother came."

Steffan's arm pressed against her shoulder. "*Ja*, and Lord Thornbeck is just behind her. Look."

Lord Thornbeck was a tall, brown-haired, broad-shouldered man on a large black horse, and riding beside him on a smaller brown horse was his wife. "Lady Avelina!"

They looked magnificent, with the bright-colored trappings covering Lord and Lady Thornbeck's horses. His knights also wore the Thornbeck colors. Mother and her few men looked drab compared to them.

"They're coming to help us." Magdalen's heart swelled. "Thank you, thank you, Avelina and Lord Thornbeck," she whispered, tears in her eyes. "See how angry my mother looks?" She stifled a nervous laugh. "I can hardly wait to greet Avelina. Do you think it's safe now to go downstairs?"

"We should wait a few minutes. We don't want to risk getting seized by Lord Hazen's guards before our friends are inside the castle."

"Oh, that makes sense."

They watched out the window until everyone had passed through the gate. Steffan's arm pressed against hers. He gently pulled her shoulder around so they were facing each other.

"Magdalen, I have something to say to you." His eyes were so intense, staring straight into her, it seemed. His forehead was creased and his mouth tense.

She raised her hand to touch his beard. A lump in her throat forced her to swallow, while her heart beat erratically. She moved her gaze from his lips to his deep-brown eyes.

He bent his head closer until their foreheads were nearly touching. "I've been waiting for the right time to tell you, and I don't want to wait anymore."

"This is a charming sight."

They spun around. Lord Hazen stood in the doorway with three guards.

Chapter Thirty-Four

Steffan placed his body between Lord Hazen and Magdalen, heat flowing through his veins, setting every muscle and nerve on alert.

"My mother is here," Magdalen said. "You had better not think of harming us. And Lord Thornbeck. He will—"

"Guards," Lord Hazen growled.

The guards moved toward them. Magdalen screamed. One guard grabbed her and placed a hand over her mouth. Steffan eluded a second guard and leapt at the one holding Magdalen. He slammed his fist into the guard's face.

A third guard landed a blow to Steffan's head. He fell back, the room going black for a moment. Then the guard grabbed his shirt front and dragged him across the floor.

Magdalen was fighting and clawing the guard holding on to her. Steffan opened his mouth to tell the guard he would kill him if he injured her, but another guard stuffed something in his mouth and held his hands behind his back. Steffan, with one great effort, surged to his feet and fell on top of the guard.

The guard scrambled up, still holding Steffan's wrists in a

painful grip, and slammed Steffan's head on the floor. The blackness returned. He was losing consciousness. *God, please. Save Magdalen.*

⸎

Magdalen watched in horror as the guard took hold of Steffan and slammed his head on the floor. Steffan went still.

She tried to scream, but the guard's hand was clamped over her mouth. She struck at him with her fists. Another guard grabbed her wrists and pinned them behind her back. Then the first guard took his hand from her face and stuffed a cloth in her mouth.

She tried to kick him but missed. Still holding her wrists with one hand, the second guard picked her up by her waist and carried her across the room.

Lord Hazen was opening the trapdoor. He must have known about it after all. The other two guards were carrying Steffan toward the trapdoor as well.

"Now you cannot trouble me. You can stay down there until you rot."

While she struggled against her guard, they lifted Steffan's limp body over the dark hole, then dropped him inside. Magdalen's stomach sank as she watched him fall.

The guard lifted Magdalen and lowered her in. When her feet touched the ladder inside, the man let her wrists go, and she scrambled to take the gag out of her mouth. She took a breath and screamed as loud as she could, just as the trapdoor came down and shut out every glimmer of light.

A groan came from below her. She hurried down the ladder,

which was only a couple more rungs, before her foot touched the bottom, then brushed against Steffan's body.

She fell to her knees, grasping in the dark for Steffan, following the sounds of his groans.

"Steffan, are you all right? Tell me what hurts."

"Where are we?"

She touched his bearded chin and managed to lift his head and shoulders and set them in her lap. "We are in the room under the trapdoor."

He moaned. "My worst nightmare. To die in a dark hole." He was breathing hard.

"We will not die here. Someone will find us. Don't worry." That was what he was always telling her—don't worry. "Everything will be all right. Now tell me how badly you're injured. Are you bleeding anywhere?"

His breathing became calmer and more controlled. "No, no, not much."

She felt stickiness on the back of his head, but it was hard to tell how much blood he was losing.

"Are any limbs broken?"

She heard the movement of his legs on the floor.

"I think I am well. Just a headache."

She remembered she had a cloth in her pocket, pulled it out, and pressed it to his head. She exhaled a long breath.

"We should see if we can open the trapdoor." He sat up, then moaned. "I hope they didn't hurt you."

"No, I am well." The truth was, she had hurt her ankle in all her struggling with the guard. It was throbbing, but she would be well enough, as long as they were able to escape.

Hazen eyed Agnes. "You did well, telling me where the duke and Lady Magdalen were hiding."

She lowered her gaze to the floor. Did she think she could fool him? He knew she hated him and that she gave him the information only because he threatened to kill Alexander. "Now go and find my son and tell him to come immediately to the Great Hall. He has to greet our surprise guests: the Baroness of Mallin and the Margrave of Thornbeck. And be sure to tell him that both your lives are forfeit if he breathes a word that is disloyal to me."

She hurried away without even looking at him.

It was so laughably easy to manipulate people who were in love. He'd discovered that many years ago when his now-deceased wife had still loved him.

But there was no time for savoring past victories. Lord Thornbeck would be coming inside at any moment. Agnes could not fool Lady Magdalen's mother, and probably not the margrave and his lady either. Which was why he would have to have Agnes disappear. He would also poison the baroness when she drank her first goblet of wine. They'd think she'd had an attack of the heart or some sort of apoplexy, and he'd have his physician attest to it.

Even now he had the vial of poison inside his waistcoat pocket, which he carried with him everywhere.

"Guards."

Two of his soldiers stepped forward from where they were guarding the back door of the castle.

"Go to the north tower, to the very top. I have two prisoners under a trapdoor in the floor. You will see it when you move the table that is sitting upside down on top of it. Kill the man and bring the woman to me."

"Yes, Lord Hazen."

He motioned to Tideke. "Take Alexander's wife to the dungeon. If my son tries to stop you, knock him unconscious."

"Yes, my lord."

Steffan couldn't stop thinking about the old well. He was five years old again, and his heart beat so fast it hurt his chest.

But he had to get control of himself. Magdalen's life was at stake. He could not bear it if something bad happened to her.

He had to stay calm and save them both. He had to, for Magdalen.

When he sat up, he lost the knowledge of which way was up and which was down, but the dizziness gradually faded. Magdalen held on to his arm as he groped around for the ladder, which turned out to be a short but steep set of wooden steps.

Magdalen stayed beside him as they groped their way up on their hands and knees. They reached the top, and he put his hand on the wooden door above him. "Do you hear anything?" he whispered.

"They must be gone."

"Help me push, but be careful."

They both braced their shoulders against the door, and he pushed with all his might with both his hands.

Magdalen grunted. "It's not moving at all. What should we do?"

"Beat on it."

They pounded on it with their fists. He beat so hard his knuckles were probably bleeding, and his heart was pounding as hard as his fists.

"Nothing's happening."

"I have to get us out of here." He growled at himself for saying that out loud and for letting the panic well up and threaten to overwhelm him. His heart raced, and sweat ran down his back.

Magdalen's arms surrounded him, and he felt her hair brush his chin. "Don't worry. We'll get out."

He felt her cheek against his, and his heart calmed. He buried his face in her hair. She was so small, so dear and fragile, and yet so strong. He took several deep breaths.

"Are you praying?" Magdalen said softly by his ear. "Because all I can think to say is, 'God, please help us.'"

He laughed, a hoarse sound, but it filled the tiny room.

They sat on the steps holding each other, with Steffan's back against the steps and Magdalen nestled against his chest, her forehead on his neck.

They took turns saying short, whispered prayers: "God, please let someone find us."

"God, give me the strength of Samson to push open this door."

"God, please don't let us have to spend the rest of the day in here."

"God, send Your mighty angels with their fiery swords to rescue us."

"God, give Lord and Lady Thornbeck wisdom to find us."

"God, how long before a person goes mad from not being able to see a thing?"

Magdalen squeezed his shoulder.

"I think I hear something." Magdalen crawled up a step and

beat on the door. Steffan joined her. They pounded for a few seconds, then stopped and listened.

"I hear someone."

Steffan heard it too—footsteps getting louder.

They both beat on the door and yelled. More noises, like something heavy being dragged overhead. A few moments later, the door was yanked open.

Hands reached down.

"Who is there?" Steffan demanded, holding Magdalen behind him.

Alexander's face appeared in the opening. "It is I."

Steffan lifted Magdalen up and let his cousin take her by the wrists and haul her out. Moments later, Alexander's face reappeared.

"Make haste. My father's guards are coming to kill you."

Loud footsteps sounded on the stairs. Alexander was holding a knife. Steffan took it from him, then glanced around. He leapt to the pile of old junk that had been stored in the room and snatched up a large table leg. Magdalen did the same.

"Magdalen, get behind me."

Two guards appeared in the doorway.

"You are not supposed to be here," Alexander said to the guards. "Go back downstairs."

"We take our orders from Lord Hazen. Step aside."

Steffan hid the knife and table leg behind his back. The guard pushed Alexander out of the way and unsheathed his sword. Steffan stepped forward.

The guard swung his sword, and Steffan swung the table leg, slamming it into the guard's wrist while sidestepping his blade.

The guard yelled and dropped his sword. Steffan snatched

it up. He glanced behind him. The second guard was lunging for Magdalen. She screamed and ducked out of his way, holding the broken table leg out in front of her.

Steffan went cold all over at the menacing look on the guard's face. He could not let him kill Magdalen. He leapt across the room, yelling as loud as he could to draw the guard's attention. But the guard ignored him and raised his sword to strike Magdalen.

Steffan would not be able to reach her in time. He threw the knife that was in his other hand. It flew across the room and impaled the guard in the back.

The guard stopped, his sword in midswing, and slowly turned around. He took a step toward Steffan, then fell forward.

More footsteps were coming up the stairs. Lord Hazen's voice echoed from the stairwell. "Kill them! Now!"

Magdalen jumped toward the window, opened it wide, and yelled, "Help!"

Alexander ran to the guard who had fallen, took his sword, and he and Steffan greeted the first guards who appeared in the doorway and started beating them back, striking furious blows.

As he fought, Steffan was able to lift his foot and kick one of the guards in his groin. The guard fell backward into the men behind him, and they all fell down the spiral staircase, at least a dozen men. Steffan went after them.

Until he heard Magdalen screaming his name.

He ran back into the room. The guard whom Steffan had originally defeated stood holding Magdalen, a knife to her throat.

The air rushed out of Steffan's lungs. *Don't take her away, God, please.* Magdalen's face was ashen, her eyes fixed on his.

"Throw down the knife and let her go." Steffan still gripped his sword.

"You will kill me if I do." The guard's voice shook.

"I won't. Just let her go." *God, please. I can't lose her. Please don't let her die.* Icy fingers gripped his insides.

Alexander stepped up beside Steffan, breathing hard and using his sleeve to wipe sweat from his face.

"You can't get away," Alexander said to the guard. "Lord Thornbeck is here. Lord Hazen will be apprehended and punished. But if you let her go, we'll make sure your life is spared."

Steffan took a tentative step toward them. The guard pulled Magdalen closer to him. The hand shook that held the knife to Magdalen's throat. The blade touched her skin. He could end her life in a moment.

"Swear to me you won't let them kill me," the guard said.

"I hereby vow, as the rightful Duke of Wolfberg, that you will not be killed if you do not harm this girl," Steffan said.

There was scuffling and footsteps behind them in the doorway.

Steffan said quite loudly, never taking his eyes off the guard and Lady Magdalen, "I demand that this guard's life be spared."

The guard took the knife away from her throat and let his arms go limp by his side.

Magdalen hurried away from her captor, and Steffan opened his arms and pulled her close.

So many thoughts and emotions went through him as he held her tight, glorying in the way she clung to him and buried her face in his neck.

Magdalen lifted her head, and they both turned around to face several of Lord Thornbeck's guards.

Lord Thornbeck stepped toward them, his brown eyes focusing on Steffan. "You are the Duke of Wolfberg, are you not?"

"I am, my lord. Thank you for coming to our aid. Did you receive Lady Magdalen's letter?"

"I did not receive a letter. I am here because the Baroness of Mallin sent for me and asked for my help in rescuing her daughter. It seems her loyal servant, a mute boy named Lenhart, wrote down a very interesting tale explaining what had been happening here in Wolfberg. His description was so detailed, she decided it must be true and sent a messenger with this young man's explanation."

That was when Lenhart stepped out from the crowd, looking shyly at Magdalen. She in turn smiled and waved at him, excitement animating her as she still held to Steffan's arm.

"Thank you, my lord. We owe you a great debt of gratitude."

"It is my pleasure to lend my assistance to friends who are being wronged. I was in a similar predicament myself two years ago, as you might remember."

Steffan had nearly forgotten about that, some sort of treachery from the Duke of Geitbart that was resolved in Lord Thornbeck's favor.

"We have apprehended Lord Hazen, and my men have placed him in the dungeon. Can you point out his son and his son's wife, Lady Magdalen's imposter?"

"My lord, as it turns out, my cousin Alexander has been assisting us. In fact, he saved our lives a few minutes ago. If you could spare him, I would be very obliged."

"Of course."

Alexander's gaze met his. Steffan nodded to him, and he nodded back.

They were free. All of them.

Magdalen watched as Lord Thornbeck's guards began to carry the dead and wounded guards from the room. Lord Thornbeck was barking orders, and Lenhart and Alexander also turned to leave. Probably Magdalen's mother and Lady Avelina had not been allowed up the stairs where the fighting was happening, as they were nowhere to be seen.

She was suddenly aware of Steffan standing beside her, looking down at her, as the last of the guards left. They were alone.

What could she say? What would he say to her? After all the closeness they had shared, the embraces, the near-death moments, and fighting for their lives . . . now she would be expected to leave Wolfberg with her mother. Steffan would forget about her and marry someone else, and he'd probably think she didn't care.

Just a few moments before, she had been overwhelmed with joy and relief that they were both safe. Now tears stung her eyes and her insides quaked with fear that he would let her go . . . that he would never love her.

"My mother will be downstairs. I must go and see her." Magdalen could not look at him as she said the words and started toward the door.

"Magdalen," he called after her.

She quickened her step and did not answer him, her insides churning.

"Magdalen, wait." He caught hold of her arm, but she couldn't face him. The tears were swimming now, threatening to fall, and the lump in her throat kept her from speaking.

He tugged gently on her arm, trying to get her to turn around, then he came around in front of her.

"What is wrong? Are you angry with me?" He leaned down,

trying to see her face. Then he touched her cheek, and she had to turn away as the first tear fell.

She shook her head, trying to swallow. She still couldn't speak. Did he think she was being ridiculous? She must seem quite strange. If only she didn't care for him so much, didn't feel so much like her heart was breaking. She should be happy that he was getting his place back in Wolfberg, but instead, she could only think how he would forget about her.

"Please tell me what's wrong."

She finally managed to swallow. "Nothing is wrong." But even as she said the words, another tear fell. She tried to turn so he wouldn't see, but he kept moving in front of her.

"Magdalen, I—"

"You should not worry about me. You have a lot of people downstairs. You should go to them." A sob was on the verge of erupting, on the verge of humiliating her even more. She clamped her lips shut.

"I'm not going anywhere. You are the person I want to talk to now."

He had seen her tears, so she wiped them quickly with the back of her hand.

"Tell me why you're crying."

"It is nothing. Please don't ask me." Why was he tormenting her? Why couldn't he just leave her in peace? "They will be waiting for you. You should go." The statement of fact seemed to calm her and dry her tears.

"I'm not leaving until you tell me why you're crying. Is it because that guard held a knife to your throat? Did he hurt you?" His voice conveyed sudden fear.

"No, I am not hurt."

"I think I saw you limping."

"It is nothing, just a little twinge in my ankle."

The tenderness and concern in his voice were making her feel as if she were two halves being pulled apart. Did he want to see her lose her self-control? She started toward the door again.

"You cannot leave until you talk to me." He hurried to block the doorway with his body.

She turned her back on him as the tears flowed down again. "This is your castle, and you can order me . . . to do . . ."

"Magdalen, I don't know why you won't tell me what I did to make you upset, but you are the sweetest, most beguiling woman I know, the kindest and the most noble and courageous."

His hand touched her shoulder. The sob broke free from her throat.

"I know I am selfish and cowardly sometimes, and my fear of marrying for love must have made you dislike me, and rightly so. But I refuse to live in fear any longer. If you will marry me, Lady Magdalen, I vow to cherish you as long as I live."

Another sob escaped. She turned her body toward him. Steffan put his arms around her shoulders and pulled her to his chest. She did her best to wipe her face and whispered, "You want to marry me?"

"Yes." He caressed her shoulder.

"You said a person should have a better reason to marry than love. Are you only marrying me for my mines?" Would he be angry? Or would he admit his motives were materialistic?

He pulled away enough to look into her eyes. "It is a fair and just question." He sighed and didn't speak for a moment. "I watched my father grieve over my mother. He was so heartbroken, he forgot he had two children and a region full of people who needed him. I was afraid of ever loving anyone that much, of ending up like my father. But I just could not help loving you, Magdalen. And that is why I wish to marry you—because I love you."

Her heart swelled more with every word he spoke, with each emotion that shone in his eyes. Surely she could trust this man to love her.

"Magdalen? Will you marry me? Will you let me love you?" There was so much hope in his expression.

"Yes, I will marry you."

He smiled jubilantly.

She couldn't wait any longer. She put her hand on his shoulder to keep her balance, rose onto her tiptoes, and pressed her lips against his.

Steffan's heart soared at her boldness and at the thought that she was willing to be his wife. He caressed her cheek as he kissed her. The sweetness of her touch, of her lips, her skin, her nearness . . . his gentle, sweet Magdalen.

She pulled away slightly. He kissed her cheek as she stroked his beard. Then he gazed into her half-closed eyes.

"Now will you tell me why you were crying?"

"I thought you didn't want me. That I would go home and you would forget me."

He brushed his thumb over her chin. "I could never forget you. But are you sure you want to marry me? I thought you were excited about not having to marry at all."

"Of course I was excited." She smiled as she slipped her arms around his neck.

"You've said you would marry me and I'm not letting you out of the agreement."

Her smile widened. "I don't want out of it."

She leaned forward and they kissed again, his heart pounding.

She ended the kiss and said, "Of course I was excited about being able to help my people without marrying a stranger or an old man. And you had already told me you never intended to marry me."

"I'm sorry. I was daft." He wished she would forget about that and kiss him again.

"You should not be sorry. It was your uncle's fault. You were only telling me the truth."

"Yes, but I should have wanted to marry you after meeting you two years ago in Thornbeck. You were obviously sweet and very lovely, though you are even more beautiful now than you were then."

She rewarded him with another kiss. How good it felt to kiss the girl he loved. Perhaps he *could* believe Alexander was a changed man after falling in love. He certainly felt different after being with Magdalen the last few weeks. Maybe they'd all learned some important lessons.

Magdalen had never felt anything like kissing Steffan. And she hadn't even told him . . .

"I love you," she whispered against his cheek.

He inhaled sharply, kissed the corner of her mouth, then her lips.

A few moments later, he said, "How can you love a selfish man like me?"

"We are all selfish. Everyone wants what they want. But you . . . you defend the helpless and weak and put yourself through pain and hardship to help others." She rubbed his beard with her fingertips and sighed.

He touched his forehead to her temple. "You say the sweetest things."

Sweet was the word for how it felt to stand here with Steffan. But it seemed all a dream.

"Magdalen, there you are."

She looked up to find her mother staring at them from the doorway.

"Do you not think it is time to go downstairs?" She sent a sharp, confounded look at Magdalen and then Steffan.

They separated, and Steffan bowed to her mother. "Lady Mallin."

Mother nodded coldly and turned to Magdalen. "Let us go. Now."

Magdalen cleared her throat. "We shall be down in a moment, Mother." Her face burned at the reprimand that was surely coming for not immediately obeying her mother.

Without a word, Mother turned and started down the steps.

Steffan squeezed her hand and whispered, "I wish we didn't have to go down."

"You do?"

"I wish we could stay here and talk." He leaned down and kissed her lips.

"We shall *talk* later." She smiled and they went down together.

Chapter Thirty-Five

Magdalen sat upright in a feather bed with all the curtains drawn back while the fair Lady Thornbeck sat beside her on a cushioned chair and nursed her baby.

"And the duke saved you and killed your attacker?" Avelina's mouth was as wide open as her blue eyes.

"Yes, thankfully."

"How terrifying it must have been for you, to be attacked at night in the forest." Avelina's brown hair was just as lovely as Magdalen remembered it. Her baby's eyes were closed in a blissful-looking slumber. "She's finished. Let me fix my gown."

"May I hold her?"

Avelina stood and laid her baby in Magdalen's arms.

"She's so sweet." Magdalen held her up and kissed her forehead, careful not to wake her.

Someday, God willing, she and Steffan would have a baby. The thought was strange, yet appealing. She had wondered a few days ago if she would ever marry or have children, and now the thought of having them with Steffan gave her a warm, tender feeling.

But she should not be dreaming about her future children while Avelina was with her.

"Did Lord Thornbeck not mind you and the baby traveling so far?"

"It is only a two-day journey. He had everything planned, every inn where we would stay the night, and we even brought our own physician in case the baby became sick."

They both laughed softly and shook their heads. How sweet that Avelina's husband loved her and took such care of her and their baby.

Someone opened the door of her bedchamber and Magdalen's mother walked in.

"So there you are." Mother's brow was wrinkled, her usual signal of disapproval. "All laid up in bed."

"Yes, Mother. I'm resting."

"I don't know how you manage to get into such difficulties as you do."

She wanted to say, "Well, it was certainly not my fault." But instead she said, "So it seems."

"Hm." Mother wrinkled her brow even more, crossed her arms in front of her, and then noticed the baby in Magdalen's arms. "And here is that sweet baby. I believe she resembles Lord Thornbeck, his eyes and forehead." Mother leaned down and examined Avelina's daughter.

"Yes, she does look a lot like her father," Avelina said.

Mother glanced back at Avelina. "Isn't motherhood such a joy? Having a baby brings a new and wonderful purpose to a woman's life, doesn't it?"

To prevent herself from rolling her gaze to the ceiling and

letting her thoughts show on her face, Magdalen looked down at the baby.

Avelina said, "Our baby has been the greatest joy to Lord Thornbeck and me."

"Oh, men never concern themselves with their girl children, especially when they're so young."

Magdalen stared hard at her mother now. Should she ask her how she could forget that it was her father, and only her father, who showed any love for Magdalen and her young siblings?

"Since you are taking your ease"—Mother suddenly looked at Magdalen and quirked one corner of her mouth down in a half frown—"I shall go downstairs, as the duke has informed us that the feast will begin shortly. You must be there."

"Of course."

Mother left and Magdalen heaved a sigh. She had thought, when she saw her mother riding into the castle bailey, that perhaps her mother loved her after all. But Mother was her usual disapproving self. Still, she had come, and Magdalen pushed away all sad thoughts and smiled at Avelina.

"I am so glad you are here." She had longed to see her friend. How good it was to see her and Lord Thornbeck so joyful together, as they always should have been.

"Oh, Magdalen, I am delighted that you and the duke are in love and getting married."

"Thank you, Avelina."

Her friend stood and hugged Magdalen. "And that you are both safe after such a terrible ordeal. It must have been terrifying."

"It did seem dangerous and frightening at the time, but now that I look back on it . . . it seems rather like one of the best times of my life."

Their gazes met and they burst out laughing.

They talked some more, catching up on what had happened to them in the last two years. Then someone knocked at the door.

"Come in."

Lord Thornbeck and Steffan entered the room. Her gaze was immediately arrested by Steffan, who had shaved his beard. How handsome and youthful and healthy he looked! He wore a blue velvet waistcoat with bright-white sleeves. His hair was clean and still damp as it swooped perfectly across his forehead.

Her heart skipped a beat.

"We came to escort our ladies to the Great Hall," Lord Thornbeck said, "if you are both feeling well enough."

Magdalen was fully dressed after her own bath, so she swung her legs off the bed, still holding the baby, and walked toward Steffan.

"Isn't she beautiful?"

"She is." But Steffan was looking at Magdalen.

Lord and Lady Thornbeck spoke quietly to each other as a servant gathered the baby's things.

"Are you well?" Magdalen said in a low voice, leaning close to him.

"I am very well."

"Your head? Does it still hurt?"

"Only a bit. Lord Thornbeck's own physician said I was well enough to be up and walking around."

"I am glad. And I must say, even though I liked your beard, you look just as handsome clean shaven."

He glanced over her shoulder at Lord and Lady Thornbeck. He must have found them looking away, because he bent and kissed her on the lips.

"Not in front of the baby," Magdalen whispered, her cheeks growing warm.

"The baby is asleep. Don't worry." He winked at her.

She smiled, his oft-spoken phrase sending a jolt to her heart.

"Let me hold the baby." Steffan reached for the precious bundle.

Magdalen helped transfer her to his arms, carefully making sure her head was supported.

Steffan held her against his chest, staring down into the baby's face. "We will be good parents, do you not think?"

"I think so."

"I think so too." Avelina came up behind them.

The four of them, plus the baby, walked down the stairs.

Steffan looked around the Great Hall, where his great-grandfather's sword and battle-ax were prominently displayed, as well as the banner and shield bearing his family's colors and coat of arms.

Steffan was back in his familiar place at the head of the table. Lord and Lady Thornbeck and Magdalen sat in the nearest seats around him, while Alexander and Agnes, who had been released from the dungeon, sat at a lower table with Lenhart.

How strange it was that Alexander, the person who had seemed his biggest enemy, had decided to help him and actually had a hand in saving their lives. Steffan's cynical side said it was due mostly to his knowing that Lord Hazen would not get away with what he had done, and Alexander had helped Steffan and Magdalen in an effort to save himself. But now that he knew what it felt like to be in love, he couldn't help believing that love had played some part in Alexander's decision to do the right thing.

Thinking of love made him turn his eyes on Magdalen. She was radiant in a pink gown and pink ribbons in her hair. She smiled nearly every moment, but that was mostly due to having Lady Thornbeck here with her. But when Magdalen turned her glowing countenance on him and touched his arm, he somehow felt taller.

Steffan had Lenhart brought up to the dais, and he stood beside him and announced that he had something to say to all their guests—the Baroness of Mallin, Lord and Lady Thornbeck, and all of the knights and guards they had brought with them.

"This young man, Lenhart"—Steffan set his hand on the boy's shoulder—"risked his life in loyalty to his mistress, Lady Magdalen. He was able to explain, even without the ability to speak aloud, all the treachery that was taking place in Wolfberg. He is the one who brought help, and Lady Magdalen and I will always be grateful to Lenhart."

Everyone cheered, and smiles beamed on every face. People congratulated Lenhart as he walked back to his seat, clapping him on the back and raising their cups of wine in salute.

When the meal was nearly over, Steffan leaned closer to Magdalen as she gave him her full attention.

"What will happen to Lord Hazen, Erlich, and Alexander and Agnes?" she asked. "Have you spoken about it?"

"Yes. Lord Thornbeck and I discussed it—your mother also had an opinion. We will send Lord Hazen to the king's castle in Prague to let him decide his punishment. It could be some time before the king returns, as he is visiting the pope in Avignon, but he should be secure in the king's dungeon until then. We will have Erlich banished, and we will ask the king to pardon Alexander and Agnes since they helped us. If the king strips Alexander of his property in Arnsbaden, I will make sure he is not destitute, at least."

"That is kind of you. What did my mother think should be done?"

"She thought Lord Hazen should be made to walk in leg irons all the way to Prague and that Alexander and Agnes should be locked in the dungeon until the king pronounced their punishment."

"Oh my."

"You are not much like your mother, are you?"

"No." She giggled. "And Katrin?"

"She'll be sent back to Arnsbaden with most of Lord Hazen's other servants—unless you have another preference."

"No, I don't want her to be punished, even though she did betray us to Lord Hazen. At least she warned us."

He smiled and caressed her cheek with his thumb. "I want to ask you something."

"Oh? Another interesting proposal like the one from earlier today?"

"Yes, as a matter of fact." He cleared his throat. "The guests who are coming in a few days will be expecting a wedding celebration."

"Shall you let Alexander and Agnes have their wedding celebration after all? That is generous of you."

He opened his mouth to protest, then saw the smile on her lips. "You are very amusing. I was about to ask you . . ."

"Ask me what?" A twinkle glittered in her eye.

"Will you marry me while the guests are here?"

"Yes, I believe I will."

He liked this flirty, self-confident, cheerful Magdalen.

She looked behind him. "Is that your father's portrait up there on the wall?"

"Yes, it is."

"He was almost as handsome as you."

He squeezed her hand under the table, then winked at her. "Yes, it is fortunate that Lord and Lady Thornbeck were able to recognize me."

"And that I was here to vouch for you?"

"Yes." He leaned down and kissed her.

A thought suddenly came to him—the other place where he used to play as a small child. "I just realized where my portrait is."

"What? Where?"

"In Gertrudt's room."

Magdalen leaned over and told Lady Thornbeck, who told Lord Thornbeck. And when the meal was over, the four of them went up to his sister's room to see if his guess was correct.

During the meal Lord and Lady Thornbeck's baby had been put to bed, and Magdalen and Lady Thornbeck were talking softly, following behind the men on the stairs.

Lord Thornbeck had been giving Steffan advice about how to help Wolfberg recover from what his uncle had done, to build up his guard once again, and to acquire more knights and soldiers to defend Wolfberg.

"I hope you will stay," Steffan said, "for as long as you feel comfortable. I very much value your opinions and advice to me, especially now that I no longer have my steward, Jacob."

Lord Thornbeck stopped and looked him in the eye in the light of the torches on the wall. "I shall be happy to help you in every way I can, not only for your sake, but for the sake of the Holy Roman Empire."

"Thank you, Lord Thornbeck." The sincerity in his tone and eyes touched something in Steffan's heart. If he'd had an older brother, he'd have wanted him to be like this man.

They reached his sister's door and they all went inside.

"What makes you think the portrait is here?" Magdalen asked.

"I used to play with my sister in here. There's a little door behind her bed." He walked to her bed, which was in the corner against the wall. "Jacob used to find us here, hiding and play-acting our own pretend stories, and when I was older he would talk about what good friends Gertrudt and I were, how we made up such interesting stories." He pulled aside a curtain and revealed a decoratively carved wooden door.

"What is in there?" Magdalen asked.

He turned the little handle and opened it. "It's a closet where my sister kept her toys and favorite things." It was completely dark inside.

Lord Thornbeck went into the stairwell and returned with a torch. He held it while Steffan stooped slightly to go inside. He moved aside some old toys, and in the back against the wall he found something large and rectangular covered with a velvet cloth. He took hold of it and brought it out.

Magdalen gasped.

He pulled the velvet cloth off, and there it was. Jacob had hidden it where his uncle would never look—Gertrudt's storage closet.

Magdalen took it from him and held it up. "It is very like you, I must say, though you look a bit younger—just as you did two years ago."

She and Lady Thornbeck discussed the portrait, comparing it to him, and how clever a hiding place it was.

Steffan had been stripped of everything for a short season, but it turned out for his good: so he might discover love and life and joy, and so God could take away all his fear.

A week later, when all the guests that Lord Hazen had invited arrived, Steffan and Magdalen made the walk down the castle mount to the Wolfberg Cathedral to say their marriage vows on the church steps before the priest. Clouds had overspread the sky from early morning, but as they walked down the street toward the church, the sun came out, the clouds continued to disperse, and soon it was a bright, clear day.

Magdalen gazed up at her soon-to-be husband and sighed.

Steffan waved to several people as they walked toward the church. He had managed to round up and bring back almost all of his old servants and guards whom Lord Hazen had sent away. His smile was genuine, and the crease between his eyes was seldom visible anymore. It was completely gone today.

They held each other's hand during the speaking of the vows. She tried to listen to what the priest was saying, but her thoughts kept wandering to Steffan and what he was thinking, to how thankful she was to be marrying him.

When the priest declared them man and wife, she kissed her husband to seal their marriage, and the crowd cheered. They partook of the Holy Eucharist with the people of Wolfberg, with Lord and Lady Thornbeck, and with several other noble men and women from the northern regions who had been invited.

Once they were outside the church in the bright sunshine again, Magdalen caught sight of a group of wild geese flying overhead in a perfect V shape. One of the birds honked to keep the others following in perfect formation.

Magdalen wondered if those birds felt the way she had once felt—following and obeying but always feeling as if she was going in the wrong direction. But now it seemed all of her fears had come to naught and her true direction was clear. And through every hardship, she could be still and know the One who was guiding her way.

Acknowledgments

I want to thank my editors, Becky Monds and Julee Schwarzburg, who took a very rough draft and helped shape it into something a whole lot better. So thank you, Julee and Becky and all the copy editors and others who helped to polish it up.

I want to thank my oh-so-competent and hardworking agent, Natasha Kern. She is a sweetheart to me, and I am grateful to her. May God bless her always.

I want to thank my uncle, Roy Lawrence, who helped me with my questions about raising geese. I'm not the only person who thinks he knows a lot about a lot!

As always, thanks to my family, Grace, Faith, and Joe, for helping me brainstorm, and to friend and brainstormer Terry Bell. And I want to send another big shout-out to my readers, who encourage and support me in ways that I truly cherish. Thank you all.

And thanks to God, who gives every good and perfect gift. His light shines in the deepest darkness.

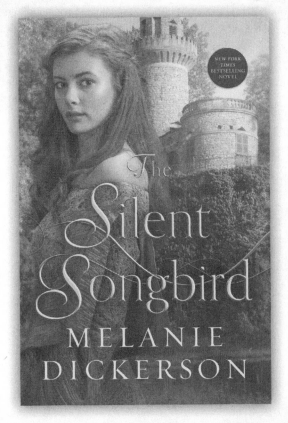

An Excerpt from
The Silent Songbird

Chapter One

Summer 1384. Berkhamsted Castle,
Hertfordshire, England.

ervants may marry whomever they want, but a king's ward has no freedom at all."

Evangeline broke off the song she was singing. A lump rose in her throat. Through her open window facing the castle bailey she watched the servants talking and laughing and milling about, finishing their morning chores.

A kitchen maid was drawing a bucket of water at the well in the center of the bailey. A young man approached her.

Alma gave him the dipper, and he lifted it to his lips.

The stranger's hair was brown and fell over his brow at an angle. He was tall, and even from Evangeline's bedchamber window on the third level of the castle, she could see he was handsome, with a strong chin and a sturdy stance.

He passed the water around to the other men who had followed him to the well. Evangeline leaned out the window to try to catch what they were saying.

"Thank you," the man said as he handed the dipper back to

317

the servant. He wore the clothing of a peasant—a leather mantle over his long linen tunic.

"Where are you from?" Alma asked.

"Glynval, a little village north . . . brought . . . to sell . . . and wheat flour . . ." Evangeline couldn't make out all the words.

The man wasn't like most peasants. Not that she had seen very many. But this man held himself upright with an air of confidence and ease she had rarely seen before.

Evangeline leaned out a little farther, hanging on to the casement. The man was moving on as the cart started forward, Alma still staring after him. He turned to say something to the other men and suddenly looked up at Evangeline.

"Evangeline!"

She jumped backward, her heart crashing against her chest.

"What are you doing, hanging out the window like a common—? Don't you know better than to behave that way?" Muriel hurried to the open window and peered out, then closed it and clamped her hands on her hips.

"Am I not allowed to look out the window? I'm no better than the prisoners in the dungeon. You know, I feel much pity for them. I daydream sometimes about releasing them and running away with them." She tipped her face to the ceiling as if turning her face to the sun and closed her eyes. "How good it would feel, walking free through the fields of wildflowers I read about in a poem once, breathing the fresh air, free to go wherever I want."

"You think your jests are amusing," Muriel said, "but when the king of England is your guardian and is planning your wedding to a wealthy nobleman, you should not expect pity. Envy is more likely."

"Wedding? What do you mean?" Evangeline's heart seemed to stop beating. "What do you know?"

"It is only gossip, but it is said that the king has promised you to one of his closest advisors."

"Who?"

"The Earl of Shiveley."

Evangeline reached out and placed a hand on the stone wall as the room seemed to teeter from side to side. How could the king betroth her to him? Lord Shiveley was old—almost forty—and Evangeline was barely seventeen. She had only seen Lord Shiveley a few times when he had accompanied the king to Berkhamsted Castle. He stared at her in a way that made her stomach sick, and he always managed to put a hand on her—on her shoulder or her back, and even once at her waist. She would always writhe inwardly and step away from him as quickly as she could.

Besides that, it was rumored that Lord Shiveley's first wife had died under mysterious circumstances.

Evangeline shuddered.

"The king and Lord Shiveley will arrive tonight, and you must be ready to greet them." Muriel bustled over to the wardrobe where Evangeline's best dresses were kept. She opened it and rummaged through her clothing. "You should wash your hair. I have ordered your bath sent up, and I shall—"

"Muriel, stop!" Evangeline stared at the woman who had been her closest companion and confidant for ten years. Though Muriel was nearly old enough to be her mother, she could not be so daft.

Muriel stared back at her with a bland expression. "What is it?"

"Surely you must see that I cannot marry that man." Her voice was a breathy whisper.

"My dear," Muriel said, not unkindly, "you know, you have always known, you must marry whomever the king wishes you to."

Evangeline's throat constricted. "The king does not care a whit about my feelings."

"Careful." Muriel's gaze darted about the room. "You mustn't risk speaking against the king. You never know who might betray you."

"I shall tell the king to his face when he arrives that I shall not marry Lord Shiveley, and it is cruel to ask it of me."

"You know you shall do no such thi—"

"I shall! I shall tell him!"

"Evangeline. You are too old to get in such a passion. Sit down and calm yourself. Breathe."

Evangeline crossed her arms over her chest and ignored Muriel's order. She had to think of some way to escape. Women often married men they did not particularly want to marry, but she could not marry Lord Shiveley. She was not like other women. They might accept unfair treatment, but Evangeline would fight, argue, rebel against injustice. Other women conformed to what was expected of them. Perhaps they did not dream of freedom and a different life.

"You must listen to reason," Muriel said. "Lord Shiveley is rich and can give you your own home. You will finally have the freedom to do whatever you wish. You will have servants and your own gardens and even your own horse. Many ladies enjoy falconry and hunting. You can have as many dresses and as much jewelry, or anything else your heart desires."

Only if her husband allowed it.

Muriel knew her well enough to know what might sway her. But a husband did not give freedom. A husband made rules. He took away his wife's control and replaced it with his own. A wealthy, powerful husband could order his wife around, beat her, do whatever he wished to her, and she could do naught.

Peasants, if they were not married and were free men and women, might be poor, but was it not a hundred times better to be free than to have fancy clothes and expensive food and servants to do everything for you? Freedom and independence were worth more than all the gold a castle could hold. Freedom to choose whom to marry, freedom to walk about the countryside unhindered, to drink from a cool, clear stream and gaze up into the trees, to ride a horse and eat while standing up. To bathe in the river and laugh and sing at the top of her voice—that was freedom.

And now King Richard was about to force her to marry an old, disgusting man.

"But you said it was gossip." Evangeline began to breathe easier. "Perhaps it was only idle talk."

Or if it was true, once she was able to talk to King Richard, he would understand. They'd been friends since they were very young, being cousins and only six months apart in age. Although she had not seen much of Richard in the past few years, surely he would listen to her pleas.

Her stomach sank. She was fooling herself. Richard would not listen to her if he had made up his mind. His loyalty to his advisors came before any childhood friendship he might still feel for Evangeline.

"At least Lord Shiveley is taller than you are." Muriel arched her brows.

"Just because I am taller than half the men I've ever met doesn't mean I want to marry this man." Evangeline turned away from Muriel and sat on the bench by the window, placing her head in her hands. Perhaps if she were able to cry, it would relieve this terrible ache in her chest.

"There now." Muriel sat beside her and placed a hand on her

shoulder. "Do not fret about something that may not even be true. We shall wait until the king arrives and let him tell you why he's here and if he has aught to say to you."

But the gentle warmth of Muriel's hand did not feel comforting. Muriel was fifteen years older than Evangeline, but they were both illegitimate daughters of important men—Evangeline's father was the king's uncle, while Muriel's father was an archbishop. Both of them were dependent on the kindness of King Richard.

Fortunately for Muriel, she was not valued as a pawn in the king's political maneuverings, to be married off to a man the king wanted to please or bribe. It was easy for Muriel to tell Evangeline not to fret about marrying a repulsive man.

A knock came at the door. Muriel opened it to a man wearing the livery of the king.

"A message for Evangeline, ward of the king, daughter of Lionel of Antwerp, Duke of Clarence."

Evangeline stood. Muriel brought her the missive, which had been sealed in dark-red wax with the king's signet ring. She tore it open. The words leapt off the page at her:

> Evangeline, I and the Earl of Shiveley would enjoy hearing you sing for us with that famous, incomparable voice of yours. I believe you are acquainted with my advisor, which is more than most noble brides can boast of their betrothed. He became quite enamored of you the last time he heard you sing.

Betrothed.

The note slipped from her hand and fluttered to the floor.

The story continues in *The Silent Songbird* by Melanie Dickerson.

The
GOLDEN BRAID

The one who needs rescuing isn't always the one in the tower.

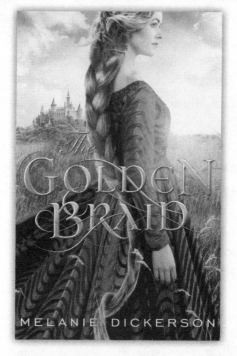

Rapunzel can throw a knife better than any man around. And her skills as an artist rival those of any artist she's met. But for a woman in medieval times, the one skill she most desires is the hardest one to obtain: the ability to read.

Available in print and e-book

THOMAS NELSON
Since 1798

Don't miss the Medieval Fairy Tale novels also available from Melanie Dickerson!

Available in print and e-book

About the Author

Jodie Westfall Photography

Melanie Dickerson is a *New York Times* bestselling author and two-time Christy Award finalist. Her first book *The Healer's Apprentice* won the National Readers' Choice Award for Best First Book in 2010, and *The Merchant's Daughter* won the 2012 Carol Award. Melanie spends her time writing stories at her home near Huntsville, Alabama, where she lives with her husband and two daughters.

www.MelanieDickerson.com
Twitter: @melanieauthor
Facebook: MelanieDickersonBooks